DARKNESS BOUND

THE WITCH'S REBELS BOOK TWO

GW00578162

Darkness Bound
Copyright © 2018 by Sarah Piper
SarahPiperBooks.com

All rights reserved. With the exception of brief quotations used for promotional or review purposes, no part of this book may be recorded, reproduced, stored in a retrieval system, or transmitted in any form or by any means without the express permission of the author.

This book is a work of fiction. Names, characters, places, businesses, organizations, brands, media, and incidents are either products of the author's imagination or are used fictitiously. Any resemblance to actual events, locations, or persons, living or dead, is entirely coincidental.

ISBN-13: 978-1-948455-07-7

ALSO BY SARAH PIPER

THE WITCH'S REBELS

Shadow Kissed

Darkness Bound

Demon Sworn

Blood Cursed

Death Untold

Rebel Reborn

THE WITCH'S MONSTERS

Blood and Midnight

VAMPIRE ROYALS OF NEW YORK

Dorian & Charlotte

Dark Deception

Dark Seduction

Dark Obsession

Gabriel & Jacinda

Heart of Thorns

Heart of Fury

Heart of Flames

TAROT ACADEMY

Spells of Iron and Bone

Spells of Breath and Blade

Spells of Flame and Fury

Spells of Blood and Sorrow

Spells of Mist and Spirit

ONE

ASHER

It was always the same damn nightmare.

Her, turning to me with the sun in her eyes, grinning like we were the only ones in on the secret.

Me, chasing her through that golden field, hungry for her touch. Her kiss.

I always let her take the lead. It made the reunions that much sweeter.

I chased her for hours, neither of us running out of breath, until she finally stopped and turned to look at me once more. The wind blew her hair into her eyes and she laughed, pinning her dark waves back with her hands, taunting me until I finally caught up.

"Touch me," she whispered then, and I obeyed, reaching for her face with the barest brush of my fingers.

The moment we connected, she was gone.

Incinerated by my deadly touch.

I dropped to my knees, a thousand screams trapped in

my throat. The sun faded. The sky turned black. The field around us burned to ash.

The wind blew the dust of her bones into my mouth, and I woke up coughing, limbs tangled in my sheets, my body on fire with the fever I'd never quite shaken.

I sat up against the headboard and sucked in air, counting backward from a hundred until my heart stopped trying to bust a hole through my chest.

Son of a bitch.

Every time was like losing her all over again. *Killing* her all over again.

I kicked free of the sheets and stumbled out of bed, desperate to feel the solid wood floor beneath my feet. From one end of the room to the other I paced, trying like hell to loosen the nightmare's grip.

The chill October breeze blew in through the open window, and the only thing I had on was a pair of gym shorts, but sweat trickled down my back anyway. My hair was damp with it, too.

The room felt like a damn sauna, and every one of my nerves buzzed with pent-up energy. My fingers twitched, already reaching for the cup of charcoal pencils on my drafting table.

Dropping into my chair in the pitch dark, I flipped open my sketchpad and grabbed a pencil. I didn't bother turning on the light; I'd drawn her so many times I could do it with my eyes closed. Sometimes, she appeared whole and unbroken, as beautiful as she'd been on the day we'd met. Other times, she was as black as night, with glowing red eyes that burned right through me.

I never knew which version I'd see until I revealed her face on the page.

Thankfully, she was turning out whole and beautiful tonight.

Her memory was a drug to me now—painfully tearing me apart inside, yet impossible to resist—and I sank deep into the process. The ritual. Drawing her face night after night was as much my punishment as my salvation, and no matter how much it hurt, I wouldn't let myself forget it.

Manically I brought the dream to life, shading in the hollows of her cheekbones, highlighting the soft sheen along her upper lip, trying to capture just how the light had danced in her eyes, the first time and the last.

Eventually, my nerves calmed. My heart rate slowed. The sweat evaporated from my skin, leaving goosebumps in its wake.

I had no idea how much time had passed, but my hand was stiff and cramped, and I'd worn the pencil down to a nub.

Tonight's penance paid, I tossed the sketchbook back on the table and yanked open the blinds. Moonlight leaked in through the slats and landed on her face, and I stared into her eyes, once again begging for the forgiveness I didn't deserve.

It was my version of jamming in the needle, and for those brief seconds, the ache in my chest dulled.

There was just one problem.

The woman staring back at me tonight wasn't the brunette beauty that had haunted my dreams and filled the pages of my sketchbooks for centuries, but a curly-haired blonde with a soft, seductive mouth and eyes like the twilight sky.

The woman who'd seen into the deepest, blackest parts of my soul and decided I was worth saving anyway.

It never should've happened.

"*Fuck!*" A roar exploded from my chest, unannounced and unwelcome. I attacked my table, flipping the damn thing over. My art stuff crashed to the floor.

Didn't help.

Never did.

And fuck my life and the horse I rode in on, because on top of all that shit, now I had company.

"Ash?" The hall light clicked on, spilling in around the doorframe, and Gray knocked, her muffled voice edged with concern. "You okay?"

We were the only two holed up at the safe house—a massive timber-framed cabin about an hour outside of the Bay, fully stocked and big enough for all of us.

Tucked away in a thick patch of woods well off the beaten path, the whole place was spelled with some fancy fae mojo Ronan and I had spent a small fortune on, making us impervious to GPS and confusing anyone who accidentally wandered too close to the property line.

It was a sweet setup for sure—one I liked a lot better when I was crashing here alone.

But this week I was on babysitting duty while the rest of

the crew sifted through the mess we'd left at Norah's placc, cleaning up the evidence of the vampire massacre and searching for any clue that might lead us to the hunter who'd taken Haley Barnes.

My gut churned just thinking of that bastard. What he'd done to those witches. What he'd done to Gray as a kid.

What he probably still had planned.

Pray you die before I find you, fuckface...

"Asher?" Gray tried one more time.

When I didn't answer, she opened the door and waltzed right in, blasting me with light.

I'd been dodging her gaze pretty much since that kiss in the attic, and tonight was no different.

Turning away from the door, I said, "If you're here for the show, you just missed it."

I felt her eyes on my back, burning right down to my bones.

"What happened?" she asked.

"Earthquake. You didn't feel it?"

"Asher—"

"You need something, Cupcake, or are you just here to practice your Spell of Endless Torment?" I finally grew a pair and turned to face her. Sheet marks creased her cheek, and her hair was a tangle of messy curls that I ached to bury my face in.

Clutched against her chest, she held the book of shadows we'd dug up from her yard.

Damn thing had barely left her sight since.

"Pretty sure I've perfected that one by now," she said.

Her smirk stayed firmly in place, but her eyes widened a fraction as she drank in the sight of my bare chest and arms. "Holy... wow."

I cracked a smile. "Did you just *holy wow* me?"

"What? No. No! I just meant..." Her cheeks darkened. "You... um... have a lot of tattoos."

"Nothing you haven't seen before."

Like when you climbed on top of me in that attic, kissing me like the world was about to end...

"It was... darker then," she said. "And you were basically dying, so..."

"So I was."

She swallowed hard, and the scent of her desire washed over me, flooding my senses and heating my blood all over again.

Sometimes I liked knowing when a woman wanted me. The nifty little incubus trick came in handy when I was running low on energy and needed to find a willing partner all too happy to feed my particular brand of hunger.

But other times—like, right-now times—it just fucked me up inside, because no matter how badly Gray might've wanted me—no matter how badly I might've wanted to return the favor—there wasn't a damn thing I could do about it.

"Anyway, I..." Gray faltered, finally tearing her gaze away from my chest. Focusing on the pencils scattered across my floor, she said, "Sorry. I was about to raid the fridge when I heard the crash. I thought something was wrong."

"Couldn't sleep, huh?"

"Not really." She bit her lip, still staring at the floor. In a whisper I could barely make out, she said, "Bad dreams."

"Makes two of us." I stooped down to pick up the table I'd upended. I took my sweet-ass time about it, too, because otherwise I might just go over there and scoop her into my arms, drag her back to my bed, and give us *both* something to chase away the nightmares…

"Well, if you'd rather be alone…" Gray cleared her throat, but she didn't finish the thought, and I wasn't in the mood to make it easy on her.

"Too late now, Cupcake." I snapped.

I righted the table, shoving it back into place with another crash. She didn't flinch—just kept staring at me like I was supposed to grab a knife and open up a vein.

"Actually, *dick*, it isn't." Gray took a step forward, hip cocked, lips pursed and ready to battle. It was a look I'd gotten to know quite well these past couple days—one I liked to think she'd perfected just for me. "Did you forget where the front door is? Because I'd be more than happy to escort your ass right on through it."

I flashed her what I'd been told was my panty-melting grin. "Is that so?"

"Bet your tattooed ass it is." Panties seemingly unaffected, she said, "Maybe then we'd both find a little peace."

I pinched the bridge of my nose and lowered my head, trying like hell to stifle the laughter bubbling up.

No such luck.

All that pent-up emotion roiling inside me, good and

bad and everything in between, and the dam finally burst. The woman had thrown me off kilter once again, and now I was damn near busting a gut.

A good belly laugh was nothing if not contagious, and soon a crack appeared in her hard shell, too.

"First of all, I don't have a tattoo on my ass. And second of all, I can't leave you, Cupcake," I said, wiping the tears from my eyes and finally regaining my composure—not an easy feat when you've got a beautiful woman standing less than two feet from your bed and you're already half-naked, but somehow I managed. "You'd miss me too damn much."

"Oh, totally." She pressed a hand to her heart, fluttering her lashes. "My life just wouldn't be the same without your constant dickishness dicking me around on a daily basis. I guess I should be thanking you."

"Don't mention it." I gave her a little bow. "What are dicks for, right?"

Now she really lost it. "Asher O'Keefe, if you haven't figured *that* out by now, you'd better get back to incubus school. You missed a *very* important lesson."

Our laughter faded into a dead silence, as if we'd both just noticed how supercharged the moment had become. The air seemed to crackle with it—that strange, electric chemistry that bubbled up between us whenever we spent more than a minute in the same room together.

I'd always found her beautiful. Annoying as hell, yet strangely compelling. But ever since the other night in the attic—since the kiss that'd saved my soul—things between us had gone from an occasional flirty simmer to a full-on boil.

And I still couldn't stop myself from cranking up the heat.

"No, Gray Desario," I said, voice low. "I *invented* the lesson." I stepped closer—close enough that my breath made the halo of frizz at the top of her pretty blonde head stir. She backed up against the doorframe and held up that book like a shield, but she was all out of escape options, and I wasn't about to relent.

Hooking a finger under her chin, I tilted her face up and leaned in, my lips brushing her ear. "Let me know if you ever need private tutoring."

A soft mewl stuck in her throat, and I pulled back and stared at her lips, seconds ticking between us like a bomb waiting to explode. I brushed the pad of my thumb across her mouth, her lips parting ever-so-slightly.

The intensity of her desire hit me head-on again, making me dizzy.

In the absence of sexual energy to feed on, her physical responses were generating just enough juice to sustain me. To help me heal from the beating I'd taken in the Bay.

I could live on it, sure.

But my cock was in absolute agony.

If ever a woman wanted to be fucked, it was this woman right here, right now, standing just stumbling distance from the very bed in which I could make all of her hottest, filthiest dreams come true.

And mine, if we were being honest.

Unfortunately, she wasn't the only one haunting my dreams, and the rest of them served as a harsh reminder of just how dangerous this game could get.

I closed my eyes, focusing entirely on the feel of her hot, velvet mouth, trying to pin it down in my memory. Trying not to kiss her. Trying not to completely lose my shit.

Whatever Gray had going on with Ronan and Darius? Whatever "family" she thought we could all be? I was all in. But unlike the crossroads demon and the vampire and even the shifter, incubuses came with a built-in hard limit—cross it, and she might just end up dead.

I dropped my hand and walked out of my own bedroom without so much as a backward glance, bound for a shower.

A fucking cold one.

TWO

GRAY

Was sudden onset attraction to someone who annoyed the hell out of you a symptom of cabin fever, a symptom of magical burnout, or a symptom of one too many blows to the head?

It had to be a symptom of *something*. I refused to believe there was any other explanation for the rush of heat I felt whenever Asher got too close—a scenario that was getting harder to avoid since we'd been sequestered together at the safe house.

I understood why the guys had left us behind—Ash was still recuperating from the damage of the devil's trap, and as the group's resident human and seriously depleted witch, I needed some extra R&R, too.

But it was hard to relax when three of the four men I'd come to care about most in this world were putting in long hours at the house where we'd been ambushed by opportunistic vampires working for the monster who'd killed my best friend and countless others.

And things between Asher and me? Oh, how I wished I could go back to those halcyon days when hating him came as natural to me as breathing. But how could I hate him now?

Whatever we were to each other when this nightmare began—whatever he'd thought of me years ago when he'd helped bring me back from the brink—springing him from the devil's trap had bonded me to him in ways that went well beyond the kiss we'd shared.

I'd felt his soul. Glimpsed the darkness there.

And in that darkness, some black, cold thing inside me had recognized a kindred spirit.

Maybe that should've frightened me.

It doesn't.

Maybe I was getting used to the darkness.

I am.

Maybe I was starting to like it. To like *him*.

I am...

I shivered, the salt of Asher's skin still lingering on my lips. He'd been in the shower for twenty minutes already, and in that time the only thing I'd managed to accomplish was filling the teakettle.

I hadn't even turned on the flame.

Scolding myself, I turned on the gas range and grabbed my mug from the cupboard—the chipped one Sophie had painted for me—grateful Ronan had thought to grab it from my kitchen in South Bay. It was a little piece of home—a reminder of my best friend and the safe, normal life we'd once shared—and I clung to it.

Words like safe and normal were no longer part of my vocabulary, but thinking of Sophie always grounded me, even when my current roommate was doing everything in his power to drive me to an early grave.

"Darlin', your love is my poison," he sang out from the bathroom down the hall, "and I'm dying for another taste."

"I've got your poison right here," I grumbled, though I doubted he could hear me.

"You make me bleed," he belted out, "a little more for every kiss. But baby don't you know by now I'd bleed myself dry for one last hit?"

Goosebumps rose on my arms.

I yelled at them.

"Can't you hear me?" he sang, louder and more passionately with each word. "I'm out here in the cold, banging down your gate. I'll never leave you, darlin', I'm just begging for my dose of fate. 'Cause oh-oh-oh, your love is my poison, and I'm falling out for—"

The kettle whistled, muffling his next words. I whisked it away from the flame and tried to catch another note, but it was too late. Asher's serenade had stopped.

"Thank God," I said, though my voice lacked conviction.

I pictured Sophie teasing me with a hearty laugh and a swift roll of her eyes.

You are soooo crushing on him, Gray…

I poured the hot water over a sachet of chocolate pu-erh

tea, letting its sweet scent calm me as the image of Sophie's smile faded.

Asher started up a new tune, but I knew better than to give him any more attention. Leaving him to it, I headed into the living room with my tea and my book and an unflappable resolve to carve out some peace, even if there *was* a sexy-as-sin incubus tormenting me from behind the bathroom door.

Where he was currently in the shower. Naked.

Dripping wet over all those muscles and tattoos.

Singing rock ballads that gave me goosebumps.

Figures he can actually sing, too…

I caught myself before I got sucked into another pointless fantasy, refocusing on the task at hand.

Which was…?

Oh, right.

Peace and quiet in the living room.

While the kitchen was a sleek affair with vast granite countertops, glass-front maple cabinets, a big island in the center, and stainless steel appliances, the living room was much homier, featuring huge bay windows, a vaulted timber-framed ceiling, lived-in leather furniture, and a massive stone fireplace that took up almost an entire wall.

Setting my stuff on the coffee table, I knelt before the hearth and loaded in some crumpled newspapers and a few logs, kindling new flames to life.

Asher's voice dimmed to background noise as the fire popped and hissed, and I grabbed the butter-colored afghan from the back of the worn leather couch, curling up in what was quickly becoming my favorite spot.

I'd left Sophie's tarot cards on the coffee table, and I reached for them now, thinking as always about my best friend. Lately, her presence had been a constant in my life; real or imagined, memory or vision or magic or plain old pie-in-the-sky hope, she'd been with me, making me laugh and cry, offering advice, and keeping me company through the loneliest hours of the night.

I'd always felt especially close to her when I read with her cards, but tonight, something seemed to shove my thoughts in a different direction. The instant my fingers touched the deck, a fresh image appeared in my mind: Haley and the other witches from Bay Coven.

Someone was sending me a message.

I centered myself, tuning out everything but the warm glow of the fire on my face, letting my intuition take the wheel. I shuffled quickly and pulled six cards, placing them face down in two columns of three cards each.

"Tell me what I need to know," I said softly.

I flipped the first two cards at the top of each column, revealing a four-handed Magician performing for an audience of shadows, followed by the reversed King of Swords. The same cards had turned up in Sophie's last tarot reading —the one she'd shown me in my magical realm after I'd discovered her book of shadows.

"Hunters," I said, eyeing the King's massive sword. But unlike that day with Sophie's reading, I now realized the cards were speaking about one hunter in particular.

One whose lips had turned words of love into weapons and curses the day he vowed to burn me alive.

I was certain he was behind the Bay's recent string of witch murders and kidnappings. But what was his ultimate plan? Why had he left some alive? Why had he left *me* alive?

Swallowing the bile that rose in my throat, I turned the next two cards—Seven of Pentacles and Eight of Swords.

In the eight, a sinister moon lured a nude woman to an open window, impelling her to lean out. A garden of eight sharp swords bloomed beneath her. One more inch, and she'd fall to a brutal death.

The seven—a young witch drawing blood from a tree blooming with silver pentacles—was the card that had clued me in a few weeks ago about Sophie practicing witchcraft in secret with the Bay Coven.

Showing up here with the Eight of Swords, it was clearly a warning.

"He's forcing them to do his bidding," I said, letting the messages wash over me. "He needs them alive, but scared—too scared to run. He needs them to work their magic."

The fire popped and sparked, as if confirming my hypothesis.

I turned it over in my mind. If it were true, it meant that Haley and the others were still alive—that they still had a chance at surviving this thing. But between the options of death and survival, a thousand more possibilities lived... and most of them weren't good.

Hastily I turned the bottom two cards—Queen of Swords and Nine of Wands.

Dressed in robes of gold and red, the fierce queen held two swords, one tipped with blood. It dripped onto the ground before her. Sometimes this card spoke to me of a badass, take-no-prisoners woman getting shit done.

Tonight? She scared the hell out of me. She was out for blood, and she'd do everything in her power to get it.

Like the woman in the Eight of Swords, the figure in the Nine of Wands also suggested imprisonment. She sat on a stone pedestal, her head bowed in apparent defeat, a black mask covering most of her face. A staircase marked by eight wooden wands loomed behind her—a possible escape—but it remained hidden from view. The only glimmer of hope came from the ninth wand, flaming like a torch, ready to light her way home.

I shivered, pulling the blanket tight around my shoulders. The positioning of the bottom two cards worried me. The sword-wielding queen seemed to be threatening the girl on the pedestal, refusing to let her leave.

"Where are you?" I whispered, brushing my fingers over the Nine of Wands. The girl on the steps seemed so scared, so defeated. I wanted to tell her not to give up. That she wasn't forgotten or alone. That somehow, she'd be found and brought home and made safe once again.

I picked up the card for a closer look, and a gust of warm air blew out from the fireplace, stirring my hair.

A small voice sounded in my head.

Help us…

I sucked in a breath. The fear I was sensing in the card suddenly manifested inside me with a heart-wrenching terror that sent real waves of panic cascading through my limbs. Sweat broke out across my forehead, and my chest heaved, my mouth filling with salty air that tasted like the sea. I gulped it in greedily, as if it were the first chance I'd been given to breathe in days.

Black smoke curled out from behind the flames, reaching for me, drawing me in. The magic inside me stirred in response, and I held out my hands, determined to strengthen the connection despite the discomfort. Smoke twirled and danced around my fingers, caressing me with a warm, inviting touch, calming the dread that had gripped my heart.

It pulled me from the couch, urging me closer, and I knelt at the hearth again, staring into the fire as some unseen force compelled me to look deeper. To see. To know.

Images appeared in the flames, frantic and disjointed at first. I held up my hands, and the fire dimmed at my command, the images slowly coming into focus.

Women and girls. Witches. Dozens of them locked in cold, cramped cells with no windows, no natural light. The glow of magic flickered all around them, throwing eerie shadows on the wall.

The image reminded me of the Magician card.

The vision zoomed in on a single prison cell, and the girl inside turned to face me, her eyes widening as if she could see me, too.

"Help us," she said, her voice weak, yet determined.

"Where are you?" I shouted, but she was already fading, the flames roaring up once again, taking her away from me.

"Gray! Her frantic call echoed, the sound of my name in her frightened voice like an arrow to my heart. *"Gray!"*

* * *

"Gray!"

The bark of a man's voice yanked me out of the trance, and I whipped my head toward the sound just in time to see Asher charging at me from across the smoke-filled room in nothing but a towel.

The fire alarm screeched overhead.

I'd barely had time to process the visual when he started shouting again

"Open the damn door!"

I bolted for the front door and hauled it open, then moved on to the windows.

Immediately, the smoke began to dissipate.

Blinking away the last of my confusion, I headed into the kitchen and grabbed the broom, using it to hit the reset button on the smoke alarm.

The house fell silent once again.

When I turned around again, Asher was at the fireplace, one hand holding up his towel, the other messing with the damper on the chimney.

"What happened?" he demanded.

When I didn't respond, he crossed the room and

grabbed my shoulders, peering into my eyes. Despite the frustration in his voice, his face was pinched with worry.

"Gray," he said, softer this time. "You looked like you were about to dive right into that fire."

I looked at my hands. They were trembling, and it wasn't because of the smoke.

"I saw her," I whispered.

Asher ducked down to meet my gaze. "Who?"

"Reva Monroe."

THREE

GRAY

Asher handed me a glass of water, his eyes boring into me like a dad scolding an errant kid. "So now that we can breathe again, you wanna tell me what I walked in on?"

I dropped onto the sofa and took the glass, holding his gaze as I gulped down the water. He'd managed to put on a pair of sweats, but he was still shirtless, his wet hair dripping into his eyes.

"Gray?" he pressed. "What *was* that shit?"

"I'm pretty sure I was scrying." I set down the glass and grabbed my book of shadows, flipping through to the section I'd kept on divination techniques. "Calla used to do it with candle flame and mirrors. I took lots of notes, but I never quite got the hang of it."

He took the seat next to me and leaned in close, inspecting the sketches I'd made of Calla's setup.

"Maybe because you're using a roaring fire to do the job of a tea light?"

I braced myself for a lecture, if for no other reason than Asher's incessant need to pester me. But instead, he draped his arm over the back of the couch behind me, totally calm. Borderline comforting.

"Tell me exactly what you saw."

I closed my eyes, reaching for the parts of the vision that still lingered.

"There were at least a dozen witches. They were trapped in some kind of prison."

"Did you see the hunter?"

"No, but it's his doing. I can *feel* it." I let the images flicker through my mind, trying to take in every single detail, searching for clues about their exact location. "Reva, the one I connected with? She's the youngest Bay Coven witch. Norah took her in a while back, but as far as I know, the two of them left town last week. Norah told Haley she wanted to go somewhere safe." I shook my head. "If what I saw was real, they either didn't make it out—"

"Or Norah lied, and handed her over to the hunter." Asher blew out a breath. "Were you and the kid close?"

"No, I'd only met her the one time at Norah's, and we barely spoke."

"Are you sure it was her in the flames?"

"Definitely." The tarot cards were still spread out on the table, and I glanced down at them now, focusing on the girl in the Nine of Wands. *Reva.* "She was terrified, Ash."

"What else can you tell me?"

"I swear I could taste the sea," I said, remembering the saltiness that had filled my mouth right before I'd slipped into the trance. "I heard it, too—like a constant roar, but muffled. Like I said, I think they're in some kind of prison. No windows. Now that I think about it, it looked like a giant… cave." I filled in the rest of the details, giving Asher a moment to turn it all over in his mind.

"This prison," he finally said. "You think it's here in Washington?"

It was a good place to start. I pulled out my phone, flipping to the maps app. "The coast is only two hours from here. And there are plenty of places to disappear out there without anyone noticing."

"Two hours… That's just far enough for the hunter to slip out of range, but close enough he could still zip back into the Bay and grab more witches." At this, he turned to look at me again, his ocean-blue eyes serious. "Or grab you."

"Well, that's not happening now." I shook my head, forcing a smile. Anxiety in a situation like ours could easily lead to paranoia, and paranoia was as contagious as a yawn. "I'm out here in the middle of nowhere with my very own demonic bodyguard."

Asher nodded, but he didn't look convinced.

I broke his gaze, turning to look out the windows at the front of the house. It was pitch black outside, silent but for the occasional rustle of dried leaves in the breeze.

The logs shifted in the fireplace, sending a cascade of sparks shooting upward, and I flinched.

"Relax, Cupcake," Asher said softly, a trace of humor

slipping through his concern. "Your demonic bodyguard will keep you safe from all threats, great and small."

"I suppose so. After all, you *did* rush out of the shower to save me from scrying-induced smoke inhalation."

"All in a day's work."

"Thank God you had time to grab your towel." I nudged him in the ribs, trying not to pay too much attention to the drop-dead sexy tattoos snaking across his arms, chest, and abs, disappearing behind his back. Now that most of the wounds from his ordeal in the devil's trap had healed, the designs stood out much more clearly. They were all done in black ink, no color in sight—a mix of ancient-looking symbols, mesmerizing patterns, and words written in a language that might've been Latin. The tattoos on his abs rippled when he laughed.

"No shit," he said. "You have a hard enough time keeping your eyes off me as it is."

I wonder what it would feel like to touch his stomach...

"Uh, case in point," he said.

Probably smooth and hot, his muscles rock-hard underneath that perfectly painted skin...

"So basically, you're saying you want me," he said. "Right here on the floor, no holds barred. Right?"

"Yeah…"

"Uh, Gray?"

"Mmm?" I blinked, tearing my gaze away from his body and up to his face. "I mean… Wait, what?"

He cocked an eyebrow, but said nothing, waiting for me to catch up.

His words crashed into me all at once.

My cheeks flamed.

Totally busted, I turned away from him, looking out the dark windows again. "Maybe if you weren't prancing around here half-naked all the time, I wouldn't have to see your goods on display every five seconds."

"Okay, first of all? I don't prance. Second of all, I don't fucking prance."

I smiled and bit my lower lip, not willing to give him the satisfaction of a full-on laugh.

Our flirty teasing felt good, though—almost as if we'd broken through another one of the walls between us.

Not that I was ready to pick out china patterns or anything.

The brush of Asher's fingers on the back of my neck recaptured my attention. His touch was unexpected but not unpleasant, and I waited a beat before facing him, worried the movement would make him stop.

When I finally turned, he caught me in his gaze. This time neither of us looked away.

Tell me about her, I wanted to say. *The woman who haunts you. The ghost that put that look in your eyes…*

But I couldn't bring myself to ask about her, and after another beat, he blinked and looked away.

"What do you want to do about the witches?" he asked. His tone was serious again, but his touch remained gentle, his thumb stroking the side of my neck.

What did I *want* to do? That was easy. Grab the keys to Asher's bike and ride out to the coast, blast apart every hole and haunt and hovel until we found that bastard. Then I'd rip out his throat.

But going off half-cocked wouldn't help anyone. Even if what I'd seen in the vision was real—and that was a big if—there was no guarantee it wasn't a setup. The only thing I really knew about Reva was that Norah had taken her in when she'd had nowhere else to go. Whatever its motivation, kindness like that usually bred loyalty, especially in a city like the Bay.

I should know. That's how I'd ended up with my rebels.

If Ronan or Darius were accused of murdering innocents, would I automatically turn on them? What if I discovered Emilio was a crooked cop? And the dead woman I'd seen in Asher's memories… what if that had been intentional?

Would I walk away from him? From any of them?

My heart ached at the thought.

Regardless, when it came to tracking down the witches, we had to tread carefully. We needed a solid plan, we needed the element of surprise, and most importantly, we needed the rest of the gang.

So, despite my instinct to jump in headfirst and think about it later, I said, "We're not making a move without the guys. I'll text them later and let them know what I saw, and we'll take it from there."

Asher blew out a breath that sounded an awful lot like relief. "Fair enough."

I wondered if he'd been testing me.

I wondered if I'd passed.

My head hurt.

"They should be back any day," he said.

"I know," I said, but I wouldn't truly relax until they were back here with us, all in one piece. "But the best thing I can do now—for the witches *and* for you guys—is to keep working on my magic."

"You still haven't gotten this creepy old relic to work, huh?" He nodded at the book of shadows still sitting open in my lap, peering over my shoulder at the scrying page. The smell of his shampoo did nothing to mask his spicy demon scent—a seductive blend of ground cinnamon, hot pepper, and candle flame that made my stomach flip whenever he got too close.

Like now.

"It's not a creepy old relic. But… no." Sighing, I dragged my finger down the center of the page. There was a time when doing so would've elicited warmth and light, a shimmer of magic connecting me to it and it to me, but lately my touch had no effect.

The instant connection I'd felt upon digging it up from my backyard the other night had cooled, and no matter how hard I'd tried since then, I hadn't been able to tap back into its inherent magic.

After so many years apart, it seemed our bond had degraded.

"Whatever happened with the fire just now," I said, "it had nothing to do with the book."

"Why do you need it, then? Obviously, you've got plenty of mojo to work with."

"Sure, but it's mostly out of my control."

"Do you *have* to control it, though? Isn't it just a part of you? Magic in the blood and all that?"

"Yes and no. All witches are born with magic in our blood, we also have natural gifts for different kinds of magic. It takes a lot of practice to unearth our unique talents and hone them into something useful."

Something that helps rather than harms.

At that thought, my gut tightened, a low murmur of magic humming inside me.

"So, everything you've done so far was just an accident?" he asked.

"Kind of? I mean, I was learning things as a kid, but the —" I still couldn't bring myself to say *necromancy*, so I opted for Liam's much less offensive term instead—"the Shadowborn stuff is new to me. I guess it's kind of like that whole sex-vibe you've got. It's an inherent part of you, right? But you still had to learn how to control it."

Asher's normally cocky grin grew into a full-on laugh. "Excuse me, but… *sex vibe*? Really?"

Oh, hell. I did not *mean to take us down this road.*

"I'm paraphrasing!" I said. "I'm talking about your… whatever you call it. Your magnetic… force… thingy. The one that erases women's brains so they'll throw themselves at you."

"That's not magic, Cupcake. That's just my natural charm." He grinned, taking a little more pleasure in my awkward discomfort before finally moving on. "Can't you just write some new spells?"

"It's not that simple. A spell is just part of the equation. Controlling magic is largely about intent. The words and ingredients in a spell can help focus that intent and amplify its effects, but that's all."

I paged through the book, settling on a section on the properties of crystals.

Smoky quartz is a good grounding stone, I'd written. *Apophyllite helps with my tarot readings. Calla says it opens up the channels to allow me to receive messages more clearly. I'm not sure what the amethyst does, but it's purple, so I automatically love it.*

I smiled at my younger self. Like most witches' books of shadows, mine was equal parts spellbook, scrapbook, workbook, and diary. Every page was wrinkled with age, indented from the frantic scribbles of a teen witch who'd embraced hyperbole and melodrama as if they were long lost sisters.

Some of it was insightful and interesting. Some of it was downright mortifying. But all of it was mine. Part of me. Part of who I was, who I became, who I was still in the process of becoming.

It was a time machine, simultaneously bringing me back to my yesterdays and launching me into my tomorrows.

I couldn't believe I'd left it buried for so long.

"Okay, now I'm totally confused," Asher said. "If it's mostly about intent, why do you need spells at all?"

"I don't *need* spells," I explained. "But a witch's book of shadows is deeply personal, and that in itself is magic. There's a little bit of my soul in here, and reconnecting with that will only strengthen my magic, waking up the parts I put to sleep. It'll make me a better witch, Ash."

I didn't want to say the rest, and fortunately, Asher didn't push. I had a feeling he already knew what I was thinking, anyway.

Reconnecting with my magic, tapping into that power—it would make me a more attractive target for the hunter. That's what this was all about now. Saving the other witches and making that vile man pay for what he'd done to Sophie. For what his father had done to my mother. For what their family—their kind—had done to the entire trajectory of my life.

"What about the whole personal gain thing?" Asher asked, peeking at a prosperity spell I'd flipped to.

"Urban legend perpetuated by TV."

"Seriously?"

"There's nothing inherently wrong with using magic to make your life better—that's kind of the whole point. The thing we have to remember is that magic has consequences, and they're not always predictable." I considered him a moment, wondering again about his past. About what his life had been like before he'd come crashing back into mine. "I take it you don't know a lot of witches?"

Asher shook his head.

"Not even from… before?"

"Before I became a big scary incubus?" He wriggled his eyebrows in jest, but it was too late—I'd already seen the flash of hurt in his eyes.

I lowered my gaze, unable to bear the intensity of his.

"You're not that scary, you know. Especially after a little soap and water. A few more showers, and who knows? Maybe one day you'll be a real boy again."

I'd meant it as a joke, but Asher didn't find it funny at all.

"I'm not like your loverboy, Ronan," he snapped. "I was never human, Gray. I was *born* this way. Throw me in a tub of boiling water and bleach and set my ass on fire, and guess what? There's still no changing what I am. Sorry if that bothers you."

My mouth hung open, my total shock chased quickly by the rush of embarrassment that followed. For all the time I'd spent reading up on monsters in the Bay, I hadn't bothered to delve much deeper than what I'd considered the necessary facts—their strengths and weaknesses, common hangouts, and most importantly—how to kill them.

Questions flooded my mind. Was that typical of incubuses? Incubi? Was that even the right word? Were they all born that way, or just Asher? Were his parents demons as well? Is that how it worked? Had he always known, or did they sit him down for "the talk" the way human kids learned about where babies came from? Did all of them stop aging in their thirties? Could he have children? Did he *want* children?

And who was the woman I'd seen in his memories? Was she a succubus? Or was she a human who—

Oh, no...

"Don't," he said firmly, his voice breaking just a little. He faked a cough to cover it up, then said, "Look. I know

31

where your mind is heading, and I'm asking you—*telling* you—just don't."

"Ash—"

"I can't," he whispered, not bothering to hide the pain in his eyes.

I closed my eyes and sucked in a deep breath, his scent still lingering all around me.

Asher had just cracked open the door on his past, and everything in me wanted to step right in and make myself at home. But that tiny opening was still just a crack, and the last thing I wanted to do was slam it shut again by invading his privacy and scaring him off.

I still wasn't sure how much I actually *liked* him, but I respected him enough to honor his wish.

"The point is," I said, eager to get us back on track, "witches who use magic just have to be aware that there are lots of other forces at play, and things rarely go according to plan."

Asher folded his arms across his chest, his brow furrowed in concentration. "So that night at Norah's, when you—"

"Saved your ass from eternal oblivion?" I shot him a half-smile. We seemed to do better with teasing, especially when we got anywhere near the serious shit. "Is that the night you're referring to?"

Asher nodded, the tips of his ears turning red. "That was your magic, right?"

"Yes, but it wasn't a spell. That was Shadowborn magic.

Removing your soul was the only way to get you out of that trap. There were no other options."

"Wrong." Asher shook his head. "You could've just left me, Gray."

"Yeah," I whispered, my stomach lurching at the thought. He'd been so bruised and beaten, so close to death. "I could have. But I didn't."

"Thank you."

It was so soft, I wasn't even sure I'd heard him, but I didn't want to ask him to repeat it. We sat side by side, no longer touching, no longer teasing, no longer even looking at each other.

The fire had dimmed, the last few embers glowing red as the logs turned white with ash.

I felt him shift beside me, and when I turned to face him again, his ocean-blue eyes were cloudy with concern.

"You said all magic has consequences," he said. "and they're not always predictable."

I nodded, my gut already churning in anticipation of what was coming next.

"So here's the million-dollar question, Cupcake. What are the consequences of messing with a demon's soul?"

I'd been so caught up in saving his life, in getting him out of that damn trap, I hadn't thought about the consequences at *all*. Not that night. Not after. Not until right this moment.

Forcing a casual shrug, I cocked my head and smiled, hoping he couldn't see through it to the real fear beneath. "For starters, I was forced to kiss you. On the *mouth*."

I faked a shudder.

Asher waited a beat, then rolled his eyes, some of his earlier playfulness returning. "You think that's a *consequence*? I got three hundred years' worth of sleepover dates who'd beg to differ."

"Three hundred years' worth? Sounds like fake news to me."

"You keep telling yourself that, Cupcake." Asher leaned in to poke me in the ribs, and my book tipped forward. A photograph slipped out from between the pages, landing on the table.

"Is this your mom? Calla?" Asher asked, his voice surprisingly gentle. He picked up the photo by the edges, careful not to smudge it.

The agony of her death freshly speared my heart whenever I thought of her, but I'd been staring at that picture for days, and this time I was finally able to smile through the pain, more grateful than sad. Grateful she'd adopted me. That she'd loved me. That I still had this connection to her through the book she'd gifted me as a child.

From the moment she'd first told me about magic as a toddler, she'd been with me through every step of discovering and nurturing my own, right up until the night she died and I turned my back on the craft. On myself.

"I took that picture on her fiftieth birthday," I said. "I'd made her these horrible black cupcakes as a joke, but she loved them, even though the frosting turned her teeth green."

Asher smiled, and Calla seemed to return it, her eyes sparkling as always.

She looked happy, green teeth and all.

"What was she like?" he asked, returning the photo. Our fingers brushed as I took it from him, and a spark of awareness skittered up my arm.

It felt shockingly intimate, sharing this moment with him. But at the same time, it felt right. Natural.

I blinked back tears, smiling. "She was sarcastic and funny and she didn't take any shit from anyone. She could do complex magic and cook a gourmet meal with nothing but clippings from her garden, but she couldn't figure out how to work the DVR or find her way around the town she'd spent her whole life in. She was tough and fair and kindhearted and the best person I knew."

Asher nudged my knee with his, stopping me from slipping under a fresh wave of grief. Ten years after her death, they still snuck up on me, doubly so now that Sophie was gone, too.

"Was she as much a pain in the ass as you, too?" he teased.

"Absolutely."

"I think I would've liked her."

I laughed, imagining her standing in front of us, giving him the stink-eye. She'd never trusted demons to begin with, and Asher was his own special brand of crazy.

"Hate to break it to you," I said, "but Calla would've *hated* you."

Asher shrugged. "I have that effect on parents. I think it's the tattoos."

"Yeah, that must be it." I tucked the picture back inside the book, closing the cover and smoothing my hand over the triple moon design on the front.

"Hey." Asher nudged my knee again. "You'll figure it out, Gray. You just got the book back, and it's only been a few days since the shit hit the fan. You probably just need a recharge."

"I guess so." I shrugged, appreciating the vote of confidence, even if I didn't quite believe it myself. "I was just hoping I could—wait. What did you say?"

"That you'll figure it out."

"After that."

"You, ah, need a recharge?"

"Oh my God." Frantically flipping to the first entry, I read over the details of the ritual I'd performed when Calla had first gifted me the blank book. "I can't believe I missed this. It's so obvious!"

Magical tools worked best when they were properly cleansed, consecrated, and dedicated. Regular use and care kept them charged.

After spending the last several years buried in my safe in the backyard, the book had simply gone dormant.

The book seemed to think I was on the right track, too, suddenly warming in my hands.

Beaming, I turned to Asher and said, "Put a shirt on, Sex Vibe. We're going outside."

"Now?"

"Full moon tonight. There's no better time for a ritual."

"A ritual? You've gotta be kidding me." Asher rolled his eyes, but there was no trace of annoyance there. Smirking, he said, "What are the chances that we figure this out on *exactly* the right night? Coincidence?"

"Witches don't believe in coincidences." I zipped into the kitchen and ransacked the cabinets until I'd found everything I needed.

"Eye of newt? Hemlock?" Asher asked, following me. "I don't think we're stocked for rituals."

"I'll make do."

Asher watched skeptically as I put everything into a canvas grocery sack.

"We're good to go," I said. "Come on."

"That's it? No magic robes or anything?"

"It's best if I do this skyclad."

"Sky *what*?"

Grabbing the bag off the counter, I slipped past him and headed for the front door, not wanting to see his expression.

Not wanting him to see mine.

"Gray, what's—"

"Naked, Asher. I need to be naked. But *you* don't, so please put something on and stop gawking at me like you've never seen a woman without her clothes on."

I was nervous enough for the both of us.

But for the first time in days, that fragile, soap-bubble of a thing that'd been so doggedly eluding us was finally making an appearance: hope.

FOUR

GRAY

The demon could not stop smiling. That should've been my first clue that bringing him along was a terrible idea.

But it'd been years since I'd done a ritual, and neither the nudity nor the companionship were optional. I wasn't an earth witch—my power generally came from my realm —so in order to tap into the earth's energy, I needed an unobstructed connection. I also needed to know someone had my back in case things went sideways.

My magic was highly unpredictable these days, and I couldn't afford to take chances. There were too many lives at stake now.

About a quarter mile into the woods that backed up to the house, Asher helped me find a level spot nestled between two large sugar pines, and I set my stuff down and took a deep breath, filling up on the damp, earthy scent of the Pacific Northwest. Autumn had arrived early in the Bay area this year, and though it was still October, the oak and sycamore trees had already shed much of their coats, giving us a clear view of the full moon.

"This is perfect," I said. "Thank you."

Asher nodded and leaned back against a tree, folding his arms across his chest. He'd thrown on a faded red sweatshirt, but he'd left it unzipped, the dark lines of his tattoos still visible. "What happens now?"

"Now you do a perimeter check to make sure we're alone, then find a quiet spot at a safe distance to keep an eye on things."

"And you're just going to strip down to your birthday suit, say a few magic words, and roll around in the dirt?"

"Something like that."

Asher grunted, but he didn't move away from the tree.

"We're clear that you're to stay at least twenty feet away from me at all times unless I'm literally bleeding or on fire, right?" I asked, my cheeks burning at the thought of him seeing me up close. Naked.

"Define bleeding or on fire."

"Severed-artery-level blood loss and/or actual flames shooting from my eyeballs. Got it?"

"Now that you've given me a visual, yes." The smile he'd worn since we'd left the house disappeared, and he stepped forward, his eyes gleaming in the darkness. "Do what you gotta do, Gray. But the minute I sense anything even *remotely* fucked about this, I'll haul you back to the house before you can say frostbitten nipples."

His voice was harsh in the secluded midnight woods.

There was a time I might've bristled at his tone.

But that time had long since passed.

"It's not cold enough for frostbite," I informed him, "but yes, I'm with you. Anything goes wrong, we bail. I promise."

Asher nodded once, then headed off, leaving me to it.

Taking another deep, steadying breath, I shucked off my clothes and folded them into a pile behind another tree. The air was crisp, the chill breeze raising goosebumps all over my body and turning my aforementioned nipples into stiff peaks, but any discomfort was quickly overridden by the absolute rightness of the moment.

Beneath a pile of dried leaves, a thick layer of moss carpeted the ground, soft and welcoming under my feet. I closed my eyes and curled my toes into the earth, shedding everything that stood between me and this pure, uncorrupted connection. My mind stilled. My fears, my obsessions, my worries, my thoughts… All of them melted away until there was only *this*. Only now.

Kneeling on the ground, I got comfortable and got to work, laying out all the supplies I'd brought.

First, I poured a circle of sea salt around me, enclosing myself inside the ritual space and asking for protection from anything that sought to do me harm.

There were no sage bundles at the house, but I'd found some dried sage in the pantry, and now I poured it into a stone bowl and lit it, visualizing the smoke carrying away any negative energy. I'd also brought two taper candles—one white, one black, representing the forces of light and dark—and after clearing away a few leaves and sticks, I stuck them in the ground inside my circle and lit them.

Aside from tonight's impromptu scrying, I hadn't been able to access my magic since we'd come to the safe house, and I wasn't sure I'd be able to do it now.

But I had to try.

Picking up the book of shadows, I passed it back and forth through the sage smoke, cleansing away the negativity, the fear and hatred I'd felt toward my magic after losing Calla, the secrecy, the neglect.

"Release," I whispered. "Release, release."

The book felt instantly lighter.

After the sage cleanse, I set the book on the ground before me, pressing one hand to the cover. With my other hand, I drew a pentacle into the air, then closed my eyes, visualizing the moonlight on my skin, bathing me in her pale blue beauty.

I called upon my magic, remembering how it felt when it swirled low in my belly, its embers sparking to life inside me.

And then I waited.

And waited some more.

When I finally felt called to open my eyes, the scene before me remained static, but the familiar heat of my magic swirled, gently stirring to life. It yawned and stretched, and then it ignited, filling me with a tingling warmth.

It's working!

I closed my eyes again and pressed my hands to the

41

earth, the moss plushy and cool on my palms. Patiently I waited again, sending pulses of my magic deep down into the ground.

Seeking.

It wasn't long before I felt the earth's energy—her heartbeat—pulsing beneath my hands, connecting to my own magic and sending up waves of strength that spread up my arms and across my back, recharging me from the inside out.

It wasn't imagined or metaphorical or new age dreaminess. It was *real*, and so beautiful it made me ache.

The earth's innate magic was fueling my own, bonding with it and creating some new, powerful whole so much greater than the sum of its parts. It filled me completely, expanding inside me until I feared I wouldn't be able to contain it.

Slowly I leaned back, breaking the connection and moving my hands back to the book. The energy still flowed into me though, ropes of glowing green that wrapped around my hands and crept up my arms, similar to the black tendrils I'd so often encountered with my own magic, only this kind was pure and incorruptible and good.

I'd brought Sophie's blade—a connection to my best friend, a witch who I'd always carry in my heart—and now I used it to slice the tip of my finger. I squeezed a few droplets of blood onto each candle. The flames flickered at first, then surged brightly.

I'd rushed out of the house so fast I hadn't stopped to prepare a dedication, but now I thought of Calla and

Sophie, of all the witches that had walked this path before me, and the words flowed out effortlessly.

> *"By light of moon, 'neath shadow of tree*
> *Let all I once was join all I shall be*
> *Open this channel so that I may see*
> *And come to embrace this destiny*
> *By blood and by fire, I bind you to me*
> *Above and below, so mote it be."*

The book heated at my words, its own energy warm and buzzing.

A grin stretched across my lips, butterflies rising in my chest. It was coming alive again. Waking up after its long nap.

"Thank you," I breathed, wishing now that I'd brought an offering to leave behind—bread and wine, or maybe something sweet. I'd have to come back out later and give my proper thanks.

I sat back on my knees, clapping once to dispel the lingering earth magic. But instead of dissipating as it should have, the green light intensified, undulating across my skin in eerie waves.

I tried again, clapping harder this time.

The waves pulsed brighter. Faster. Deep inside me, my own magic began to swirl and spin.

High overhead, thick clouds skated in front of the moon, blanketing the woods in darkness. A stiff breeze blew into the circle and extinguished both candles.

Everything stilled. I cupped my hands in front of me, energy flaring into a blinding indigo flame between my palms. It didn't burn.

Of its own accord, the opalescent shield I'd first seen in the alley and in Sophie's bedroom the night of her murder appeared again, encasing me in its protective bubble.

Fear crept into my chest, spreading its icy fingers up and down my spine, but I took a deep breath and held my ground.

This was my magic, strengthened by that of the earth. There was nothing to fear. No harm would come to me.

The magic flared in my hands, and the book flipped open at my knees, pages shuffling so quickly all I saw was a blur.

It came to a dead stop at the first blank page.

By some invisible hand, words appeared across the top, glowing the same indigo blue as my magic.

The handwriting wasn't mine.

What are the consequences of messing with a demon's soul?
What are the consequences of messing with a demon's soul?
What are the consequences of messing with a demon's soul?

The line repeated a dozen times, faster and faster, then a dozen more, consuming the entire page before moving on to the next.

The dam inside me burst, my confidence crumbling beneath a wave of fear, unleashing a desperate scream.

I caught a flash of Asher's red sweatshirt. He was moving toward me, but when I tried to call his name, something cut off my words. My head snapped backward, and my eyes opened wider, staring up at the bare branches as the world began to spin. I felt the ground beneath me come alive, sensing rather than seeing hundreds of nightcrawlers and centipedes churning through the dirt, wriggling toward me as if I'd compelled them.

"Gray!" Asher called, but I couldn't respond. Couldn't move my head. Couldn't even shift my gaze to see him.

Calling on my meditation lessons from Liam, I took a deep breath, attempting to slow my heartbeat and stave off the adrenaline pumping through my veins. Focusing on the dark sky and the ground beneath my shins, I counted backward from a hundred, anchoring myself to this place. This time.

Above and below, so mote it be…

Slowly, the world stopped spinning. The force that had taken control of my body released me. Everything was still, just for a moment.

I tilted my head down and found Asher staring back at me across the distance, my magical shield keeping him at bay.

I was certain my own expression mirrored his.

Shock was the only word for it.

Where moments ago the woods had been quiet, now it hummed and chittered with life, animals of all kinds slinking out from burrows and hollowed logs and shadows.

After a beat, Asher's eyes widened, and I turned my head to find the source of his new concern.

A gray wolf loped toward us, her eyes milky white. Her once-gray fur was dingy and matted, her skull caved in at the top. One of her legs was caught in a rusty metal trap, the teeth of it embedded deep in her bone, the chain dragging behind her.

Too small to be a shifter, she looked like a regular wolf, once majestic and awesome, brought down by a human hunter's greed.

I didn't even think there were wolves around here. I wondered where she'd come from.

Unfortunately, she wasn't the only unexpected visitor.

The stench of rot and ruin filled my nose, making my eyes water.

Behind the wolf, a coyote and her pups followed closely. The pups were bloody and mangled, the mother's head bent at an odd angle, her neck obviously broken.

I whipped my head back around, trying to take it all in. Raccoons. Mice. Ground squirrels. Deer. There must've been two or three dozen animals encroaching on us, each one more mangled and decayed than the last.

They should've been dead.

By the looks of things, they *had* been.

Until now.

The realization slammed into me, forcing the air out of my lungs.

"Oh my God," I gasped.

Pain split my skull, and I grabbed my head, trying to alleviate the pressure. Asher pounded on the shield, his eyes wide with horror, but there was nothing he could do but wait.

My vision dimmed. Blood trickled from my nose and

into my mouth, dripping onto my book, the pages still glowing with that eerie script.

What are the consequences of messing with a demon's soul?

I didn't know if it was related to Asher's soul, but it was clear I'd brought these poor creatures back from death. And unlike what I'd done to Bean—and what I'd tried to do to Sophie—the animals appeared to have been dead long enough that their souls had already moved on.

I'd simply reanimated their empty, rotting corpses.

I slammed the book shut and jumped to my feet, willing the connection to break. To end this magical nightmare.

Finally, the protective shield dropped away.

"Gray!" Asher charged forward.

"No! Don't!" I held up my hands to stop him, but he ignored my feeble attempt at a barricade, crashing right through the perimeter of salt I'd poured.

Right through the very last thing that might've kept us safe.

FIVE

GRAY

Shambling.

That was the only word to describe their disjointed, unnatural movements.

Ignoring the pet cemetery, Asher whipped off his sweatshirt and wrapped it around my nude body.

"Remember when I said I'd haul your ass home the minute I sensed anything even *remotely* fucked about this?" He pulled a bandana from his back pocket and shook it out, then pressed it to my nose, squeezing gently. "Pretty sure this qualifies."

I grunted an acknowledgment, but a bloody nose and a bunch of mid-sized, half-decayed animals were the least of our worries.

Ten feet away, a pair of cougars emerged from the shadows. Unlike the others, their bodies were sleek and muscled, their eyes alert. If they'd been dead at all, it hadn't been for very long.

"Fuck *me*," Asher whispered.

"What do we do?" I asked.

"Get behind me." He dropped the bandana and reached for my arm, but the movement caught the cougars' attention, their heads following the motion of his hands.

Together they stalked toward us, the dead October leaves crunching beneath their paws. Taking a cue from the cougars, the rest of the animals crept closer, too. Some of them didn't even have eyes—just dark, rotting holes crawling with maggots.

"Don't make a sound," Asher warned, keeping me at his back. It was just as well; I wasn't sure I could've screamed, even if I'd wanted to.

I dug my nails into his forearm, frantically scanning the woods for an escape.

But there was no easy way out of this.

The female cougar growled, a wheezing sound that fell somewhere between a hiss and a moan and made every hair on my arms rise.

"Ash," I whispered. "I think she's—"

"Move!" He shoved me backward just as she lunged for him. Asher went down hard, struggling against her determined attack. With a snarl, she bit into his thigh. Blood seeped through his sweatpants.

"Asher!"

He howled in pain, shouting at me to stay back, but fuck that.

I glanced around for something sharp and heavy, but my book of shadows was the only thing within reach. I grabbed it and hauled it against my chest, my hands glowing a faint blue-green.

Magic surged through my arms, and I smashed the book down over the cougar's head, the power of the hit reverberating through my muscles. She yelped and slunk backward away from Asher, but her retreat was short-lived.

She came toward us again, slower and less certain now, her skull caved in, black blood dripping from her nose. I didn't think she could do much damage in her current state, but unfortunately for us, her male companion was right behind her. In a blink, he dove for Asher, catching him around the calf, tearing out a huge chunk of flesh from his already injured leg.

He was much more tenacious than the female, shaking off my hits as if they'd barely registered. When he made a move for Asher's throat, Asher blocked with his forearm.

The cougar sank his teeth in deep, right down to the bone.

Asher growled in pain, punching the animal with his free hand as I called forth my magic. My arms and hands tingled again, the blue-green glow surging bright as I slammed the book down over the cougar's head one last time.

Finally, the animal released him. He stumbled toward his mate, both of them wobbly on their legs but still standing.

Thankfully, they weren't in any shape to mount a counterattack.

"I *hate* fucking cougars." I dropped to my knees and

grabbed the bandana Asher had pressed to my nose earlier, wrapping it around the top part of his arm and tying it extra tight, hoping to slow the bleeding. I tore a strip of fabric from his ruined sweatpants, tying that one around his upper thigh. It was a temporary fix for what would quickly become a permanent tragedy if I didn't get him back to the house soon.

"Have you ever actually *tried* fucking a cougar?" he grunted out. "Older women can be quite… entertaining."

Clearly, the blood loss was already affecting his cognitive abilities.

"How can you think about sex when you're bleeding out?"

"Hi, I'm… Asher O'Keefe," he said, his breathing becoming more labored, despite his devilish grin. "Friendly neighborhood… incubus. Maybe you've… heard of me?"

"You do realize you're probably going to turn into a zombie cougar shifter now, right?"

Asher forced another smile I knew was for my benefit, the pain evident in his eyes. "No such… thing."

"Says the incubus to the witch." I grabbed the salt and tried to reform the circle around us, but there wasn't enough, leaving the area in front of us totally exposed.

Ditching the salt canister, I sat back on my heels, scoping out the situation. The cougars were severely weakened, but the rest of the animals were still shambling around us, their bodies twitching.

The smell was ferocious. I bit back another gag.

Asher let out a soft groan.

I checked on his wounds, struggling to keep my expression neutral. The beasts had done a number on him, shredding flesh and muscle. The bleeding had slowed, but only a little.

"We need to get you home."

"Don't bother," he said, gritting his teeth against a fresh wave of pain. "Unless you're… in the mood… for a quickie… I'm not strong enough."

One of the cougars ambled toward us again, taking a half-hearted swipe at Asher. I smashed the book down on its paw, flattening it.

There was no way we could keep this up all night.

Damn it.

I couldn't believe I was about to say this, but…

"How quick is a quickie?"

Asher cocked an eyebrow. "You serious?"

I rolled my eyes and reached for the zipper on my borrowed sweatshirt, telling myself I was only doing this to save our lives. "You're saying this will work, right? That if I give you my… energy… you can juice up in time to make a break for it before something else attacks us?"

"Oh, hell no." Asher coughed out a laugh, the bastard. If the animals didn't maul me first, that bad-boy grin was going to be the death of me. "But at least I'd die a happy man."

"Great." Not sure whether I was more relieved or flustered, I zipped back up, getting to my feet. Looked like I was in for a solo fight. "I'll be *very* happy to facilitate your demise later. Right now, I've got other priorities."

Like that wolf, and the other animals trailing in her wake.

Something seemed to be riling them up. The wolf staggered toward me, unsteady but no less menacing. The coyote nudged her pups closer, and a half-dozen mice followed, a nightmare formation of tiny skeletons striped with patches of matted, sticky fur.

A flightless seagull, way out of his element here in the woods, paced before us. With one wing and a smashed beak, the poor thing looked wasted.

"Get the hell out of here, Gray," Asher said. He was fading fast.

"I'm not leaving you, dick." I jumped in front of him just in time to stomp on two coyote pups. Their skulls collapsed like wet papier mâché under my bare feet.

God, I really hope they can't feel anything.

"I'll buy you some time," Ash said. "Get back to the house."

"No way. You'll die out here."

He shrugged, but his brave face was slipping fast. "Come back later… Give me another one of your… magical kisses."

"Forget it, O'Keefe. *That* was a one-time deal."

The milky-eyed wolf lunged for me, and I jumped out of the way just as it snapped its jaws. I leveled it with a swift kick to the side of the head, but it shook off my attack and circled back for more.

"They're… everywhere." Asher cursed as an army of mice swarmed over his legs.

I bent down to grab the book of shadows. The moment I turned my back, Asher was shouting again.

"Gray! Look out!"

The wolf leaped on top of Asher's chest. I swung the book with everything I had, decimating what was left of its skull.

Its skull. Not hers. I could no longer think of this abomination as a once-beautiful wolf.

It wobbled again, undeterred as I hit it repeatedly. After a last, crushing blow, it finally stumbled backward, dropping into a heap next to Asher.

I wondered how it'd gotten to this place. My throat tightened.

"I'm so sorry," I whispered.

But there was precious little time for guilt. Mama coyote was nosing the ground where I'd smashed her babies, and another group of coyotes emerged from behind the sugar pines—three adult males, big and ferocious. All of them dead. Or undead. Or whatever the hell these abominations were.

"Ash?"

No response but a groan. His eyes were half shut, sweat beading across his forehead. His skin was so pale he looked blue.

Fuck. *Fuck*!

"What the hell do I do?" I shouted.

As if it heard my call, the book heated in my hands, suddenly pulsing with that soft, blue-green light. I let the book fall open, watching as it flipped itself to a page near the beginning.

An unraveling spell.

It was one of the first Calla had taught me, mostly used in potion-making for fixing simple mistakes like using the wrong ingredient or going a bit overboard with the hemlock.

Not exactly the same situation here, but I had to try.

The book *wanted* me to try.

I quickly scanned the verse, then closed my eyes, reciting it out loud as I walked backward in a counter-clockwise circle:

> *"Backward I step, like time rewound*
> *Unravel the ties I've thusly bound*
> *Unmake my mistakes one by one*
> *And what I've made wrong is now undone."*

As I spoke the words, I visualized the animals back-tracking into the woods where they'd lain before my magic had disturbed them. I imagined each one lying down on the sacred earth, resuming the long process of decay until they were once again at rest.

I repeated the verse three times, completing a backward circle for each recitation, directing all of my focus and will into the desired outcome.

Into unraveling this horrible mistake.

"It's… working…" Asher whispered, barely conscious.

I opened my eyes. A spark of excitement zinged through

my body when I realized he was right. The animals were retreating.

When the last of the skeleton mice had finally left us, I dropped to my knees and checked Asher's injuries. His arm wasn't too bad, but his sweatpants were drenched with blood, his leg trembling.

I wasn't sure how much time he had, but there was no way I could get him back to the house or go for help now.

Sweeping the chestnut fall of hair from his eyes, I leaned over him and offered a gentle grin. "Guess I have to make an exception on that one-time deal, huh?"

Without another word, I lowered my head, pressing my lips to his.

Unlike the night in the devil's trap, he didn't pull away this time. His lips parted, and I deepened our kiss.

My hair fell into his face, and he moaned softly, sliding his hands into my curls and cupping the back of my head.

His tongue swept across mine, and despite the dire situation, a groan of pleasure escaped my mouth. The electric heat of his kiss fluttered all the way down to my toes.

Pulling back just for an instant, he met my eyes and whispered, "Are you okay?"

I nodded, nudging my nose with his. "I'll tell you if anything feels off."

It didn't though. Not when he tightened his hold on my head, pulling me closer. Not when I stretched out next to him, hooking my leg around his uninjured one, losing my mind as he broke our kiss again and made his way down my chin, my jaw, dragging his teeth across the sensitive skin on my neck.

The sweatshirt he'd given me was long enough to cover me from neck to knees, but underneath, I was completely naked. It would've been so easy to let this happen. To climb on top of him, tug down the waistband on his sweatpants, and welcome the hot slide of him inside me…

"Damn, Gray," he whispered against my neck, his kisses becoming more fevered. He wasn't a mind reader, but the incubus could absolutely sense the very hot, very dirty direction of my thoughts.

I didn't try to bury them, though. My desire, my touch, my body's responses to his kisses… All of it was healing him.

He was feeding on me. On my energy. My magic. It went on long enough that I should've felt drained, or at the very least tired.

Instead, I felt absolutely *amazing*.

Which was a clear sign it had to end.

What am I even doing?

He'd moved back to my mouth, but I broke our kiss, slowly pulling myself to a sitting position. Slowly willing my heart rate back to normal.

Asher sat up behind me, his hand on my shoulder. "Shit, Gray. Did I hurt you?"

"No."

"Why are you panting?"

I closed my eyes, taking a deep breath. Taking in the sounds of the woods—living nocturnal creatures skittering through the underbrush, the soft sigh of the pine boughs in the breeze—all of it natural and expected once again.

My lips throbbed from his kiss.

Why did he *think* I was panting?

"Gray?"

I turned and shot him a glare over my shoulder, waiting for the barrage of jokes. The innuendos. The reminders about how sexy he was, how he didn't even have to use his incubus "sex vibe" on me to get me all worked up.

But Asher seemed genuinely oblivious, the opportunity for poking fun passing us by. Instead, his eyes were full of worry.

He really thought he'd hurt me.

I sighed. "Asher, I'm good. Really."

"But I took… a lot." He tugged his pant leg up, peeling the sticky fabric away from his skin. The wounds were still there, but the bleeding had stopped. His flesh had already begun healing.

"It's weird," I said. I didn't know how to explain it, but rather than weakening me, sharing my energy with Asher had only made me stronger. "I feel like I could run a marathon."

"Are you sure?" He cupped my face, staring at me with wonder in his eyes.

"Okay, maybe a *half*-marathon. But still. I feel… Wow."

"Funny," he said, stroking my jaw. "I was about to say the same thing."

Heat crackled between us again, and I let out a nervous laugh, nudging him away. "Happy to hear it, Ash, but here's a hot tip: Next time you want to make out with me, just say it with flowers or chocolates like a normal guy."

His smile was back with a vengeance. Tugging on one of my curls, he said, "A normal guy wouldn't know what to do with you, Cupcake."

I lifted a shoulder. "I'm not that hard."

"*I* am."

I laughed, but then my gaze trailed down to his lap.

Holy hell.

Sweatpants left very little to the imagination on most men. On Asher, they were downright *obscene.*

"Quite a conundrum," he teased.

I was about to tell him to go wander off behind a tree and deal with that conundrum himself, when a new arrival captured my attention.

"What's wrong?" Asher asked, following my gaze to the raven that had landed on a sugar pine bough a few feet away.

"I'm pretty sure that's Liam."

"Seriously?" Asher groaned. "First a zombie cougar decides I'm a snack plate, and now I'm getting cock-blocked by Death himself? I should've stayed in bed tonight."

I got to my feet, glad to see Ash was feeling better, and glad that after days of radio silence, Liam had finally found his way back to us.

Glad that he'd interrupted what could have been a *total* disaster. The worst.

My unmet desire turned into relief that turned into

giddiness, and it quickly overtook me, filling me with a warmth and lightness that bubbled out in a laugh.

"Sorry, Liam," I called out. "You missed all the fun."

"More like you *ruined* all the fun," Asher added, but he was on his feet and smiling, too.

The raven vanished, and a black shadow slunk forth from behind the tree, skipping the usual explosion of feathers and fluidly morphing into a man with sun-kissed blond hair and glowing blue eyes that blazed with…

Anger?

Oh, shit.

"Gray Desario and Asher O'Keefe," Liam bellowed, snatching a fallen leaf from his shoulder and crushing it in a way that made me feel completely insignificant. "What against all that is holy have the two of you done now?"

SIX

LIAM

The stench of death was heavy in the air, tinged with the sweet, electric hum I'd come to associate with Gray. Her magic was as much an aroma as a feeling for me, yet it was becoming harder to distinguish from the scent of decay, as if the latter were attaching itself to the former like a parasite.

That was… worrisome.

"I was doing a rededication ritual for my book of shadows," Gray explained. "When the earth magic connected with mine, it all kind of…" She made a starburst gesture with her fingers.

"Define *this* for me." I mimicked her gesture. When she didn't further explain, I reached for her hand. "Come. We have much to do and little time in which to accomplish it."

The incubus stepped in front of her and folded his arms across his chest. "I don't think so, Spooky."

"Your protective instincts are admirable, yet wholly

misplaced, not to mention detrimental to Gray's education as a witch and—"

"Yeah?" He didn't budge. "Ever had a boot wholly misplaced up your—"

"Okay, boys." Gray placed a delicate hand on the demon's bulging bicep, which I was certain he'd flexed on purpose, and offered me a pleading glare. "Let's all take a deep, cleansing breath."

Reluctantly, we did as she asked.

"Better?" She nodded, as if answering for all of us. "Okay. So, Liam? I'm *really* glad you're back, and I'm sure you've got some concerns. Ash and I would love to tell you all about our wildlife adventures, but maybe we can move this party inside? Where there's plenty of tea and cookies and blankets and best of all, no dead things shambling around?"

"You make a compelling argument, little witch." I nodded and lowered my hand, but I didn't enjoy the soft pulse of emotion her pleading look had engendered inside me.

Perhaps I needed to consider alternate vessels.

"Could I get that in writing?" Gray asked. Her face, which had been pinched with worry in the wake of my admittedly rude opening remarks, transformed with a smile.

"That won't be necessary," I assured her. "The word of Death is more powerful and binding than ink on a page. I am everywhere, from the smallest speck of dust to the tallest mountains and—"

"Beyond. Yes, we're all aware." Gray smiled again, looping her arms around my neck and pressing her body against mine in an unexpected show of pure affection. "I was seriously starting to think you'd forgotten about us little people."

I patted her back awkwardly, still unaccustomed to my human vessel. Unaccustomed to her very warm, very human touch.

"I haven't been able to sense you until this evening," I told her, disengaging from the embrace. "I worried you'd left this realm altogether."

"What?" she asked.

At this, the demon finally showed a modicum of concern. "You're saying you couldn't get a read on her at the house?"

"If said house is where she's currently spending the majority of her time, then yes, that is what I'm saying."

"It's spelled," he said, snapping his fingers as the realization dawned. "Fae magic obscures it."

"A worthwhile investment," I said. "It's impervious even to me."

"But tonight isn't the first time I've been outside the house," she said. "I go out every day."

"Not this far from the property line, though," Asher said.

"And likely you weren't using your magic," I said, "so there was nothing for me to pick up on, so to speak." My mind clouded with frustration once again. "Unlike tonight, during which you could not have sent a brighter beacon if you'd—"

"Clearly we have a lot to catch up on." Gray smiled at me once more, then turned her back, heading toward a tree where it looked like she'd left her things. "Just give me a sec to get my clothes, and then—"

"Gray!" A male voice crashed through the woods, followed by a second, and then a third, each calling out for her as though she'd been lost to them for years.

I recognized them immediately. The crossroads demon, the vampire, and the wolf shifter.

Stealthy her friends were not.

"Ronan? Guys?" Gray called, squinting into the trees. The smile touching her face far outshone the one she'd offered me, and again some foreign unpleasant feeling overtook my vessel.

The trio burst forth like water breaking upon the shore, and she ran to them, letting them envelop her. It seemed an overdue reunion.

"How did you know we were out here?" she asked them.

"I scented you guys," the shifter said, offering the incubus a brief nod of acknowledgment. "And something that smelled a hell of a lot like death. And I don't mean Colebrook."

Gray wrinkled her nose. "It's… kind of a messed-up story."

Ronan took her hand, pressing a kiss to her palm. "You're okay though, right?"

"Better than okay."

Confused by the relief I sensed among them at their reunion, I asked the incubus whether fae magic had kept the others away, too.

He shook his head and laughed, placing a hand on my shoulder. "Stick around, Spooky, and you might just learn something here."

"Save your patronizing for another being, demon. A single eyelash on my vessel contains more knowledge than all of your feeble minds put together."

He laughed again, and I'd meant to ask him what he found so humorous, but that would've been a waste of time. I needed to know about Gray, not the company she kept. I needed to understand what had happened here. What her magic had created… and destroyed.

It was the first I'd seen of her since they left the city. For her protection, they'd kept her under magical lock and key. I couldn't fault them for that—in fact, I appreciated the caution.

But I *could* fault them for this.

"She should not have been encouraged to perform such a powerful ritual unsupervised," I said, glaring at the incubus. "Magic has consequences, and—"

"And Gray is perfectly capable of handling them," he said. "With or without supervision. Or permission, for that matter."

Gray lowered her eyes, blushing at his comments. "Thank you."

"The natural order is not something to interfere with

lightly." I took a step closer to her. "She could've been seriously injured or killed. Would we still be standing here arguing about permissions if that had been the outcome?"

"Dude. She took out a pair of zombie coyotes with her bare feet and bludgeoned two cougars and a wolf with a spellbook." Asher wrapped his arm around her shoulders, pulling her close. "Give the girl some credit."

"Come again?" Ronan said, glaring at them both. "And what the fuck happened to your leg?"

"Yes, clearly we've lost the plot somewhere along the way," Darius said, looking from Asher's torn and blood-stained pants to Gray's still-bare legs with a mixture of confusion and unchecked desire.

Emilio, her wolf shifter, remained silent, eyes and ears scanning the woods for danger.

Obviously, he was the smart one of the operation.

"I didn't mean to bring them back," she said, her earlier confidence dimming a bit. "The magic was a lot more powerful than I expected, especially since my book seemed completely dead before tonight."

"Not unlike the creatures who'd nearly killed you," I said.

"Hey!" She broke away from the demon and jabbed a finger into my chest. "The book is part of my magical heritage. You're the one who kept telling me to embrace it. So I did."

"Yes, but my intention was for you to do such embracing under the proper supervision."

"You mean under *your* supervision," Asher said. "Why is that, Colebrook?"

"The answer to that question is more complicated and multifaceted than your mind could ever hope to comprehend, and so is she."

I allowed him to interpret that as an insult, but the truth was, there was still so much *I* didn't even comprehend.

I'd made many assumptions when I'd selected this particular Shadowborn for my plans, and ever since her birth, she'd unknowingly challenged every one of them, forcing me to revise and improvise, to keep my ideas as fluid and fleeting as smoke.

She was, quite simply, like nothing I had ever known.

"Try me," Asher said now.

"Primarily," I said, quickly losing patience, "to ensure something like this doesn't happen."

I nodded behind the group, where two raccoons approached, trailed by a family of woodchucks. All of their eyes were vacant, their bodies in various states of decomposition.

Gray gasped, taking a step back. "I must've missed a few stragglers."

"Gray, what are you talking about?" Ronan asked.

Ignoring him, she grabbed her book of shadows and searched through the pages. "I'll try the unraveling spell again."

"That won't be necessary." I swept my hands across the expanse, instantly ending the last few resurrected lives she'd missed.

They dropped to the ground, animated no more.

"Show-off," the incubus muttered.

"Yes, well… I don't have a bludgeoning spellbook," I said. "I had to improvise."

No one made a sound.

"That was… a joke," I explained.

"I wasn't aware Death had a sense of humor," the vampire said.

"We have the *ultimate* sense of humor, vampire."

"*We?*" Ronan said.

I waved away his comment. How I chose to self-identify in my present form was none of his business, and this was hardly the time for philosophical discussions about the multidimensional nature of beings unconstrained by the physical rules of the prime material plane.

The tension among us still lingering, Gray finally set down her book and excused herself again to finish dressing. I noticed she put the demon's sweatshirt back on over her clothes, inhaling its scent as she did.

I shook my head. Humans were an odd creation indeed.

The men watched her closely as she jogged back over to us, each lost in his own private thoughts—thoughts they probably believed they were hiding.

Wherever the three new arrivals had been, they were clearly pleased to be reunited with Gray and the incubus. Nevertheless, I couldn't let this most recent incident go unmentioned.

"Gray," I said when she rejoined the group, "I'm not

sure I've impressed upon you the severity of what happened here tonight."

She opened her mouth, then closed it, nodding somberly. "You're right. That could've been a lot worse than it was. I didn't realize I had the power to do... whatever that was. Not with animals."

"It's another form of necromancy, of which there are many," I said. "And this was not the first time you've done such a thing."

"What? But I've never..." I watched as she combed through the archives of memory, the realization slackening her jaw. "Oh my God. The mice? But... I thought I'd healed them."

"No, Gray. You merely brought them back, like you did tonight."

She sat on the grass and pulled her knees to her chest.

"Gray?" Emilio sat down next to her. "What's he talking about, *querida*?"

She pressed her forehead to her knees and sighed. "Back in Phoenicia, before everything... you know. There was this stray cat that used to come around, blind in one eye, skinny as hell. Calla wouldn't let him in the house—she'd said he'd been around for years, and that he simply preferred to be wild. But I used to leave food outside for him anyway."

"Of course you did," Darius said fondly.

Gray lifted her head and smiled, but it quickly dimmed as she continued her story.

"One time I went out there to leave him some milk, and I found he'd left something for me instead—six dead field mice and a robin. I know it's supposed to be this great honor when cats do that, but I was horrified." She pulled her hands inside the sleeves of her sweatshirt and hugged her knees close again. "I tried to do a healing spell on them. I just focused all my intent on making them okay, so when they started moving again, I really thought I'd... God. I can't believe I resurrected them. I turned them into those... those *things*."

Gray shuddered at her memory, and the human vessel I'd chosen began to malfunction. Why else would I feel a sharp pain in my chest at her words? What was it in this collection of bone and muscle and blood that made me ache to touch her, to comfort her as the others did?

No matter. Her destiny was more important than the whims of my very human, very fallible body.

"Gray, we must leave now," I said. "You're at a critical point in your magical learning, and if we don't—"

"I can't," she said simply. "Not until I help my friends. The hunter has them in some kind of prison. I'm sure of it."

"How can you be certain they're even alive?" I asked.

"Can't you feel it?"

"I'm not... connected to them in the way I'm connected to you. I feel many things, all at once, backward and forward. Time is irrelevant. Only you are clear."

"Wait." She got to her feet, looking at me with new eyes. "How long have you... known me? Or sensed me like that?"

"Twenty-five years, seven months, four days, and nine

hours, give or take a few hours, adjusting for differences in local time zones and seasonal—"

"My entire life. You've been watching me my entire life." Her sadness turned suddenly to anger, though I couldn't comprehend why. "Well, you've got Ronan beat there."

The demon in question sighed. "Gray, it's not—"

"Show of hands," she said, raising her own. "Who here *doesn't* know my life story?"

No one moved.

"So just me, then," she said. "Great. Hey, my birthday's in a couple months. Here's a fun gift idea—maybe you could all put together a little scrapbook for me."

She swiped at her eyes with her sleeves, then crouched down to pick up her book. I thought one of the others would go to her, touch her as they always did, try to take away her pain.

But they remained still.

"You are Shadowborn, Gray," I said matter-of-factly.

"So you keep saying."

"I am connected to all Shadowborn beings, across all realms and time periods. It's not a choice, but it *is* a privilege. One I take quite seriously."

She lowered her eyes, seemingly unconvinced.

"None of us knows your life story," I assured her. "That is something only you can know."

"But I don't, Liam. That's the problem. My memories are faulty—you just proved that with the story about the mice. I don't even know how I got to the Bay or what led up to it—only that these guys found me and took me in. Which, by the way, I also don't remember. So much of my life is just a big… blank."

"Memories do not exist," I assured her. "Not in the way you believe."

"They don't exist for *you*, because you don't live in one time and place like we do," she said. "That doesn't mean they aren't important."

"They are only important because you make them so. Memory is a time-bound construct that has no more bearing on *this* moment than anxieties about a future you cannot possibly know."

"That's real Zen of you, Liam, but that's not how humanity works. We are made by our memories. Shaped by them, every time we take them out and polish them up again for another look, hoping to see something we missed the first time around. We change them as much as they change us, and the cycle never ends."

"And that, little witch, is your fatal flaw." I offered a sad smile. This was not the first time I'd had this conversation with a human, and it would not be the last. I feared that when their world finally ceased to exist again, it would not have been war or famine this time that proved to be their fatal undoing, but their inability to live in the present, haunted endlessly by a past that no longer existed for them and a future that hadn't yet dawned.

"Alas," I said, certain I'd no more change her mind than I had anyone else's, "life stories are just that. Stories, constantly created and revised, moment by moment. And no matter what anyone tells you, no one can write yours but you."

She was quiet a long moment after that—all of them were. As fiercely protective of her as they'd been, they seemed to be waiting for her to make the next call on her own.

"Well, here's the story we're dealing with right now," she finally said, her voice heavy with exhaustion. "The witches are still alive—you'll have to take my word on that. I've managed to bond with earth magic and reconnect with my book, which means I'm more powerful than I was even a week ago, though I still can't control it, obviously. And the hunter has to know we're looking for him. Best guess, he's either licking his wounds after you guys decimated his vampire squad, or he's focusing on the captive witches. Either way, I have no doubts he'll come after me again soon."

"Agreed," Darius said, and the others nodded. "You're safe at the house here, but staying at the house means you can't help us search for the witches."

"Not an option," she confirmed.

"Well, the bastard doesn't know you've leveled up," Ronan said. "So we've got an advantage there."

"He also doesn't know I can scry," she said.

Darius raised an eyebrow. "Excuse me?"

"More plot," Asher said. "We'll fill you in later."

"I was able to see Reva in the flames tonight," Gray continued, "and I believe she and the others are being held in a cavern, probably close to the ocean."

"So now that we're all here," Asher said, "what's the next play?"

Gray locked eyes with him, some new understanding passing between them.

I had no idea what, if anything, had happened since I'd last seen them, but it seemed they'd worked out their differences.

"The play is... I need training," she finally said. "Serious, hardcore, dedicated training."

"That's what I've been saying," I said, relieved she'd finally come around. "We can begin with—"

"Magical *and* physical," she said. "And I'd really love it if you guys could help."

"That goes without saying, *querida*," Emilio said, and the others grunted out their agreement.

Her earthly concerns were not my priority, but they *were* hers. As much as I wanted to ferry her away to the realm, I knew she'd never come to embrace her *true* destiny if she didn't accomplish her tasks here first.

So when she looked at me for my response, I nodded brusquely and said, "I believe this is the first time all five of us are in agreement."

Gray smiled, but there was no humor in her eyes, and the earlier exhaustion in her voice was quickly giving way to the fierce determination I knew she was capable of.

"We need to find that prison and save the witches," she said. "Their lives are the priority. But once I know they're safe?"

She met my gaze as if the answer was intended for me

alone. The look in her eyes sent a shockwave through my vessel—some icy, primordial emotion that tightened my chest and raised the hairs on the back of my neck.

Fear.

It was a human response to a perceived threat, though I couldn't understand why my body suddenly found her threatening.

"Gray?" I prompted. "What is it?"

The breeze whispered through the pines and stirred her hair, gently blowing the curls away from her face to reveal the grim set of her jaw. She clutched the book of shadows to her chest. Then, as smooth as water flowing over stones, she held out a hand before her, and a flame ignited in her palm, blue and beautiful and brighter than the moon.

The ferocity in her eyes took on a sinister cast in the glow, and in a voice all the more treacherous for its eerie calm, she made her proclamation.

"I'm going to watch him burn."

SEVEN

GRAY

Back at the house, the walk from my bedroom to Ronan's at the other end of the hall felt like a thousand miles, and when I finally reached up and knocked on the door, the sound of it made me jump.

"Come in," he said, and my heart rate kicked into overdrive. I'd just showered and changed into clean pajamas, but already I was sweating again.

Ronan and I hadn't been alone since we'd spent that one blissful night in each other's arms, just before we'd rescued Asher from Norah's attic.

There hadn't been time to talk after that.

But now there was.

Taking a deep breath, I stepped into his room.

This side of the house had high, slanted ceilings, and through a row of skylights over the bed, the full moon winked down at us from above.

He'd also lit candles, always preferring them to artificial

light, and I shut the door behind me, taking in the welcome sight of him in the flickering glow.

His thin beard had filled in a bit more, but his cheeks looked hollow, his eyes haunted.

"Hey," he said softly, a smile touching his lips.

All the time we'd spent together, all the years we'd been friends, I'd never felt as nervous and awkward as I did just then, suddenly conscious of dumb things like whether I was slouching too much or my shirt was too see-through or what I should've been doing with my hands. They'd made incredible, awe-inspiring magic tonight, yet now they felt like two slabs of ham dangling at my sides.

Why didn't these useless pajamas have pockets?

"You okay?" he asked.

"Yeah, it's just... It's been a long couple of days."

"Asher giving you a hard time?"

I shrugged and leaned back against the door, not even sure how to answer that question. "I don't want to talk about Asher right now. I came to say... I mean, I wanted... I was thinking..."

I closed my eyes, searching for the words again.

There was a time in our relationship—not that long ago, actually—when being around Ronan didn't leave me tongue-tied and stupid. But when I opened my eyes and found his autumn-hazel gaze looking back at me now, those days felt like a million years ago.

Being friends was different. I could be my fumbling, imperfect self and know that Ronan would still be there, looking at me as he always had.

But love? Love made me want to be better. To be perfect. To stoke the embers in his eyes into a red-hot, roaring fire.

Just-friends made me feel safe.

Love was making me feel crazy.

Maybe that was part of the package.

Ronan stepped closer, pressing his hands against the door and boxing me in with his arms. The fire in his eyes had already kindled, and as he swept his gaze down to my mouth, the flames spread straight to my core, heat licking between my thighs.

"I, um… I wanted to apologize about before," I stammered. "I didn't mean to bring up that stuff about my past and—"

"Apology accepted." The fire in his eyes blazed, and he leaned in close, capturing my mouth in a kiss.

Relief mingled with pleasure, and I sighed, parting my lips and welcoming the now-familiar taste of him on my tongue.

Ronan lifted me up and carried me to the bed, crashing down on top of me, kissing every inch of the skin he exposed as he peeled off my pajamas. Moments later he was naked, too, settling between my thighs, exactly where I needed him most.

I closed my eyes and whispered his name, threading my fingers into his silky hair as my body relaxed under the delicious weight of his, and it felt so, so right.

I knew how this would end. It might not happen tomorrow, or in a month, or even in five years. But it would happen. Ronan was my demon guardian; when I died, he'd have no choice but to deliver my soul to the demon who held my contract.

Ronan knew it, too.

But despite our already-scripted end, I could no more have walked away from him than I could've stopped the magic bubbling inside me. Both were part of my destiny, however tangled and complicated it may have been.

I suspected Ronan felt the same, and here in his bedroom, tangled up in the sheets as he finally slid inside me, kissing me as if the world were burning, there was no more awkwardness between us. No distance or discomfort. Only love and friendship and connecfedness and the warm, familiar touch I'd come to know.

To crave.

After spending the last handful of days apart, neither of us seemed capable of prolonging the exquisite end, and it wasn't long before I felt my muscles tightening around him, my body so, so close to the edge. Ronan let out a low growl, thrusting harder and faster, the pressure building until we had no choice but to tumble right over that sheer cliff together, spiraling down into pure, white-hot bliss.

Perfection.

After, I lay my head on his chest and closed my eyes, once again finding my home in the strong, steady beat of his heart.

"I hate being away from you," he whispered into my hair, his arms tightening around me. "Always have."

"Me, too." I relaxed into his embrace, letting out a soft sigh. "Did you guys find anything at Norah's?"

"Nothing that can't wait until tomorrow," he said. Then, with a low chuckle, "What about you? I was worried Asher would have some kind of bullshit incubus meltdown just so you'd kiss him again."

"No meltdowns." I laughed, rolling my eyes. "Only a nasty bite from a zombie cougar, and yes, I kissed him again, but that's *definitely* a story for tomorrow."

"If you keep insisting on collecting boyfriends," he teased, "we're going to have to start wearing name tags."

I sat up at that, pulling the sheet up to cover my bare breasts. "Okay, first of all, Asher is *not* my boyfriend."

"Mm-hmm." Ronan tugged the sheet back down, his lips buzzing lightly over my nipple before trailing up to my earlobe. "And Darius? Is he your not-boyfriend, too?"

"Darius is also *not* my boyfriend. But… he *is* someone I care about, yes."

Ronan didn't say anything, and my chest tightened.

"Does that bother you?" I asked, hoping I hadn't hurt his feelings.

Ronan nuzzled my neck and snuggled closer, his hand sliding across my belly, his touch so tender and protective it made my heart swell. "I could never be bothered by anything that makes you happy, Gray. That's all I want for you. For all of us."

"Even Asher?"

"Especially Asher." He sighed against my skin. "He's had a rough life. Same goes for Darius and Emilio. I know we've all had our differences—and I spend more time fantasizing about beating their asses than is probably healthy—but they're my brothers. No matter what fucked-up shit happens between us or how much time passes, that won't change."

In the short time we'd all been together, I'd sensed that bond among them, rekindling now after many years. It was one of the few silver linings in the black cloud of the witch murders and kidnappings; somehow, it had brought them closer.

A pang of longing hit my chest, but it was short-lived. Ronan, who always seemed to know exactly what I needed, kissed my shoulder.

"You're part of that now, too," he said. "Part of *us*. You have been for a long time." Ronan grinned, nudging me with his nose. "So if you wanted to start collecting boyfriends…"

I flashed him a devious grin. "You're okay with sharing. That's what you're saying?"

"As long as I'm your favorite." Ronan bit my neck, making me squeal.

"Well *that's* hardly fair," I said. "I'll have to give you monthly reviews to make an objective determination. I'll call it the boyfriend assessment test—BAT for short."

"What? Asher's an incubus, for fuck's sake! He's got a built-in competitive advantage!"

"Better bring your A-game, Vacarro." I cracked up, surprised at the direction this conversation had taken. Surprised at the direction *I* had taken.

The intensity of my feelings for Ronan was blinding. For

so long, I'd truly believed that the heart wasn't built to contain so much love—not for more than one person.

But maybe I'd been wrong.

I hadn't known the other guys long enough to start throwing around words like *feelings* or—god forbid—*love*. But the more time I spent with them, the more I felt my heart expanding, making room for the possibility that love wasn't something that had to be contained at all.

If love was truly infinite, I reasoned, perhaps our capacity for it should be infinite, too.

"What are you thinking?" Ronan whispered, smoothing the wrinkle between my eyebrows with the heel of his hand. The glint of humor in his eyes had dimmed, leaving the familiar intensity in its place.

I smiled, brushing my fingertips over his beard. I'd never said the words out loud to him; I'd never found the courage before. But tonight—with every kiss, every touch, every kind word—he'd given me strength.

"I'm thinking I'm in love with you, Ronan Vacarro," I whispered.

And there in the flickering candlelight, when he pulled me close and kissed my mouth and whispered three little words against my lips, too, I knew that this was real. That all the twists and turns in my life had led me here, right where I was supposed to be.

EIGHT

GRAY

Snuggling beneath the sheets with my bare back against Ronan's chest, I couldn't calm my giddy heart.

I still didn't know what to make of what had happened in the woods tonight, but for the first time since Sophie's death, the night had brought more rainbows than rain: scrying, reclaiming my book of shadows, connecting with earth magic, helping Asher, seeing Liam again, and most importantly, falling asleep in the arms of the man I loved.

Trying to, anyway.

"Mmm. Why aren't you asleep?" Ronan nuzzled the back of my neck, his voice soft and gravely in my ear as his hand slid up to cup my breast.

"If you want me to sleep," I said, "maybe you should stop touching me like that."

"I'll never stop touching you like this." His thumb ghosted across my nipple, sending a new shockwave of pleasure straight to my core.

"You're not… tired?" I asked, but his touch was making it extremely difficult to speak.

God, this man's hands… Someone should write a song about them…

"I was," he said. "But now I'm… up." He stroked my nipple again and rocked his hips forward against my backside, presenting some rock-solid evidence to back up his claims.

"You are such a bad influence, demon." Arching against him, I let out a soft sigh, already imagining the hot, sweet feel of him between my thighs…

A knock on the door startled us both.

"Ronan?" It was Darius, his voice urgent. "Is Gray with you?"

"Yes," Ronan said. "Now go away."

"If I'm interrupting, I can return at a more convenient time. Though I was hoping—"

"It's fine," I blurted out, at the same time Ronan said, "You're interrupting."

Darius let out a low chuckle on the other side of the door. "Well, which is it?"

Heat rushed to my cheeks, and I held my breath, not sure what to say next. Of course Darius was interrupting—that much was obvious.

But my imagination was already serving up a slow-motion play-by-play of my vampire stripping off his clothes, lifting the sheets, and climbing right into this bed with me.

With us.

Maybe it was crazy and self-indulgent, but some part of me—okay, a *few* parts, including one in particular that was currently very hot, and very wet—*really* wanted to let him in.

"Enter if you must," Ronan said, saving me from having to make the decision. He'd done his best to sound annoyed, but I wasn't buying it. His voice was still gravelly, still seductive.

And as Darius entered the room, Ronan's cock was still pressing quite urgently against my ass.

"Gray. Are you alright, love?" Darius asked, coming over to kneel beside the bed. His honey-colored eyes were warm and golden in the candlelight. "We didn't get a chance to talk about what happened in the woods."

Ronan huffed. "And you thought *now* would be a good time?"

"The sun will be up in a few hours, demon. If not now, I'll have to wait until tomorrow evening to speak with her."

"And the fact that she's naked right now has nothing to do with your sudden need to see her?"

Darius's lips slid into a cool grin, desire flaring in his eyes. "Now that you mention it…"

Beneath the sheet, Ronan's thumb traced over my nipple, making me gasp. He was still hard and ready, his breath hot on my neck, and when he shifted closer to me, I closed my eyes and let out a soft moan.

A low growl rumbled in Darius's throat, and holy *hell*, was I turned on.

"You okay?" Ronan asked, his lips brushing my neck.

"Very," I said softly. I opened my eyes, meeting Darius's desirous gaze. "But this is a little… awkward."

"Is it?" Darius asked. His gaze shifted to Ronan, who simply replied, "If you're staying, bloodsucker, close the damn door."

Darius did not need to be told twice.

He shut the door and returned to his position beside the bed, reaching for my face. When he traced the outline of my lips, I opened my mouth and slowly took him in, sucking gently as he slid his finger across my tongue.

Darius, all-powerful immortal vampire, shuddered.

He dragged his finger from my mouth, and I let my gaze trail down his body, wishing he was already naked but unable to say it out loud.

As if he could sense my trepidation, Ronan said, "Tell us what you want, beautiful. What you need."

Despite his momentary gruffness at Darius's interruption, there was nothing in Ronan's voice now but pure, red-hot fire.

I closed my eyes, suddenly shy.

Was this really happening?

Ronan and Darius both knew that I'd been… well… *close* with the other, and Ronan had already told me he was open to the possibility that I might develop feelings for the other guys.

But this was different. This was close… *together*. At the same time. The two of them, wrapping me in a cocoon of heat and pleasure, touching me…

"I've never done anything like this before," I confessed, opening my eyes to meet Darius's gaze.

His golden eyes shone with new heat. "Never?"

I shook my head.

Despite their thirty-something-year-old bodies, Darius was a centuries-old vampire, and Ronan was a centuries-old demon. They'd probably had lots of practice with three-somes and foursomes and who knew how many other-somes. But me? Until last week with Ronan, my sex life had been hibernating since before the invention of the smartphone.

"It's just us," Ronan said, his voice a smoldering whis-per. "Darius and me. We're in this with you no matter what. There's nothing to be embarrassed or worried about."

I nodded, comforted by his words, knowing that I could trust them.

"But you have to tell us what you want," Darius said. "No one is making any assumptions here."

"I know." I bit my lip, a flush of heat washing over me. Reaching a hand behind me to caress Ronan's leg, and one in front to touch Darius's face, I finally said it out loud. "I want you—both of you—naked in this bed with me."

Darius stood up to undress. I watched as he carefully unhooked each button on his shirt, slowly revealing the lean muscles of his chest and abdomen. In typical Darius form, he hung the shirt over the back a chair in the corner, careful not to wrinkle it. The pants and boxer briefs were next, sliding down his toned thighs at an agonizingly glacial pace, giving me an unobstructed view of his perfect erection.

My core throbbed with a need so deep it ached.

Just when I feared my body might burst into flames if he didn't touch me soon, he lifted the sheet and climbed beneath it, and I closed my eyes, taking a moment to appreciate all the little things—the way his whiskey-and-leather scent mingled with Ronan's smokey cloves-and-campfire. The warmth radiating among us, heating my skin. The rapid beat of my heart. How safe I felt nestled between them, my demon and my vampire.

How much I truly wanted this. Wanted them.

Wordlessly I wrapped my leg around Darius's hip and reached for his cock, stroking his perfect length as Ronan slid into me from behind, filling me completely.

"Relax," Ronan murmured into my hair, sensing my lingering awkwardness. "Let us do this for you. Let us make you feel good."

"I just…" I squeezed my eyes shut, still a bit uncertain. I wanted this more than anything, but the moment felt big and overwhelming—at least to me. I didn't want to misread anything. "I don't want to make assumptions, either. Are you sure you guys are into this?"

"We're into this," they said simultaneously, and I laughed, the last of my doubts eradicated by another one of Ronan's expertly-positioned thrusts.

Darius captured my gasp of pleasure with a kiss that unleashed a hundred butterflies in my stomach, and I tightened my fist around him, elated that he'd finally allowed me to touch him. To *feel* him.

To make him lose a little bit of that control he prided himself on.

With my other hand, I reached behind me again, seeking Ronan, wanting him to know how much I loved him. How much I needed him. I curled my hand over his hip and squeezed, pouring everything I felt into that touch, into my kiss for Darius, into all of this.

A growl rumbled deep in Ronan's chest, his cock thickening inside me as he rocked his hips, the pleasure inside me building as the three of us created our perfect harmony of kisses and heartbeats and sighs and searing-hot caresses.

As the candles melted down to nubs, throwing the last of their dancing shadows on the wall, I inhaled the mingled scents of Ronan and Darius again, my chest fluttery and warm. I felt so close to them. So connected.

So cared for.

When the last candle finally winked out and the moon rose higher in the sky, I pulled away from Darius's kiss, finding new confidence in the darkening room.

Safe in our private bubble of pure ecstasy, in the one place where I felt free to wish for beautiful, impossible things, I said, "I want to feel you inside me."

"Mmm." Darius ran a finger between my breasts, trailing down my abdomen, dipping down lower and lower until he found the perfect spot.

Teasing my aching clit with a slow, featherlight touch, he whispered, "You are absolutely insatiable, aren't you?"

"I could've told you that." Ronan bit the back of my neck, teasing the sensitive skin at the nape with his tongue.

"For you guys? Yes. I'm…" *Oh, God.* My scalp tingled with goosebumps, and I gave in to a full-bodied shiver, which Ronan took as encouragement to deepen his thrusts.

He was going to drive me wild, and Darius was going to tease me until I begged him for more, just like he'd promised that night we'd hooked up in his car.

And despite my pride and my dignity and all the teasing I'd doubtlessly endure later, I was absolutely going to give in.

"*Please*, Darius," I begged. "I need you right… *God*, yes. Right there. I mean now. Right now. I… I want you guys to switch."

But unlike me, Darius had no trouble sticking to his principles. "As much as I'd love to indulge you, little brawler, we've already discussed how that particular moment will unfold between us. Was I not clear?"

"Was I not a control freak?" Ronan teased, doing a pretty good impression of Darius's accent.

"We will be in *my* bed," Darius continued, unbothered by Ronan's jabs. "*I* will be taking charge, and—"

"See?" Ronan said, kissing my shoulder as he worked his fingers up to my nipple again, showing no regard for the fact that I was melting into a puddle under his touch. "Control freak."

"*And*," Darius said, "the hellspawn twat will be nowhere in sight."

"Can you believe this guy?" Ronan grunted. "I let him into *my* bed, but he won't return the favor? I told you—never trust a bloodsucker."

The two of them carried on with this banter as if I wasn't about to spontaneously combust.

"I don't trust either one of you at the moment," I breathed, unable to form coherent thoughts as Ronan teased my nipple and Darius increased the pressure on my clit. "The two of you are… conspiring... against me."

"Why on earth would we do that, love?" Darius asked.

"Because you're a pair of no good, very bad—"

"Indeed." Without warning, the vampire pulled me on top of him, and Ronan followed effortlessly, kneeling behind me and urging me up onto my hands and knees. As I hovered over Darius, my hair falling into his mouth, Ronan gripped my hips and slid back inside me with a deep, delicious thrust.

"You like your boyfriends bad," Ronan said, running his palm up my spine.

"*Very* bad." Darius raised his head just enough to reach my breasts, his mouth closing over my nipple and sucking it to a tight, diamond-hard peak. He grazed my tender flesh with his teeth, and I gasped, learning a new appreciation for the phrase *hurt so good*.

Just when I thought I couldn't take another moment of his exquisite brand of torture, he moved to my other breast, flicking my nipple with his tongue until my whole body was trembling with need.

I reached for him again, wrapping my hand around him, stroking him harder and faster. Words fell away, leaving only breath and softs sighs and whispered names as the three of us balanced on the edge of bliss together, looking down over the abyss, knowing we had mere seconds before the wave washed us out to sea.

My thighs were slick with sweat, and pleasure hummed through every nerve, every cell, each one crying out for more, more, more.

Ronan was moving faster again, deeper, his fingers digging into my hips. Beneath me, Darius's abs tightened, his cock growing even harder as he claimed my mouth in a bruising kiss.

Darius was the first to go, a deep rumble starting in his chest and escaping in a final moan as he rocked into my hand. The feel of his movements set me off next, my body clenching around Ronan as the orgasm exploded inside me, bringing my demon right along with me, his growl of pleasure reverberating straight into my chest as he clenched my hips and shuddered against me.

It felt like an eternity before we finally stilled. The room had fallen silent, the moon sharing the last of her distant light through the skylights above. It felt like she was peeking at us, and I smiled to myself, basking in her muted glow as I finally caught my breath, my heart feeling full and content.

When I had no more strength to hold myself up, I gave in to my delicious fatigue and collapsed onto the bed.

Darius caught me with another kiss as Ronan pulled the sheet over us.

Together they wrapped me up in their arms, and in that moment, I gave myself over completely, trusting that no matter what else came our way, no matter what monsters awaited us on the other side, these strong, generous, incredible men would always be there to catch me when I fell.

NINE

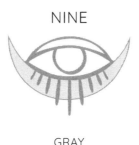

GRAY

Is that bacon?

Alone in Ronan's bed, I awoke to the heavenly scent of a home-cooked breakfast, the afternoon sun streaming in from the skylights and heating my skin. Darius had gone down to his basement quarters sometime before sunrise, and Ronan left early to run some errands in town, but I didn't mind waking up solo. I didn't need to see them to know they were still with me; my thighs burned with a delectable ache that brought back every red-hot memory of our wild night.

After a quick shower to chase the stiffness from my muscles, I wandered out into the main area, prepared to offer Emilio my first born in exchange for the breakfast of champions he'd clearly been working on.

Famed cooking skills aside, I was looking forward to spending more time with him. Of all the guys, he was the one I knew the least, and I still hadn't gotten a chance to truly thank him for the kindness he'd shown me, especially on the night of Sophie's murder.

My shoulders dipped under the weight of grief, still so fresh, so raw. Sometimes I still couldn't believe it had actually happened. That this was my life, and my best friend was no longer part of it.

Despite the hollow in my chest, I pictured Sophie's face, her brows drawn together in concentration as she painted her mandala rocks, and I smiled. Thinking of her now was bittersweet, but I'd take a lifetime of pain if it meant I got to see her face for one more second, even if that second was only a memory.

Blinking away tears, I squared my shoulders and headed into the kitchen, more than ready to join Emilio for breakfast.

"What's cookin', good lookin'?" I asked, my spirits already lifting. "It smells amazing in—"

The sight stopped me in my tracks.

To my endless frustration, the shirtless man humming at the stove wasn't the kind-hearted shifter detective who loved to cook, but the cocky incubus who loved to push my buttons.

"Good morning, beautiful," Asher said. "Or rather, good afternoon."

"Where's Emilio?"

"Supply run with Ronan." Asher lowered the flame on whatever he was sautéing and peeked at me over his shoulder, a sly grin plastered across his face. "They'll be back in time for my epic feast, though."

Giving him a skeptical eye, I said, "Since when do you cook?"

We hadn't shared a single meal together the entire time we'd been secluded at the house.

"I don't *cook*." Asher shrugged, and I forced myself to keep my eyes from wandering back down to the dark, seductive tattoos snaking across his body. "Not really. But I do make a pretty mean spinach, mushroom, and Swiss scramble."

My stomach rumbled. "I love scrambles."

"I know. Over the years I've made it my business to learn *exactly* how a woman likes her eggs in the morning." He winked at me before turning back to the pan, the heat between us cranking up from simmer to boil once again. "There's bacon warming in the oven, too. Emilio already made the fruit salad, but you can set the table if you want."

"Could you maybe… put a shirt on while you do that?"

"Hmm. Distracting you?"

More than you know…

"Yes. Health code violations are *very* distracting. I'm surprised none of your three hundred years' worth of sleep-over dates ever warned you about the dangers of unsanitary kitchen conditions."

"I guess some things are worth the risk." Setting aside the sautéed mushrooms and spinach, he cracked a bunch of eggs into a Pyrex mixing bowl and added a splash of milk, whipping it to a perfect froth with a flex of his catalog-worthy forearms.

Hot.

"I know."

"No, I mean…" Shit. Had I said that out loud? "Hot *coffee*! You didn't let me finish. I really need some hot coffee."

God, what was wrong with me? Darius was right—I *was* insatiable. Maybe I was part incubus, somewhere way back in the mysterious family bloodline, and all that magical energy I'd been burning through lately needed to be replenished with the very hot, very intense sex I kept craving…

Or maybe I just needed to up my caffeine intake.

Thankfully, a fresh pot of coffee sat on the countertop like a beautiful beacon in a storm. Helping myself to a mug full, I said, "Why the hell are you so chipper today, anyway?"

Asher laughed. "Three guesses, Cupcake. That's all you get. One, two, *three* guesses."

I rolled my eyes. "Yes, Asher. Three guesses is the usual amount of guesses one gets."

"Three," he went on, "as in a *triad* of guesses."

"Are you drinking already? It's not even noon."

"A *ménage* of guesses."

"What are you even—"

Oh, God. No wonder he's so damn happy.

Ronan, Darius, and I had generated more than a little sexual energy last night, and that was *after* Ronan and I had spent time getting reacquainted in the very carnal sense of the word.

Asher must've gotten a big fat dose of… everything.

Not to mention, he'd probably heard the sounds coming

from behind Ronan's bedroom door last night, most of which belonged to me.

"Are all incubuses total pervs," I snapped, "or is that just another one of your special charms?"

"Sex isn't perverted, Gray," he teased. He poured the egg mixture into the frying pan with the veggies, bringing it all to sizzle. "When two people love each other very much… Wait, did I say two? I meant three. Or more. No judgments as long as everyone's all in. All in! Ha! Pun intended."

Asher continued to amuse himself at my expense, but after my night of total ecstasy, the annoying incubus couldn't bring me down.

I offered him a sympathetic frown. "I'm sorry you're hurting right now, Ash. Dry spells can be rough. But it's not you. It's them. Most likely."

Asher bristled. "Dry spell? Speak for yourself."

"Mmm-hmm." I sipped my coffee, grinning behind my mug.

"I'm *not* in a dry spell," he insisted. "I'm just… selective."

"Of *course* you are."

"You know, it's not that easy to just—"

"Asher?" I joined him at the stove, placing my hand flat against his bare chest. His heart hammered beneath my touch. "I need to tell you something. It's important."

Fingers gripping the spatula, Asher swallowed hard, ignoring the pan of eggs sizzling behind us. "Yeah?"

I stood on my tiptoes and pressed my lips to his ear, and his heartbeat kicked up a notch.

"Whatever you do," I whispered, enjoying the smattering of goosebumps that rose along the back of his neck. "Don't. Burn. The bacon."

The crunch of a car rolling up the long gravel driveway was a symphony to my ears, and I set down my mug and headed for the front door, leaving Asher gaping like a fish, his mind casting for a comeback that just wouldn't come.

The guys were loaded down with grocery bags, so while Asher worked out his issues at the stove, I helped unload the car and put away the goods. Most of it was essentials—food and alcohol—but there was also a big bag overflowing with what I could only describe as girly gear.

"What is all this stuff?" I asked.

"It's for you, *querida*," Emilio said. "We didn't know what you normally used and Ronan didn't want to rifle through your bathroom drawers. We just got a little of everything."

He wasn't exaggerating. I found several bottles of shampoo and conditioners, hot oil treatments, a curly hair mask, moisturizers for day and night, peppermint foot lotion, a bunch of makeup for all different skin types, hair accessories, shower gel in every fruity combination, a shower poof, and a back scrubber thingy that looked like a bunch of shower poofs sewn together with a loop on each end.

I hadn't even finished digging through the bag yet, and there was already a big fat lump in my throat. Maybe bath and beauty products were a silly thing to get excited about, but no one had ever done anything like that for me before. Until that moment, my entire beauty routine had been built around whatever was on sale and didn't smell like someone's grandma vomiting up rose petals.

This felt like a luxury, and it'd been a long time since I'd gotten one of those.

Catching the shine of emotion in my eyes, Emilio frowned. "We can get something different if that's not—"

"No. It's perfect." I smiled. "All of it. I don't… I don't even know what to say."

"*De nada.* We just want you to be comfortable here." Emilio squeezed my shoulder, and the room fell silent. No one bothered to fill in the rest of that sentence, but I sensed we were all thinking it.

Because we don't know if you'll ever be able to go back home.

I thought of the cute little house I'd shared with Sophie, and a sliver of regret touched my heart. But despite how much I'd loved that place, deep down I knew home wasn't a place at all. Places were easier to come by; I'd had lots of them during my time on the streets, often with strings attached.

But I'd also been blessed with homes. First with Calla. Then with Ronan. Then Sophie.

Now, I was making a new home all over again. Temporary or not, that's what this place was to me.

"Thank you," I said, stretching up to press a kiss to Emilio's cheek. "For everything."

He stroked his hand down my back, and when I finally pulled away and met his eyes, he quickly dodged my gaze.

The wolf shifter was actually blushing.

"Alright," Asher said, clapping once. "I hope you guys are hungry, because I'm pretty sure I outdid myself here."

"Wow," I said, scoping out the spread he'd set up on the counter. "I didn't know this was going to be such a formal affair. You actually put on a shirt?"

"Had to." Asher flashed me his bad-boy smirk, reminding me that no matter how long we played this little game, he'd always come out ahead in the end. "You were drooling so bad, the bacon was getting jealous. Now let's eat."

TEN

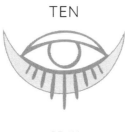

GRAY

We served up heaping piles of food, buffet style, then took our places at the dining table—a massive oak slab with polished benches on either side, centered before a row of huge bay windows that overlooked the backyard.

The eggs were cooked perfectly, the bacon nice and crisp, the fruit salad sweet and fresh. But despite our happy family meal and the beautiful home we were now officially sharing, tension had crept in and settled over us like a cloud.

Every one of us at this table—as well as the vampire still sleeping downstairs—seemed to be holding a different piece of the puzzle. I was sure they thought they were protecting me, shielding me from some new danger or painful knowledge. But the only way we were going to solve this thing—to help the witches and erase the hunter from existence—was to work together.

No longer willing to sit silently and wait for someone

else to take the lead, I said, "We need to talk about what you guys found at Norah's place, and about what happens next. I'm supposed to start training with Liam today, but that could take weeks—and that's just the magic stuff."

The guys exchanged glances, but I didn't give them a chance to contemplate.

"What are the chances the hunter will stay quiet much longer?" I asked. "We need to move on this, and we need to have a solid plan. That means no secrets, no matter how ugly the truth might get."

"Gray's right," Emilio said, pushing his plate away and leaning back in his chair.

"For starters," Ronan said, "just because he's quiet doesn't mean he's easing up. We have to assume he'll try to take another witch, probably sooner rather than later."

"Any witch in the Bay is a target," I agreed. "Neighboring towns, too. If my hunch is correct, he's keeping them on the coast, and probably commuting back and forth as needed."

I filled in the guys about what I'd seen in the flames, and though it probably didn't qualify as irrefutable evidence in the eyes of Blackmoon Bay's finest, they all agreed it was worth investigating.

"If what you saw was real," Emilio said, "and we've got no reason to doubt that, any witches west of the Bay need to be on high alert."

"Agreed," Ronan said. "But that doesn't mean other communities won't be hit, too. Gray's vision suggests he's keeping them near the ocean, but even if we narrow that down just to Washington state, we're still talking about hundreds of miles of coastline."

"It's a start," Emilio said. "We just need to move through this methodically, ruling things out and slowly narrowing our search."

"Slowly isn't an option," I said. "Witches' lives are at stake."

I took a long pull from my coffee, trying not to let the impossible odds bring me down. Despite the obstacles, there was still hope—the witches I'd seen were definitely prisoners, hurt and scared, but alive. And as long as they were alive, there was still a chance we could help them.

Haley. Reva. The others. God, there'd been so many.

We have *to find them…*

"I'll coordinate with state and local law enforcement as best I can," Emilio said, "but we have to tread lightly."

"No shit," Ronan said. "Human cops will make this even more of a mess than it already is."

Emilio nodded. "The good news is there are quite a few shifters working as cops in this state, especially on the outskirts. The bad news is the coastal communities in particular are territorial as hell. Working with them is a nightmare on the best of days."

"Even with your… connections?" Ronan asked.

"*Especially* with them," he said. He and Ronan exchanged an odd glance, but before I could ask about it, Ronan was speaking again.

"The other issue is we don't know who else this jackoff

is working with. He had Hollis and the other vamps in his pocket. He may be infiltrating police departments, too."

"And we still don't know their connection to the vamps who attacked Darius and Gray at the morgue," Emilio said. "That's another loose end, and I *really* don't like loose ends."

I took another sip of coffee, swallowing down the shame that rose in my throat at the mention of the morgue vamps. Darius kept on telling me that what I'd done—that the murder of the female vampire who'd attacked me— was self-defense, but that didn't make it any easier to accept.

Eager to move on from that particular topic, I said, "So what did you guys turn up at Norah's? Anything?"

"Not much," Ronan said. "A few basic witchcraft supplies, some notes, but nothing that raised any red flags. If Norah had any computers or phones, she either took them with her, or the vamps cleaned her out before we got there."

He got up from the table and headed into the kitchen, returning a minute later with the coffee. "Anyone need a warmup?"

"You really think she'd take everything with her?" I asked, holding up my mug. "How long was she planning to stay away? I got the impression it was a temporary thing."

"No idea." Ronan topped me off, then poured the rest into his mug, setting the empty carafe on the table. "Norah either cleaned up her tracks like a pro, or she's innocent, and she really did leave town with every intention of keeping Reva safe, no matter how long that might've taken."

"Doesn't look like that plan worked out," I said, remembering the fear I'd seen in Reva's eyes last night. Poor kid. I really hoped Norah was innocent, if for no other reason than sparing Reva the crushing pain of learning the woman who'd given her a home was a traitor.

"Neighbors were starting to ask questions about the broken windows," Emilio said, "so we cordoned off the house and told them there was a robbery. I've been trying to reach Norah to let her know about the property damage, but she hasn't returned my calls."

"What about the dead vampires?" I asked, recalling the pile of bodies they'd left, including the charred mess of one Clayton Hollis.

"Taken care of," Ronan said, and I didn't press for details.

"Alright, let's assume Gray's vision was accurate." Asher, who'd been happily shoveling food into his maw, finally jumped into the conversation. "Our best lead is still the rogue vampire. Things may have gone south between him and the hunter, but he's gotta know something about the dude's plans or hideouts."

"Yeah, but where is he?" I asked. "If Hollis was telling the truth, the hunter's blood bank bailed on him. That vamp is probably in hiding now—the hunter likely wants him dead."

"Not to mention the Grinaldi family," Emilio said. "This

rogue attempted to break their code. They won't let a slight like that go unpunished."

"Darius's people are making progress with Grinaldi," Ronan said. "He thinks he'll be able to secure a face-to-face meeting soon. We'll know more about that in the next day or so."

"In the meantime," Emilio said, reaching for Ronan's coffee mug and stealing a sip, "I'm still working the case. We're combing through security footage from all the street cams in the area between Haley's place, where she and Asher were jumped, and Norah's, where Asher was left to rot like a piece of bad meat."

"Dude." Asher, who'd returned to his fourth helping of eggs as if it'd been days since his last meal rather than minutes, dropped his fork. "I'm right here."

"Thanks to Gray," Ronan said, winking at me across the table. "She saved your ass."

"Maybe not one of my better decisions," I teased.

"Aww, you two are *adorable*." Asher grinned, but the mischievous glint in his eye told me exactly where his comments were heading. "You know, Ronan, I just realized something about that night. Technically, I've been inside your girlfriend. Is that weird for you?"

Ronan plucked a grape from the fruit salad bowl and chucked it at Asher's head. "Keep dreaming, cocksucker."

"Every night and all day long, brother," Asher said.

The demons looked at me, both laughing, waiting as if they were expecting me to hit Asher with a zinger of my own.

But I couldn't.

What had happened between us the night I'd saved him —the night I'd taken his soul inside me—wasn't something I could easily joke about. Not while the ghosts of Asher's past still haunted me.

"Anyway," I said, "we've got our work cut out for us. Until we find the rogue vamp or the hunter, we have to keep tracking down leads, training, planning for the inevitable. And I need to get a *lot* stronger with my magic."

"You're scrying now," Asher said. "And you've got your book juiced up again. That's a good thing, right?"

"It is, but you have to remember… I'm still new at this. I buried my magic for more than a decade, avoiding anything even remotely connected to witchcraft. I might as well be starting from scratch."

"We've got your back, Gray," Ronan said. "You just focus on your training and leave the rest to us. At least until we know more."

"That's the plan," I said, looking down at my hands in my lap. They looked like regular hands, no glowing, no sparks, no blue flame. If I concentrated, I could feel the magic, a low and constant current humming through my blood, but I still couldn't call it up at will. Not every time.

I needed to learn. To perfect. No matter what leads Emilio could uncover, no matter what Darius learned from Grinaldi, no matter what the demons had in store, deep down I knew this would all come down to one thing, just like it always had, for millennia.

Magic.

Witches had it, but most of us hid it. Mages had it, but lost it, and then they evolved into brutal hunters, desperate to get it back. Reclaiming what they believed was their birthright became their prime directive, the thing that drove them to every thought, every belief, every action.

It stood to reason that the stronger and more connected to my magic I became, the more desperate the hunter would become to possess it. To possess *me*. And desperation had always been the hunters' downfall. It clouded their judgment, blinded them to their flaws, and led to mistakes.

We just had to be in the right place at the right time when he made his.

"And Mr. Surfing Philosopher?" Asher blurted out, his mouth full. For someone who needed sexual energy to survive, he had a damn hearty appetite for regular food. "Where does he fit into all this? Because if we're taking a vote, mine—"

"Doesn't count," I said. "Liam's involvement is non-negotiable. None of you can help me with my magic—not like he can."

"Is that *all* he's doing?" Asher asked. "You two seemed pretty chummy last night."

"I don't know what you mean by *chummy*, but Liam has been an ally from day one, and he's given us no reason not to trust him." I rose from my chair, gathering up the dirty dishes. "Not to mention the role he played in saving your life."

Asher stayed quiet a full minute after that. But just when I thought the matter was settled, he said, "So where *is* your knight in shining highlights, anyway? Shouldn't he be here by now?"

"He's… You know." I shrugged, making my voice sound breathy and mystical. "Everywhere, all at once, within and without."

The guys laughed, but the truth was, I had no idea where Liam was. Even in human form, he couldn't stay on the earthly plane for long periods of time, and it's not like his presence in my magical realm was a given, either. He mostly just… arrived. And then departed.

He'd said he'd be here today to start my magical training, but I had no idea when, where, or in which form he might show up.

Still, I trusted that he'd come through. He'd already helped me so much, guiding me through the strange and often frightening developments of my magic. My so-called destiny. I wasn't sure if *friend* was the right word just yet, but he'd certainly been loyal and trustworthy. I didn't take that lightly.

"He's in this with us," I reiterated, feeling a sudden need to defend him. "Even if he's unpredictable and not always physically present."

"I think he's in this with *you*," Asher said, his tone implying what he didn't say out loud. "And I don't know if encouraging that is the best idea."

Why was he always such an asshole? It's like he had a built-in decency limit. Two minutes of being nice and his circuits started overloading.

"To reiterate, *dick*," I said, "he saved your life. Maybe *that* wasn't the best idea."

"Ash," Ronan warned, "you're heading for a timeout. And by timeout, I mean an ass-whooping. Gray, ignore him." Ronan reclaimed his coffee from Emilio, then said, "Death—Liam—whatever you want to call him… He's bound to Gray's power. Necromancy is his domain, and he's connected to her no matter what. Nothing we can do about that."

I dropped the stack of plates I'd gathered back onto the table, making them jump. "Stop talking about him like he's some kind of parasite! He's an ally, you guys. He wants to help us. I *know* he does."

"He's Death," Ronan said plainly. "Chaotic neutral. No alliances. No enemies. No friends. The great equalizer. By nature, he can't help us. You might inadvertently be helped by something he says or does, but it's not because he's this stand-up guy choosing to do the right thing."

"You're wrong," I said. "He's… well, he's Liam now, not just Death."

"He's wearing a *suit* called Liam," Ash pointed out. "Not the same thing."

All three of them were looking at me with pity in their eyes, like I was a little kid who kept insisting Santa was real, no matter how many times he'd forgotten our address.

It stung. Not because they didn't trust Liam—they didn't know him like I did, and trust had to be earned—I understood that. But because it felt like they didn't trust me.

No matter what I did, no matter how hard I tried, I'd always be their weakest link.

"Gray," Ronan began, but I shook my head, grabbing the stack of dishes I'd dropped. I brought them out to the kitchen and loaded up the dishwasher, then put away the leftovers and washed all the pans Asher had used.

When I'd calmed down enough to trust that I wouldn't lash out at them again, I returned to the dining room.

They were right where I'd left them, silent and unmoving.

"Okay," I said, and they all looked up. "I have a *lot* to learn, and zero time to do it. Self-defense, tactical fighting, first aid, basic survival techniques, magic... Forget crash course. I need a full-on wreck."

I pulled out a chair, taking a seat next to Emilio.

"I trust you guys," I went on. "I trust that you're doing what you think is best, that you know how to deal with certain things that I don't, and it goes without saying you have a *lot* more experience."

"It's not about experience," Emilio said, but I held up my hand.

"I know I haven't always made the best decisions," I said, "but I'm trying. Maybe I don't deserve it yet, but I'm asking for your trust, too. I'm asking you to believe me when I say I'm keeping an open mind with all of you, and I'm doing the best I can."

"You're doing *awesome*," Ronan said, and to my surprise, Asher nodded. "We understand that a lot of this is new for you. It's new for us, too, Gray. I'm sorry for what I said about Liam. I'm willing to give him a shot, but you gotta know you're our main concern."

"We get that he's helping you," Asher said. "But Death… Liam… He's still an unknown quantity. *That's* what concerns us."

"I hear you," I said, looking at each of them in turn. "And I know you guys have my back. I appreciate that more than you know. But in all this worrying about Death and hunters and rogue vamps and who knows what other monsters we haven't faced yet, you keep forgetting something really important."

Emilio slid his arm around the back of my chair, his fingers brushing my shoulder. His warm brown eyes swept down my face, then back up again, his brow wrinkled in concern. "What is it, *querida*?"

I swallowed hard, dropping my voice to a whisper. "I'm an unknown quantity, too."

Three men—all of whom I cared about—stared at me in disbelief, as if it would never occur to them that I could be anything other than the woman staring right back at them. Unpredictable, sure. A little complicated, definitely. But not a stranger. Not unknowable.

I wished I could reassure them, could crack a joke and a smile and tease them for being so serious.

But deep down, I *was* unknowable—even to myself. Every day I was unearthing new facets, new emotions, new powers, new fears, new strengths.

New dangers.

Liam had once told me I had no idea what I was capable

of. He'd said it like it was a good thing, but to me, it was a double-edged sword.

It meant I might put my skills and magic to use fighting for my friends, saving the witches, and eradicating the world of hunters and anyone else who meant us harm.

But it also meant I could just as easily turn on my so-called allies. Or lose myself in the magic. Or end a life rather than saving one. Liam had said as much that first night when I'd asked him what a Shadowborn was.

What *I* was.

They are necromancers in the truest sense of the word. They have the capacity to give life, to save it, or to destroy it. And they are, all of them, bound to me...

"Doesn't matter. We're with you either way."

The words broke into my thoughts, and I was surprised to discover it was Asher who'd spoken them.

When I met his eyes, he locked me in an intense gaze, serious and sincere.

"Don't *ever* doubt that," he said, and in that moment, despite our constant sparring and all the unresolved stuff between us, I *didn't* doubt it.

It seemed we'd all reached a new level of understanding. Hopefully, they'd give Liam a chance and we could all move forward with our plans.

I closed my eyes and blew out a breath, releasing the last of my frustration.

In its place, an image of Haley flickered through my mind, her once-glossy ponytail now dull and frizzy, her face smudged with dirt. She sat on a stone floor, huddled in the corner with a blonde woman I didn't recognize. They weren't crying, though. They seemed to be… strategizing? The blonde was sketching something on the floor with a sharp rock. A map?

"Gray?" Emilio touched my shoulder again. "You okay?"

I blinked away the vision, not sure that's what it even was. It wasn't as clear or strong as the one I'd seen in the flames, and it hadn't really yielded any new information.

Just another little spark of hope. I tucked it away in my heart, keeping it close.

Hang in there, Hay. We're coming.

"Just thinking about Haley," I said softly.

"We'll find her, *querida*. All of them."

"Then we'll neutralize the sonofabitch and finally put this nightmare behind us," Asher said.

"Nightmares," a voice echoed eerily from the living room, "are neither behind nor ahead. They are non-linear and immeasurable."

Liam stepped out from behind the other side of the fireplace.

"They are within you," he continued, "rooted in a scorched yet sacred place that lies beneath your deepest secrets, your darkest fears, your own eternal emptiness, a barren wasteland revisited endlessly despite every feeble attempt at escape."

"Um." I rose from my chair, forcing a grin. "How about some coffee, Liam? Sounds like you might need a little pick-me-up today."

"I was merely attempting to expand the collective consciousness by—"

"Dial it down, Spooky." Asher rolled his eyes. "Your people skills are even worse than mine."

"Perhaps we could address that at the next vote?" Liam deadpanned. "However, I understand you don't get one. Will you be naming a proxy to vote me off the island instead?"

Asher cocked an eyebrow. "Was that… Was that another joke?"

"Indeed, demon."

"Two jokes in less than twenty-four hours? Whatever you're smoking, I'll take two."

There was an awkward pause, and then Liam cracked up, the skin around his bright blue eyes crinkling.

It was the first time I'd ever really seen him let loose like that, and when his blond hair flopped in front of his eyes, it was easy to forget that inside that vessel, he was still Death. Chaotic neutral. The Great Equalizer.

The unknown quantity.

But then he turned to me, his smile dropping away as if I'd only imagined it, and I remembered *exactly* who I was dealing with.

"Gray." He held out his hand, and I could tell by the ice in his eyes he wouldn't be taking no for an answer today. "Come. It is time."

ELEVEN

GRAY

As much as I'd initially feared it, my realm was finally starting to feel familiar again. Lush and wild, different than it had been when I was a child, but still mine. Still *me*.

"This way," I said, reaching for Liam's black-gloved hand. He'd assumed his Death form here—something that seemed much more comfortable for him, especially this close to the Shadowrealm—but just like this place, his non-humanness no longer unnerved me.

The path that led to the meadow was crowded with new growth, forcing us to walk single file, carefully stepping over the flowers and ferns that clogged our way.

When the tangle of vines thinned and the clearing finally came into view, I released his hand and rushed ahead, eager to reach the white stone pedestal, its indigo light pulsing warm and bright in my memory.

I'd assumed it would be a good starting point for my lesson with Liam today, but the closer we got, the farther away the pedestal became until it simply vanished altogether.

Shocked into silence, I turned to Liam for an explanation.

"It is ever-evolving, Gray," he said. "Now that you've reconnected and more fully opened yourself up to it, your magic will change to best suit your needs, guiding you first toward a deeper knowledge of Self, and then toward awareness of your place in this world and those beyond."

"So, the pedestal—"

"Is no longer needed. It guided you here on your initial visits after many years, almost like a homing beacon. But now it's time for something new to take its place."

He gestured for me to look around, and I did, slowly taking in the changing landscape. In addition to the vanishing pedestal, the spring-green meadow had also begun to fade, first taking on a blue-gray hue, and then darkening as the grass retreated into the ground, revealing freshly turned earth. In its place, new growth poked through. At first, I thought it was grapevine, slowly churning up the dirt. But the vines quickly dried, transforming into dark, sharp-toothed brambles.

We continued onward, finding a grassy rise still untouched.

Liam and I sat together on the rise, my shoulder brushing against his shadowy robe as we watched the brambles twist and turn across the meadow.

The black forest surrounding us remained unchanged,

its branches draped in silver tinsel, but otherwise as stark and bare as the first night I'd seen them.

The night I'd brought Bean back from the dead.

"What about that?" I asked, nodding toward the second path, a dark, narrow trail that led to the stone arch and gateway marking the entrance to the Shadowrealm.

"The Shadowrealm remains unchanged," he said. "As ever. The two realms share a mystical border—one that remained hidden from you until your deeper powers began to manifest—but they are two different places, operating under very different metaphysical rules."

I pulled my knees up to my chest and hugged them close, fighting off a chill. "You're going to make my head explode again, aren't you?"

"Believe it or not," he said, "exploding heads are a bit outside my skill set. But I *will* ask you to ponder the greater mysteries on occasion, if that's okay."

My lips curved into a smile. As much as Death was helping me explore the depths of my magic, it seemed I was helping him explore a sense of humor.

"What happens now?" I asked, rubbing the chill from my arms.

"What would you like to see happen?"

It was a big question, one with as many answers as there were stars in this otherworldly sky. But on a fundamental level, I needed to learn control.

"I'd like you to teach me how to access the magic without taking too much," I said, thinking of the undead creatures that had attacked me and Asher. "Or too little."

"It's not enough to simply access the magic, Gray. You must reclaim it fully and continue to nurture it through dedicated study and practice. And you also must learn to protect yourself—from outside influences, as well as from your own."

I understood the part about outside influences. Though I experienced the realm as a physical place, my actual body was still on earth, in a deeply meditative state that I couldn't always control. That kind of situation left me extremely vulnerable to physical and psychic attacks, especially if anything went wrong with the shield—another aspect I hadn't yet learned to control or call up on command.

But my *own* influences?

"How do I protect myself from... myself?" I asked, more confused than ever.

"I'm referring to your thoughts. Your fears and doubts, your insecurities, your resistance. Negative thoughts are pollutants, Gray, eroding this place just as they erode your confidence and spirit. They may come to you unbidden, but you must practice letting them pass. Do not nurture and encourage them. Do not actively create an environment in which those thoughts can multiply and thrive."

I tilted my face up toward the stars, trying to take it all in. This place. His words. Everything that had happened. Everything we'd yet to face.

Everything roiling inside me.

"You're still judging your magic—your *self*—as evil," he

continued, "and until you can escape that mental prison, you will never gain the control you seek."

"I just… I don't understand why it even exists," I said. "*Necromancy*. Soul manipulation. Everything about it is unnatural."

"It is part of you, Gray. It *is* you. In the simplest terms, it can't possibly be unnatural, because *you* are not unnatural."

"A lot of people would argue otherwise."

"A lot of people would argue that hot dog carts are superior to taco trucks. Clearly, people are prone to wrong-headedness."

Liam blinked rapidly, surprised by his own words.

"Spoken like a true Californian," I teased. "I guess we know where Liam Colebrook was from. Sounds like some part of him is still with you."

"I've never had a taco," he said.

"So I gathered. We'll have to make you a bucket list when we get back. Sound good?"

"I think I might like that." Liam's eyes brightened with an almost child-like excitement, the humanness of his vessel peeking through his otherworldly form.

But it faded quickly, and he turned to look out over the vast sea of brambles still churning before us. "There are many things in your world, Gray, that man has labeled an abomination. Yet the mere naming of a thing does not make it so."

"Sticks and stones," I mumbled.

"That is what you call those things, yes. But a stone is not a stone because of you, or even because of the first human who named it such. A stone is a stone because it simply is, no matter what name it was given, in what language or epoch or realm."

"It's… just an old saying," I explained. "A thing they tell you in school when you're getting picked on—that you can be hurt with sticks and stones, but not when someone calls you a name."

He stared at me a long moment, his eerie blue eyes seeing right through me. I wondered what he was thinking about. What he saw when he looked at me like that.

"Was it difficult for you, being a witch?" he finally asked. "Knowing you were different?"

"No, actually. I never thought about it like that. Sure, there were times I wished I could've told my friends at school about the real me, but I understood it wasn't safe. Anyway, I had Calla for that. I never felt alone in it until after she…"

"And now?"

"It's different now." I plucked out a handful of grass, absently dropping it onto my legs—something I used to do as a kid. "Before, it felt like something special, full of potential."

"But not anymore?"

"Not entirely, no. I still feel that potential, that good magic. But there's something else there, too. Festering like a sickness." Shame burned my cheeks. I knew these were exactly the kind of negative thoughts Liam had warned me about, but I couldn't help how I felt. Dropping my voice to a whisper, I said, "It's dark."

I held out my palm, picturing the blue-green magic I'd conjured last night, the blend of my innate magic with that of the earth. My skin heated, then glowed, pulsing faintly before igniting in a beautiful flame that hovered just above my hand.

Gingerly I brought my other hand close, and the flame slid from one to the other. I pulled my hands apart, then pushed them together, the magic changing shape, dancing at my touch.

"Dark," he repeated, and the flame in my hand surged briefly.

Liam held up a hand, then closed his fist, the effect like dimming the lights. The moon vanished first, allowing the stars to momentarily brighten, then they faded as well.

My magic flame flickered out last, and I closed my eyes, catching the faint echo of its glow inside my eyelids.

When the spots faded and I opened my eyes, I was bathed in a blackness so complete, I couldn't even see my hands in front of my face.

The effect was dizzying, no sense of up or down. It felt as if someone had dropped me into the void.

In that dark, empty moment, words came to me unbidden, a thought that began not in my head but in my heart, taking root as the truth so often did—painfully at first, and then blooming into something so starkly beautiful it could no longer be denied.

"We are, all of us, bound for darkness."

A thrill shot up my spine as I spoke the words out loud,

and I shivered, feeling something deep inside me unfurl like a spring bud.

"Do not fear the dark," Liam said softly, his strange shadow-voice oddly comforting in the pitch black. "Fear a world in which there is only light whose radiance remains unknown, for one cannot truly exist in the absence of the other."

He was right, as always. I'd been struggling to accept this part of myself since it first began manifesting in the alley when I'd brought Bean back. Maybe even before that.

The struggle itself was holding me back. Creating another layer of resistance between me and the pure source of my magic.

"The darkness isn't just a part of me, like some separate entity," I said. "It *is* me."

"As is the light, and all the shades of gray that fall between."

"Shades of gray?" Smiling, I nudged his shoulder with mine. "Another joke?"

"Of course not. A pun, perhaps, but not a joke."

I felt him shift before me, and then the light came back, all at once and overwhelming—stars, moon, and magic, flickering once again in my hands.

I cupped my hands before me and blew, and the magic scattered, floating away like a child's dandelion seed wishes.

The ground rumbled, then shifted before us, the tangle of vines and brambles retreating to reveal a vast lake, black as night. Ripples cascaded across the surface.

I gasped. "Where did that come from?"

"The lake is your unconscious mind, and as such, will seek to give you clarity on that which you know to be true in the depths of your soul."

"It's… it's breathtaking."

The lake stilled, it's surface turning glassy, mirroring the stars so clearly it was difficult to tell where the sky ended and the water began. I was mesmerized, compelled to walk down off the rise and kneel at the water's edge.

Liam didn't follow, but I didn't need him to. This was *my* place; I wasn't afraid.

I peered into the dark water, and peace settled over me, everything inside going calm and silent. Reflected in the lake's obsidian surface, the stars began to swirl, winking out one at a time until there was nothing but blackness.

A shape appeared in the water, unrecognizable at first, then slowly coming into focus.

A face, with haunted blue eyes framed by dark, unruly curls…

"Reva!" I gasped, reaching for her. But the instant my fingers touched the cool water, the image of her face shattered, reforming in the shape of a shadow so dark and dense it swallowed up the stars.

Terror gripped my heart and I froze, but a strange, inexplicable compulsion urged me to step into the water. To feel it. To feel *him*.

Jonathan…

The name slithered into my ear, and my senses were suddenly flooded with him: His scent, like fresh-cut grass and sweat. His red hair, coarse and wavy, stiff to the touch from the gel he used to like. His voice, older now, menacing and full of hatred.

He wasn't in the water—not physically— but I could *feel* him all around me, threatening me. Taunting me.

I'm waiting for you, Rayanne…

The water turned as thick and heavy as tar, sucking me in deeper, dragging me down. It swallowed my legs, making it impossible to move. My chest, crushing the air from my lungs. My shoulders. My neck. My chin.

I opened my mouth to scream for Liam, but no sound came. Only Jonathan, shouting in my head.

You belong to me, Rayanne…

I took a final deep breath and held it as the lake surged, sucking me under, dragging me down to the depths.

When I find you, I will burn you…

I struggled to break free, legs scissoring through the viscous black water, my fingers reaching for the moonlight that still glimmered on the surface. Raw, hot fear threatened to eat away my insides, but I had to stay calm. To find a way out of this.

I didn't know how it was possible, but Jonathan was here. Changing the landscape of my magical realm. Turning it against me.

If I didn't breach the surface, I was going to die.

Still holding my breath, I forced myself to relax. I pictured my blue-green flame again, imagining it surging up inside me, then radiating outward, encasing me in a bubble of warm, pure light that lifted me up from the depths.

My body began to rise, slowly at first, then faster, the water thinning, the moon and stars becoming visible overhead.

Your friends will die, Jonathan's voice warned. *You're fighting me, and you're leaving me no choice.*

My heart skipped, but I pushed the fear aside again, still concentrating on the magic. I couldn't falter, couldn't lose my focus, or it would be over.

The little one will break first…

I punched through the surface of the lake just as his final words echoed, and I gasped for air, sucking in big gulps, spitting black water from my mouth as the sky began to spin, the world collapsing in on me from all sides…

TWELVE

LIAM

I shattered into billions of tiny particles no more significant in size than atoms, exploding first, then reassembling
in a violent collision that knocked me back to the earthly
plane.

Gray had somehow expelled me. Whether she'd done it
intentionally was another matter, but it was the only explanation for my current predicament.

I found myself deposited rather roughly into the woods
that bordered the property of her current home. In the
clearing where we'd begun today's lesson, Gray sat in the
lotus position undisturbed, her eyes closed, her body
deathly still.

Her shield encased her in an iridescent dome, impenetrable to all, including the angry incubus presently
hammering it with his fists.

I shifted into my human form and approached silently,
but he must have sensed my presence, for when he

rounded on me, his eyes were already black with demon rage.

"*Do* something," he demanded.

"There's nothing I can do until she returns."

"Returns from where?"

"She's in her realm. I assure you, she's perfectly safe." At least, I hoped that was the case. The fact that I'd been expelled didn't bode all that well.

"And you're creeping out of the woods looking like warmed-up shit with a hangover, so forgive me if I don't take your word for it."

"Death neither forgives nor—"

"Colebrook?" He stepped closer, sucking all of the oxygen from the air. "I'm only gonna say this once. Shut your damn death hole, zoom back into outer space, and bring her back to me. She's been zoned out in there for two hours already."

"Gray's magical realm is not located in outer space, demon, but *inner* space," I said. "Retrieving her is not that simple."

"Why?"

"Time and space work differently there. It's not a simple matter of packing a suitcase and catching an airplane, or—as you say—*zooming*."

I hoped the partial explanation would be enough. Lingering on the earthly plane in human form was foolhardy enough; traveling back and forth now would severely weaken me in ways that could have a ripple effect on the entire cosmos. After Gray's interference with the natural fabric last night—the overdose of necromantic magic she'd called forth—I couldn't take that risk.

Not even for the Shadowborn herself.

"The shield protects her," I said, calm and cool in the face of the demon's fire despite my own very real concerns. "We'll simply have to wait."

He glared at me, but finally relented, returning his attention to Gray. Pressing a hand flat against the dome, he said, "So why aren't you with her? I thought you two were working together today."

"We were."

"And?"

"And now we're not."

"What happened?"

I drew myself up to my full height, looking down upon him as best I could manage given the fact that Liam Colebrook was scarcely more than an inch taller than the incubus. "Death explains himself to no one, hellspawn. I am beyond comprehension, vaster than the sky, older than the sea, more infinite than—"

"Can Death die?" he asked, then grinned. "I've always wondered how that would work."

I released a breath, shrinking beneath his unwavering glare. "One moment I was by her side in the realm. The next, I was hurtling through stardust and galaxies and… In any case, I arrived in the woods through no action of my own."

"And you don't know how that happened?"

"I do not."

Fortunately, Gray's shield vanished, interrupting what could've become quite an ugly conversation.

"Gray!" The incubus dropped to his knees, taking her face between his hands. His eyes were frantic with worry, but they'd returned to their natural color.

"Asher?" She blinked at him, slowly coming back to us. "I was… I ended up in the lake, and I…" Her gaze shifted to me, her brows drawn tight together. "What happened? Where did you go?"

"There's a lake?" the incubus asked.

"I was… called away," I said. "Tell me what happened at the lake."

"I thought I was scrying again," she said. "Reva was there, just like in the fire. I tried to reach out to her, but as soon as I touched the water, it was like something just… I don't know. Sucked me in."

"Did you fall?" I asked.

She closed her eyes, shaking her head. In a pained whisper, she said, "I thought he was going to kill me."

"Who?" the incubus demanded.

"The… the hunter. He was there." She wrapped herself in a hug, her body trembling at the memory.

"Did he take physical form?" I asked.

She shook her head, and I sighed with relief.

"But he was still there," she said, blinking up at me once again. "Like a shadow almost, but… different. It reminded me of an oil slick, actually. Dark like that—like you could tell it wasn't part of the water."

"And you're certain it was him?"

"I heard his voice in my head. I *felt* him, all around me. It was like he could see me—like he knew I was there. He told me he'd been waiting for me. That he was going to kill the others. That…" Her eyes widened. "Oh, God. Reva. He said… he said the little one would break first."

The incubus brushed her tears away with his knuckles. "We'll find him. We'll destroy him. He's just taunting you, Gray."

"No, it was more than that. He… he did something to me." She got to her feet and began to pace. "The water got heavier. Thick. He was saying that stuff inside my head, and somehow, he kept pulling me down. I couldn't get free —it felt like trying to swim in cement."

"And then he let you go?" I asked.

Gray pressed the heels of her hands to her eyes, shaking her head. "I used my magic. When I finally got to the surface, everything started spinning, and then I ended up back here."

"So the hunter's turning your own realm against you?" the demon asked. "How the fuck does that even happen?"

"For him to access her realm at all," I said, "he must have a deeply personal connection to her. As for effecting physical changes there and holding her against her will…" My mind whirled with the possibilities, but each one came to a dead end. I'd never heard of such a thing happening among any of my Shadowborn.

"Sorry, but those are some bullshit rules," the demon said. "This guy's old man kills her mother, and now he can just, what? Take the reins in Gray's realm?"

"That's… not the kind of connection we're talking about." I looked at Gray, wondering if she might elaborate. She looked supremely uncomfortable.

I wished I could've made this easier on her, to say the words she was so struggling with, but hers was not my story to tell.

"I… need a minute." Gray turned her back on us and slipped deeper into the woods, where she sat down at the base of a large oak tree.

Silence descended upon us like a yoke.

When Gray finally returned, her eyes were red, her skin pale.

"Jonathan Reese," she finally said, her voice no more than a whisper. "At least, that was the name he'd gone by in high school. He was my… my first."

"First what?" the incubus asked, though I suspected he'd already put the pieces together. "Who was this guy to you, Gray?"

Gray met his eyes, her own brimming with secrets she never should've had to carry.

"*Everything*, Ash," she said, her pale cheeks darkening with shame. "He was my first everything."

He opened his mouth, then closed it, falling silent once again.

"I didn't know who he really was back then," she said. "We were kids. I'd never met his family, and we'd never talked about witchcraft or magic or any of the things that existed in my world. As far as I knew, he was just a typical boy. I mean, he was into video games and dodgeball and building forts in the woods. I never would've thought…" She shook her head, as if to clear the memories.

"You have nothing to be ashamed of, Gray," I assured her.

"I have *everything* to be ashamed of."

Her incubus finally put a hand on her shoulder, his thumb touching the side of her neck. The barest brush of his skin seemed to calm her, and I felt a strange sensation in my chest—a pinching, electric burn that followed a path down into my stomach, where it pooled uncomfortably.

"It's not just the connection, though, right?" Gray asked. "He also needs something physical from me, like my hair."

"And some skill with magical workings," I said, "regardless of his own lack of power."

The demon sighed. "He must've taken something from her house when he… The night…"

He left his thoughts unsaid, which was probably for the best. It's not as if Gray could ever forget that the hunter stalking her in her realm was the same man who'd murdered her best friend in their home.

"But I still don't understand how he even knows my realm exists," Gray said. "I never even told him I was a witch. I mean, he found out, obviously. I just can't figure out how. I've *never* been able to figure that out. No one at school knew—not even my closest girlfriends. Calla was always really strict about that."

"I wish I had an answer for you, Gray," I said.

The breeze picked up, making her shiver. The incubus put his arm around her, rubbing away the chill.

"My plan for all this was to use my magic as bait," Gray said. "To lure him out of hiding so we could eventually catch him. But all that was supposed to happen *here*, in the real world. Not in my realm." Her eyes drifted to some faraway place, and she shivered again. "He must've been the presence we felt that time, remember? The one the hellhounds were supposedly protecting me from."

"That is my understanding now as well," I said.

"So how do we make sure this asshole doesn't get his hands on her in her realm?" the incubus asked. "We can't bring the hounds back in. They're too unpredictable—they could end up killing her."

"I'm aware," I said.

"You're aware? Oh, good! I'm sure we can all rest real easy now."

"Your anger is not helping," I said.

"It's better than—"

"Please," Gray whispered. "Stop arguing." She dropped to her knees, her strength finally giving out. "He's always a step ahead of us. He's got Reva and Haley, he's accessing my realm… Can't we ever catch a break?"

I thought the demon might offer her comfort again. But rather than sharing a kind word or a reassuring touch, he grabbed her by the elbows and hauled her back up.

"Walk it off, Cupcake," he demanded, new fire burning in his eyes. "It's only the first day of training. You can't fall apart on us now."

For reasons I couldn't comprehend, she often seemed to

find the demon's brutish behavior endearing, and I waited for her smile to appear at this latest display.

But she merely shook her head.

"I mean it, Gray," he said. "Pull it together."

"Is that really necessary?" I asked. "She's been through—"

"Take a hike, Spooky," he said. "Amateur hour is over."

Gray sighed. "He's not going anywhere, Ash. He's still teaching me about my powers."

"Well, given how that turned out, I figured I'd teach you how to kick some ass instead." The demon grinned, a look as frightening and feral as the ancient pit from whence his ancestors came. "Starting with mine."

THIRTEEN

GRAY

"Again."

Asher locked his hands behind his back and closed his eyes, waiting for my epic smackdown to resume.

"This is pointless, Ash. I'm no match for you."

"You're right. You're no match for me or any other supernatural. Vampires and shifters are faster, stronger, and more agile than you could ever hope to be. Fae are master manipulators. And demons… Well." Asher grinned, enjoying this way more than I was. "We're just trouble any way you slice it."

"Then why are we wasting our time?"

"Listen." His smile dropped. "You've got innate magic, Gray. A *lot* of it. Once you learn to channel it properly, it'll make you stronger and faster. Add a few solid fighting techniques into the mix, and next time you're backed into a corner, you might have half a chance at getting out."

"Half? Not sure I like those odds."

"Half is better than zilch. Reading lore books and sparring with Ronan isn't enough. Not anymore." He gestured for me to come at him again. "Let's go."

Swallowing the very last of my wounded pride, I wound up and took a swing.

He dodged easily, surprising no one.

We'd been at it an hour already, trampling the lush backyard as I chased him in circles in the fading evening light. He'd kept his hands behind him the whole time, and I'd yet to land a single punch.

My knuckles brushed across his bicep once. That was the closest I'd gotten to inflicting any damage.

"Come on, Cupcake. You're acting like you don't *want* to hit me, and we all know that can't be true."

I rolled my eyes. I could think of nothing more satisfying than knocking that smug grin off his stupid face.

"It's not for lack of trying," I said.

"If you get into a situation with this hunter again—or another Hollis or Weston or any number of underworld assholes salivating for a chance to kill you—trying isn't gonna cut it." He whipped off his shirt and tossed it into the grass, then clapped once and gestured for me to come at him again. "Don't hold back, baby."

"What do you have against shirts?"

I waited for the smartassery, the innuendo, the flirty teasing that had become our comfortable norm. But it never came.

Asher's face twisted with annoyance that bordered on

disdain. "Stop screwing around, Gray. This is important. I need you to focus."

He closed his eyes again, his arms loose at his sides, and I lunged at him, truly believing I had the element of surprise this time.

Me and my brilliant delusions.

He sidestepped, and I stumbled, the momentum of my ill-timed swing carrying me forward. I stopped myself from face-planting, then regained my balance and spun around on my heel, throwing my hands in front of my face just in time to block his hit.

Barely.

"I had a feeling you'd come in for the kill," I said.

"Always a good assumption in a fight, especially if it looks like you're about to go down. Your opponent will always look for weaknesses to exploit. Mistakes to take advantage of."

"Makes sense."

Asher wiped the back of his hand across his brow. "That was better, but still not good. Not by a long shot."

"A long shot? I totally blocked you!"

"I wasn't even trying, Gray." He turned his back on me, walking out to the middle of the yard. When he turned to face me again, he waved me forward. "Bring it."

Determined not to let him get any deeper under my skin than he already was, I steadied myself, taking a deep, centering breath.

Then I charged.

Leading with my shoulder, I ran straight for him, slamming into his gut in a collision as painful as it was satisfying. The impact jarred my bones, but Asher showed no more reaction than if he'd been hit with a stiff breeze.

Locking a meaty hand around my wrist, he said, "Is that your best shot, Cupcake?"

"Nope." I didn't hesitate. Grabbing his hand and holding it against my wrist, I swung his arm up and around, twisting it behind him and forcing him to the ground. It was a move Ronan had taught me, and I was surprised at how effective it was against Ash.

My victory, however, was short-lived.

Jerking me forward, he broke my hold and got to his feet, grabbing me and crushing me against his chest, locking his arms around me in an impossibly tight embrace.

"Looks like you're all out of moves, witch," he said. "So what happens now?"

Arms pinned to my sides, I lifted my head and met his eyes, our mouths so close I could feel the soft, seductive heat of his breath whispering across my lips.

My body released a sigh, totally without my permission, and his pupils dilated, his lips quirking into that bad-boy grin I loved to hate.

"You tell me," I said.

Ash's gaze lowered to my mouth, lingering, his hold around me tightening. Every soft curve of my body molded against every hard plane of his, our skin hot and sticky despite the rapidly cooling temperature.

A low rumble reverberated through his chest, so soft I wasn't sure he even realized he was doing it. I closed my eyes, swooning a bit on my feet. My heart thudded hard, my breath jagged and uneven, and if Asher had tried to kiss me right then I wouldn't have done a damn thing to stop him.

I bit my lip, and he growled again.

"This… is a bad idea," he whispered.

"I've had worse."

"Trust me. You haven't." He released me and took a step back, jogging in place and grinding the heels of his hands into his eyes as though he were trying to shake off a nightmare.

When I met his eyes again, all traces of desire were gone.

"Time for a different scenario," he said, his voice as serious as his eyes. "Close combat, surprise attack from behind."

He gestured for me to turn around.

When I hesitated, he sighed and said, "I'm not going to hurt you."

That's not what I'm worried about, dummy.

Blowing out a breath, I rolled my shoulders and nodded, stamping out the last flicker of heat pulsing inside me.

The moment I turned around, Asher was on me, his arms locked across my shoulders and chest. Immediately I flailed, trying to shake him off.

"Don't struggle," he said. "I've taken control of the situation and your body—the worst thing you could do is try to fight it. You simply need to retake control."

I nodded. Finally, he was going to give me some actual pointers.

"Grab my wrists," he said, "and then drop down into a squat."

I did as he asked, feeling my center of gravity shift, and his along with it.

"Okay, good. Now let's try it again, only this time, I want you to keep your head turned instead of facing straight. That way, the dude can't choke you."

We went down again, my hands clamped around his wrists, our bodies as close as we could be without spontaneously combusting.

"Stay crouched down," he continued, "then you're gonna step behind me and grab behind my thighs, right above the knees. Then lift me up and *drop* my ass."

I blinked, trying to make sense of what he just said. "Um. What?"

"You just…" He shoved a hand through his hair. "Here, switch places."

I did as he asked, and he walked me through the whole thing in slow motion again, this time with me playing the aggressor. When he got to the lifting part, he picked me up as if I was no heavier than a sack of hair, then put me down on the grass, flat on my back.

He pressed his hand flat against my stomach, his touch warm and firm and distracting.

"You want to use your center of gravity to throw me off balance and get my feet out from under me. Once I'm on the ground, you can jam an elbow into my gut, or stake me, or do whatever the hell you need to do to buy yourself time to run." He gave my stomach a light slap. "Got it?"

Right. He'd made it look and sound so damn easy, I felt like a complete moron for not comprehending it.

Not wanting to disappoint him, I nodded anyway.

He helped me to my feet, and we switched positions, going through the motions all over again. One more time. Two more. Three. But no matter how many times I tried, I just couldn't get the leverage I needed to get him on the ground.

"Come on, Gray," he said after the fourth time. Or maybe it was the fifth. I'd lost count sometime between the ouch-muscles-burning stage and holy-hell-my-quads-are-literally-jelly stage of this little exercise. "You can do this."

"I'm not strong enough."

"This maneuver isn't about strength. It's about smarts."

"Then I guess I'm not smart enough, either." Tears of frustration stung my eyes. Ronan had worked with me a lot over the years, sparring, teaching me about monsters, helping me learn basic self-defense. I thought I'd had a pretty decent skill set—not amazing, but enough to get me out of most situations.

Asher was making me feel as helpless as a newborn.

"I need a break," I said, but Asher shook his head.

"No breaks. Not until you can convince me you're not going to curl up and die the next time some jackoff gets the drop on you."

"I'm twenty-five fucking years old, Ash. I might seem

like an insignificant speck to an old-ass demon like you, but I managed to make it this far in my life without your help."

"Doesn't mean you won't bite it tomorrow."

"What do you want me to do?"

Asher's eyes blazed, his frustration quickly degrading into anger. "I want you to show some initiative here. I want you to give a fuck about the fact that your psycho ex is a hunter, and he's out there terrorizing witches, working his way closer to you every day. If that little stunt in your realm didn't make that *crystal* fucking clear to you," he snapped, tapping on my forehead with his index finger, "I don't know how else to drill it into your rock-hard skull."

I smacked his hand away. "Oh, *I* have a hard skull? Really?"

"You're the most stubborn woman I've ever met. You're a pain in the ass who flat out refuses to open your damn eyes and—"

"Go to hell, Asher. I don't need this shit." I turned away, heading back toward the house. "I'll figure it out myself."

I felt the air shift behind me and tensed for impact, but it was too late. He knocked my legs clear out from under me.

And then the bastard let me fall.

I hit the ground with a thud and a grunt, no gentle hands to cushion my fall this time.

It fucking hurt.

I blinked up at the twilight sky. Somewhere in the distance, an owl called out, and in my head, I answered him.

Whooo-hoo are you?

Whoo-hoo am I?

I was too shocked to do anything else.

Breaking into my momentary peace, Asher loomed over me, extending a hand. "Are we done throwing tantrums?"

Tears welled up again, turning his stupid face into a blur. Ignoring his hand, I turned my face and stretched my arm across my eyes, as if that alone could hide my shame. My frustration.

Asher wasn't having it. He nudged my hip with his foot. "Get up, witch."

"No."

Asher cupped a hand around his ear. "What's that? You're giving up?"

I was a hot mess. Sweat in my eyes, the tang of blood in my mouth, my heart about to burst from my chest.

But somehow, the idea of letting Asher win felt even worse.

Growling like an animal, I rolled onto my stomach and pushed myself up.

One time. I just have to put him down one time…

He came around behind me, putting me in the lock once again. I grabbed his wrists, dropped to a squat, and then…

I gave up. My legs trembled. My knees screamed in protest.

Releasing my hold, I turned to face him, defeated. "I can't, Ash. I just can't."

"God *damn* it!" he shouted, making me flinch. The feral glint in his eyes made the hairs on my arm stand up. "What are you playing at here, Desario?"

"I'm not playing! I'm trying to learn how to defend myself. To fight."

"So defend! Offend! Fucking do *something* that doesn't end with you burying your head under a blanket and crying every time things don't go your way."

"That's not fair. I'm doing my best to—"

"If that's your best, Cupcake, you may as well go back to the Bay tonight. Find a nice secluded spot in the warehouse district, sit out there with your little spell book and a big-ass pentacle around your neck and a neon sign that says 'Come and get it, hunters!'"

"You suck," I said, tears sliding down my cheeks. I was spent. Utterly spent. My muscles were rebelling, my already-bruised ego had crossed into contusion-and-abrasion territory hours earlier, and shame was burning a hole in my stomach. I couldn't do this. Not tonight.

But Asher wasn't finished.

"His family murdered your mother, Gray. They already tried to kill you once, and this fuckface has made it his mission in life to find you. He murdered your best friend. He—"

"Stop it! Shut up!" I shoved his chest as hard as I could. He stumbled a step backward, but this demon was just getting warmed up.

"He's a ruthless witch-killer," he went on. "He's a sadistic—"

"I know what he is. You don't have to be such a—"

"Such a *what*, sweetheart? A dick?"

I folded my arms over my chest, clenching my teeth so hard I thought they might shatter, and still, he kept going.

"You think that sonofabitch is gonna be nice to you? That he's gonna get all weepy and nostalgic and ask you to the prom?" Asher stepped into my space, crowding me, over-whelming me with his spicy-hot scent. "No, Gray. He's gonna salivate like a fucking *animal* when he sees you, because that's what he is. And you know what he's gonna do next?"

"Stop," I whispered, my eyes fluttering closed, my body slowly shutting down, logic checking out. In its place, the now-familiar blackness bubbled up, filling my veins with venom. With rage. With gasoline.

Asher was the god damn match.

"He's gonna carve you up," he said, his voice low and menacing, inhuman in its abject cruelty. "He's gonna tear you apart, limb from limb, until all that's left of you are your shiny blond curls."

Asher reached for my hair, tugging on a lock that had slipped out of my ponytail.

Hurt him, the voice inside whispered. *Make him pay.*

"Fuck you!" I screamed, welcoming the fire as it licked my belly, my chest, consuming everything in its path. Instinctively I raised my hands, magic sparking across my palms, desperate for an outlet.

A car door slammed nearby, followed by the fall of foot-steps and the shouts of familiar voices, but I didn't care who witnessed this. What they thought of me. What truths they had to face.

At the moment, I could barely remember their names.

The blackness surged.

And with everything I had, I slammed my hands into Asher's chest.

He flew backward, landing hard on his back a dozen feet away.

The dark magic that had so quickly risen inside me was receding, leaving an electric hum in its wake, my body vibrating and hyper-alert, hyper-aware.

Everything came back to me all at once.

The fighting. Asher's words, as sharp and deadly as knives. The blackness churning inside me, taking control. Taking my power…

No, not taking it, I realized with a start. *Giving it.*

It wasn't some separate entity taking over. It was part of me. It *was* me.

"Gray! Ash!" Emilio darted across the lawn toward Asher, Ronan close on his heels, heading for me.

"Gray?" Ronan put his hands on my shoulders, concern mingling with terror in his hazel eyes. "Are you hurt?"

I shook my head.

"We were sparring, and things got… heated."

Ronan sighed. "I know. We got here just in time to catch the last of it."

I glanced over toward Emilio, who was helping Asher sit up.

"Looks like he's gonna live," Ronan said.

I should've been relieved. Maybe some part of me— some deeply buried, still pissed-off part—was.

But mostly, I just felt numb. The magic had faded completely, leaving me wrung out and empty.

Blood trickled from his nose.

I didn't have the energy to care.

Asher caught my gaze, his own just as fiery as it had been before I zapped him. Flashing me a bloody grin, he said, "*Now* we're getting somewhere, Cupcake."

"Don't talk, asshole," Ronan snapped. Turning back to me, he took my face in his hands and said, "I've got some shit to do for Waldrich tonight and tomorrow, so I'll take Asher back to the Bay, give you some space. You good here with Darius and Emilio?"

I hated to see Ronan leave again, but he was right; I needed the space. As much as Asher might've deserved it—and as much as he'd apparently *enjoyed* it—I never should've lost control like that. Especially not with someone who was trying to help me. To protect me.

His methods sucked ass, but I still trusted him.

Maybe that made me a fool. Jury was still out on that.

"I'll be fine," I assured Ronan. "Text me later, okay?" I leaned in for a quick kiss before heading over to join Emilio, who led me to the front door with a hand on my lower back.

His soft, gentle kindness was exactly the company I needed tonight. No pressure. No awkward sparring. No tension. Just a decent freaking guy with a killer smile and a heart the size of Nebraska—the perfect remedy for the day's disasters.

The last thing I heard before disappearing inside was

Ronan, the eerie calm in his voice belying the rage simmering just below the surface.

"Get in the van, hellspawn," he said to Asher, and I knew without looking back that his eyes had turned coal black. "We've got some shit to discuss."

FOURTEEN

GRAY

The shower wasn't quite hot enough to wash *all* my sins away, but it did get rid of the dirt and the blood, and most of my residual anger. Asher's words may have been unnecessarily brutal, but he'd been right about one thing: crying under the blankets was not a winning strategy, especially now that Jonathan had the power to reach me in the magical realm.

I didn't know how or when he'd make his move here in the physical realm—only that he would. I needed to learn how to fight, both defensively and offensively. I needed to learn how to channel that magic—to tap into that strength, let it infuse me with power, and direct it on command rather than as a reaction to being taunted. And I needed to learn it quickly, no matter how frustrated I might get at my own limitations.

Still, why did Ash have to be such a dick about everything?

Every time I thought we were making progress as friends, he put up another wall. And I just kept on slamming right into them.

Determined not to let him ruin my *entire* night, I dressed in my coziest pair of pajamas—a light blue fleece set with clouds all over them that Sophie had given me when I'd come down with the flu last winter—and followed the scent of fresh baked deliciousness to the kitchen, where Emilio was taking a pan of something out of the oven.

"Are those brownies?" I asked.

"Excellent timing, *querida*," he said with a wink. He set the pan on a cooling rack on the center island, then removed his oven mitts. "This is an Emilio Alvarez exclusive recipe, and since you and I are the only ones here, you get first dibs."

"Where's Darius?"

"He had a meeting in Seattle—he won't be back until tomorrow night. He said to tell you he'd try to call you later —he didn't want to disturb you in the shower."

The idea of Darius disturbing me in the shower sent a little thrill down my spine, and I was bummed that he hadn't tried.

Still, it didn't get much better than homemade brownies, and I took a deep chocolatey whiff. "You made these from *scratch*?"

"How else do you make sweet-and-spicy triple-chocolate brownies?" Emilio's face morphed into a mask of abject horror. "From a *box*?"

I nearly swooned.

"Don't take this the wrong way, but… Emilio Alvarez?" I batted my eyelashes. "Will you marry me?"

His smile looked as sweet as his creation smelled. "Not tonight, *querida*. But to ease the sting of my brutal rejection, I'll share these with you. Sound good?"

"Are you kidding me? That's the best offer I've gotten all day."

"They need to cool a bit, and I need to return a call to the police chief." He pulled the phone from his pocket. "Let's say we reconvene on the deck with a couple of spoons, some milk, and this whole pan in fifteen minutes."

"You got it, detective."

While Emilio went to make his call, I found a tray and loaded it up with spoons, napkins, and two big, frothy glasses of ice-cold milk, already feeling a hundred times better than I had an hour ago.

The deck was a huge wooden expanse with an unobstructed view of the moonlit sky but no furniture, so I set the tray on the railing and headed back inside for a blanket to sit on. I grabbed the butter-yellow one from the back of the couch, sending a lone tarot card fluttering down onto the floor.

It must've gotten lost in the shuffle last night.

I picked it up and turned it over, a smile instantly touching my lips.

It was the Page of Cups—a beautiful young girl with sleek ebony skin and a fish-shaped headdress, her cape and tunic the color of the sea.

She was my Sophie card, just stopping by to say hello.

"I miss you, too, my friend." Carefully, I tucked her into the shirt pocket of my cloud pajamas, inviting her along on my brownie date, knowing she'd definitely approve.

It wasn't long before Emilio joined me on the blanket outside, bringing his pan of chocolate heaven. After clinking our spoons together in cheers, we promptly dug in, steam still rising from the gooey center. He'd cooked them perfectly—crispy on the edges, soft and warm inside, the decadent chocolate taste followed by a just-spicy-enough kick of chili pepper.

We'd demolished half the batch when he finally stopped to speak.

"Feel better?" he asked.

"Aside from the stomach ache I'm working on? Yes."

He took another spoonful, licking it clean. "Chocolate fixes everything, doesn't it?"

I set my spoon in the pan and leaned back on the blanket, staring up at the moon. It was still mostly full, and the bright light blotted out most of the stars. "Almost everything."

"Gray..." He seemed to be searching for his words, but I already knew what he was going to say. Why else would he whip up a batch of scratch brownies and hang out with me on the deck?

"It's not your fault, Emilio," I said, letting him off the hook. "You weren't even here."

"Maybe I should've been."

"Asher and I shouldn't need a babysitter."

"No. A mediator, maybe." Emilio stretched out on his

side and propped up his head, facing me. "He was wrong to push you so hard. To say those awful things. I'm sorry you had to deal with that, *querida*."

"You don't have to apologize for anyone," I said. "Especially Asher. That demon can handle his own messes."

"Not you," Emilio said softly.

"He hates me," I said, the realization stinging a hell of a lot more than I wanted to admit. "Case closed."

"Asher doesn't hate you. He hates himself. That's the whole problem."

"Come on, Emilio. He's the most egotistical asshole I've ever met. Tell me that's not true."

"Being full of yourself and hating yourself aren't mutually exclusive. In fact, they often go hand-in-hand."

I turned away from his soft brown eyes and went back to staring at the moon. I didn't want to feel bad for Asher—not right now. Not after everything he'd said to me.

He's gonna carve you up. He's gonna tear you apart, limb from limb, until all that's left of you are your shiny blond curls…

"I'm not trying to make excuses for him," Emilio continued, "but I *am* trying to understand where he's coming from. I think you are, too."

"I've been trying all along," I said. "But Asher doesn't want anyone to get too close. He'd rather stew in his anger and hate the world than admit he has an actual heart in there. And you know what? Let him. I'm done."

"I don't blame you for feeling that way." Emilio unleashed a deep sigh. "This is Asher's pattern. He starts to care for someone, and the moment they start to reciprocate, he pushes them away. It's his own form of self-punishment."

"Why is he punishing himself?"

"Why do any of us? Maybe he feels like he has to atone."

Atone.

I let the word hang in the air as an image floated through my memory—the dark-haired woman I'd seen when I'd taken Asher's soul. The immeasurable pain I'd felt as I'd watched her die through Asher's eyes.

I wondered if Emilio knew about that—if Asher had ever talked about her. I wanted to ask him, but no matter what Asher had said to me tonight, deep down I still believed he was my friend. At the very least, he deserved my respect. It didn't feel right to bring up the story of the woman with anyone but Asher. In fact, it didn't feel right to bring her up at all.

"I'm not saying I want him to suffer, Emilio," I said, softer this time. "But I didn't sign up to be his emotional punching bag."

"I know. I suspect Asher knows that, too. And on the off chance he forgot, I'm sure Ronan is reminding him of that right now."

I bit back a smile. Not that I wanted anyone to fight my battles, especially with the infuriating incubus. But when it came to me, Ronan's overprotective nature ran deep. I could only imagine the earful Asher was getting right now.

I almost—*almost*—felt bad for him.

"Emilio?"

"*¿Sí, querida?*"

"Thanks for the brownies. And, you know—the rest."

"You're welcome for the brownies. And, you know—the rest." Emilio reached across the blanket and squeezed my hand, his gentle laughter fading into a sigh. "Actually… There's something else I've been meaning to talk to you about, Gray."

The tenderness in his voice made my heart go soft, and the Tarot card inside my pocket suddenly felt warm and heavy.

"Sophie," I breathed, and he tightened his grip on my hand.

An image of her danced across my vision, and I allowed myself to get swept up in the random memory. They often came like this now, unbidden but not unwelcome, and each one felt like a treasure washed up on the shores of my heart, just for me.

I knew what Emilio was going to ask me about, but I wasn't ready. Not yet. I just needed this one last chance to remember her as she was—vivacious and alive and crazy and incredible and so full of life, she almost seemed immortal.

"Wait," I whispered, closing my eyes as I tumbled headlong into the memory…

"*Um, Sophie? Do I even want to* know *what's happening in here?*"

I'd just gotten home from the grocery store, and I found her in the living room with her hands planted on the floor, her ass bobbing up and down to some kind of nightmare bubblegum pop music blasting from her laptop.

"I'm teaching myself how to twerk."

"You're a few years late for that craze."

Sophie stood up and shook her head, her red ponytail swinging in time with the music. "Twerking is timeless. Put that stuff down and get over here."

"I'm… not really in a twerking kind of mood right now."

"That's the beauty of it, Gray. Twerking automatically puts you in a twerking kind of mood. It's very meta." She waved me over and cranked up the music, and I joined her on the makeshift dance floor, caught up as always in the tide of her crazy.

"Like this?" I asked, swerving my hips. I couldn't help the smile that broke across my face.

"That's it! Get it, girl!" She clapped along with the beat, and it wasn't long before I was following her lead, the two of us working it for all we were worth, laughing our asses off the entire time.

It wasn't long before we brought alcohol into the mix, rearranged the living room furniture to make a temporary dance-hall, made a playlist we dubbed "S&G's Twerkalicious Beats," and recorded our own dance video.

"And this," I said to her just before we finally passed out, "better not ever see the light of day."

Sophie winked. "No worries, Gray. Your twerkaliciousness will remain forever our dirty little secret."

I opened my eyes and sucked in a shuddering breath, pressing a hand to my pocket where the Page of Cups still sat.

"I'm okay," I whispered, more to myself than to Emilio.

He touched my hand again, gently stroking my skin. "We're finished with the forensic exams on Sophie's body. Do you know what sort of arrangements she'd want?"

I closed my eyes again, reaching out for her with my mind, wishing she could tell me what she wanted. Wishing she was still here so that we wouldn't have to make this decision at all.

"She didn't have any family," I said. "Just me."

"There's no 'just' about it, Gray. Sophie was very lucky to have you."

I didn't really know what to say to that. I used to think Sophie and I were both lucky that our paths had crossed, that we'd become such inseparable friends. But if Sophie had never met me, she might still be alive. Twerking in someone else's living room, my life all the poorer for never having known her light, but she'd still be here.

Yanking myself back from the precipice of those pointless thoughts, I said, "I'm not sure what the rules are when someone isn't a relative."

"Don't worry about the rules," Emilio said. "I'll take care of that."

Despite the heaviness of the moment, I laughed. "I never thought I'd hear you say that, Detective Alvarez."

"Don't tell anyone. Especially not Ronan. I'll never hear the end of it."

My smile faded. "Sophie never talked about her wishes. I mean, there are always risks living in the Bay, working late nights in the warehouse district. But we'd always taken care of ourselves. Until that night in the alley with Bean, I'd never had any real problems."

But when I finally did, they'd followed me home to Sophie. To the other witches in the Bay. Now that I knew Jonathan was behind the murders, how could I not blame myself? He wouldn't have ended up in the Bay if not for his vendetta against me.

The hole in my heart started to burn as the Sophie-sized ache turned to anger. Grieving for her was like walking on a knife's edge—despair at her death on one side, raw fury at her murder on the other. I never knew where I'd end up on any given day—only that it cut deep either way.

I didn't want to think about the murder right now. About the hunter and his vampire bitch who'd poisoned her. I wanted to think about her life. What she stood for. What she would have wanted, and what kind of place was beautiful enough to serve as her final resting place.

"Sophie always wanted to see the mountains," I said, grateful for the warmth of Emilio's touch. For his under-standing. "She used to talk about planning a big hiking trip for us to Rocky Mountain National Park in Colorado. I'd like to take her there one day, when all this is over. I think she'd like that."

As if to confirm, the card in my pocket warmed again.

"That sounds like a beautiful tribute, Gray." Emilio laced his fingers through mine.

"How do you... I mean, I guess we need to have her cremated, right? God, then I need to figure out how to cancel her cell phone and close her bank accounts and stop her mail and make sure her bills are paid and… I don't even know where to start with all this."

"You just did, Gray," Emilio said. "I'll make the arrangements with the funeral home. After that, we'll just take things one day at a time. What else can we do, *querida*?"

I sat up on the blanket, wrapping my arms around myself. Emilio was right. We were never promised more than that—one day was all we ever had. What else *could* we do?

Emilio sat up next to me, placing a comforting hand on my back and offering a deep smile that swept the gloom from the corners of my heart.

I returned it, already feeling lighter.

"Should we save some brownies for the demons?" he asked, his eyes twinkling with mischief.

Now it was my turn for the mask of abject horror. I leaned across his lap and grabbed the pan from his other side, my spoon at the ready once again.

"Just because I don't want Asher to suffer does *not* mean I'm interested in sharing my brownies."

Emilio winked. "I didn't think so."

"As far as I'm concerned, those demons are on their own tonight."

Emilio didn't even hesitate before picking up his spoon. "Fair enough, *querida*. Fair enough."

FIFTEEN

RONAN

"Get out."

They were the first words I'd spoken to Asher since dragging his ass off the property an hour ago.

We'd just pulled up to the loading dock at Waldrich's warehouse after an hour of stone-cold silence, which was probably for the best. The long drive back to the Bay from the safe house gave me time to cool off.

Marginally.

I shut off the van and pocketed the keys. Without waiting for a reply, I hopped out and headed inside to pick up the delivery manifest from Waldrich, my and Gray's boss.

When I returned to the dock, I found Asher already hard at work, stacking boxes onto a hand truck and loading them into the van.

"About time you showed up," he snarled. "I'm freezing my balls off out here."

"It's not my fault you like to strut around showing off your eight-pack. Next time put on a shirt."

"For one thing, that's not where my balls are, and for two things, it's not like you gave me a choice when you ordered me off the property." Asher leaned back against the side of the van and shoved a hand through his hair. "For fuck's sake, Vacarro. I was trying to help her."

"I think you and I have different definitions of *help*." I shucked off my jacket and tossed it at him, then grabbed the hand truck to load up a few more boxes. "You were way out of line."

He didn't respond right away, though I could tell it was just eating him up inside. Ash wasn't human, but he wasn't *inhuman* either; I'd seen the guilt in his eyes as he watched Gray head into the house with Emilio.

Still, I was letting him stew in it. Whether he thought he was helping or not, he hurt the woman I loved.

I clenched my jaw, swallowing down a fresh swell of anger as Ash made himself at home in my jacket.

"Try not to sweat it all up, dickhole."

"Sweat *this*." He grabbed his balls, classy guy that he was, and the sonofabitch almost had me laughing again.

Fucking Asher.

"Look," he said, grabbing the last box and tossing it into the van. "The way things stand right now? If that cock-sucker gets his hands on her, Gray's going down, guaranteed. Not without a fight, but all the fight in the world won't matter if she ends up dead."

"Tell me something," I said, slamming the van door.

"Exactly how many times did your mother drop you on your head as a baby?"

Asher flashed his tough-as-nails grin. "Not enough times to kill me, unfortunately for you and your witchy woman."

I thought of that witchy woman earlier tonight, backed into a corner, lighting his ass up like a firecracker.

It would've made me smile if she wasn't so upset about it.

"For fuck's sake, Ash. She's human. A witch of indeterminate power, but still human." I started up the van and navigated us through the district, heading toward Black Ruby, Darius's club and our first delivery.

The load was fairly light tonight—small favors. Between collecting overdue payments and pulling other odd jobs for Waldrich, I'd been handling Gray's delivery shifts as best I could, but I wasn't sure I could keep it up much longer. I didn't like being away from her for so long, especially not while she was still struggling to get a handle on her powers, and I needed to focus on tracking down the hunter before any more witches got snatched.

Especially Gray.

"She's a fucking target," Ash said. "She's not ready for him—that much is clear. And she's way too exposed, even at the house. I don't like it. Not after… after everything." He cranked down the window as we wove through the narrow streets, keeping his eyes peeled for any bullshit.

Just another Tuesday night in the Bay.

But Ash, who'd ridden shotgun on shifts with me before and knew the drill, seemed antsy tonight.

"You got something else on your mind, demon?" I asked.

He didn't say anything right away, but I caught the tick in his jaw, the tightening of his hand on the doorframe.

I punched his thigh. "Out with it. Or I'm taking back my jacket."

"Some serious shit went down tonight," he said.

"What shit?"

Ash closed his eyes, shaking his head. "He showed up in her realm, Ronan. Held her against her will. She had to bust out on her own."

"He fucking what?" I slammed the van into park. "How the hell did he get in?"

"It's a long story—one she needs to tell you herself—but he's definitely upping his game."

"Motherfucker." No wonder Ash pushed her so hard. If the hunter could reach her there, where else could he reach her? What other help—or powers—did he have?

"She's a sitting damn *duck*." He slammed his hand on the dashboard, his rage continuing to build. I could feel it emanating from him, as hot as sunbaked pavement. "You think I *like* hurting her? You think I get off on watching her heart break into a thousand pieces because of shit that *I* said? Fuck you, Ronan. Fuck. You."

He threw himself out of the van and went to the back, hauling open the cargo doors and yanking out the hand truck.

I let him have five minutes to cool off before joining him out there.

"I get it," I said, shoving my hands into my pockets, not wanting to get too close. A pissed off incubus wasn't someone you wanted to snuggle with. "I don't blame you for trying to help her learn how to defend herself."

"No, you just blame me for making her cry. Right? Because that's my thing. Biting people's heads off. Being a grade-A dick." He slammed the van door shut, and I took a risk, reaching for his shoulder while his back was still turned.

Mistake.

He whirled on me fast, punching me hard in the shoulder. He hadn't done it to hurt me—he could've easily cold-cocked me in the face if he'd wanted to cause serious pain—but it still pissed me off.

I grabbed the front of his—*my*—jacket and shoved him back against the van, bracing a forearm across his throat. "You really wanna do this, asshole?"

His black eyes bore into mine, but I felt his body relax, his fury receding as quickly as it had risen.

"I don't know what the fuck is going on with you and Gray," I said, releasing him and smoothing out the jacket. "But you need to make it right with her. And with yourself."

When he looked up at me again, his eyes were back to blue. He nodded.

"We good?" I asked, squeezing his shoulder.

He returned the gesture and nodded once, then pulled

me in for a hug. I hugged him right back; I wasn't sure which one of us needed it more.

"We're good," he said.

"I wouldn't be too sure about that," a voice said.

I turned around and caught a wiry, sniveling vamp slithering out from behind the other side of the van.

Ash and I exchanged a quick glance that basically said, *this motherfucker is going down in about three seconds...*

"I hope you brought your friends," I said, turning toward him. He was maybe five foot four, a hundred and ten pounds on a good day.

"And your lunch," Asher said, joining me at my side and folding his arms across his chest. "You look a little... malnourished."

"In that case," I said, "better bring your friends' lunch, too."

Ash scratched his head. "Pretty sure his friends *are* his lunch."

"That poses a problem when one is about to get his ass handed to him. Still, I don't see anyone else jumping to his defense, so..." I whipped the stake out from the back of my waistband and shoved the guy up against the van, pressing the pointy end to his chest.

He didn't resist. Didn't even try.

"I'm not here to fight," he said, raising his hands in surrender. "Just delivering a message."

"Try the post office," Ash said, offering a helpful smile. "They're the most reliable. Texting also works, especially if your solar sensitivity prevents you from accessing postal services during normal business hours."

His mask of calm detachment shattered, his lips curling back in a sneer. "Darius won't be able to protect you forever, hellspawn."

"Wait, was that… Was that the message?" Ash cupped a hand around his ear and leaned in close. "Or just you talking shit?"

"If you're smart," the vamp said, "you'll disassociate from him now."

"Damn," Ash said. "I'd hate to be *your* friend."

"Oh, you think you're his friends?" the vampire spat. "Beaumont's already betrayed his own kind. How long until he decides demonic company is no longer worth the trouble?"

I pressed the stake a little harder. "You don't know shit, bloodsucker."

"I know your friend is no more than a witch's lapdog."

"And you think you know something about *her*?" I tightened my grip on the stake, shifting it up to his throat. His Adam's apple bobbed nervously, but that was the only indication that he was remotely concerned about it.

"Dude." Ash faked a yawn. "I'm tired. And bored. I say we ice this asshole."

"Good call. You got a match?"

Asher patted down his pockets. "Picked a hell of a time to quit smoking."

"Now that's a damn shame," I said, knowing Ash had never smoked a day in his life. "Guess we'll just have to stake him and leave him for some other poor son of a bitch to find."

"Hope it's one of his friends," Ash said, "and not one of ours. Gosh, I'd really hate to think what a witch's lapdog could do to this piece of shit."

"Or the witch herself," Ronan said. "I hear she's pretty brutal when provoked."

The vampire hissed. "Fuck you, d—"

He might've meant to say dick, or dude, or devilish demon dickbags, but Ash and I would never know. I'd shoved the hawthorn stake clear through his voice box.

Blood oozed out over my hand and down my arm, soaking my sweatshirt.

The vamp dropped like a bag of rocks.

"That was… bloodier than I expected." I tried to shake the gore from my arm, but it was pretty well soaked.

Asher wrinkled his nose. "Dude. Nasty."

"Shut him up, didn't it?" I shook the blood from my hand. "If only I had another one for you."

"Make it a dozen," another voice said, "and you might stand a chance."

"Guess he brought a friend after all," I said to Ash, rolling my eyes as the two of us whipped around to face the latest bullshit threat.

Only this time, the threat was real.

Fuck.

At least a dozen vamps stood in formation, ranging in stature from small and willowy like our messenger there, to one guy roughly the size of a dump truck.

All of them were poised to attack.

One scrawny vamp we could take. But a whole damn platoon?

My stake was currently embedded in someone's voice box. Asher wasn't packing. And we were seriously outnumbered.

"This is gonna suck," Asher said to me out of the corner of his mouth.

"Understatement."

"Alright, let's do it," he said. "You go left, I'll go—"

"Ash," I sucked in a breath, taking a closer look at the crowd. "They're not all bloodsuckers. Half of them are humans."

"What the serious fuck?" he whispered.

I couldn't decide whether that upped the odds in our favor or not. Chances are, we were going to die anyway.

"Just… try not to kill any of them," I said. If humans died on Beaumont's turf—at the hands of two demons who were known associates of his—the Council would be up his ass in a heartbeat.

Asher flicked his gaze over to me and grinned, his eyes two smoldering black pits, and I knew any chance at getting out of this cleanly was long gone. "No promises, Vacarro."

SIXTEEN

GRAY

"I hate that this is your path," Darius said, holding out a hand to help me up.

It was the night after my disastrous battle with Asher, yet I'd made Darius promise he wouldn't go easy on me. I needed to learn how to fight; treating me with kid gloves wasn't going to cut it.

As much as I would've loved to take another shot at Asher, he and Ronan were lying low at Ronan's apartment in the Bay, giving me a couple days to recoup.

It sounded nice in theory, but recoup time felt like a luxury none of us had earned—least of all me.

I blinked away the pain and sucked in a breath of cool air, preparing myself for another round.

Respect was the only ground rule Darius and I had set— a concept as foreign to Asher as wearing a shirt.

Ignoring the vampire's outstretched hand, I pushed myself off the ground and got to my feet, spitting out a mouthful of dirt and blood. "Doesn't change the fact that it *is* my path."

"No, I suppose not." Darius slid out of view, but this time I anticipated his appearance behind me, throwing my elbow back just in time to catch him in the ribs. It didn't hurt him, of course, but it bought me just enough time to spin around and duck down low, dodging his next blow.

"Good," he said, sliding away again.

Figuring he wouldn't make the same move twice, I tucked myself into a tight ball and rolled to the side, then swept out my leg, catching him in the shins just as he reappeared in front of me.

He stumbled a bit, but quickly recovered, lunging straight for me before I had a chance to get back on my feet. He came at me hard and fast, barreling into me and knocking me flat on my back. He pinned me down, his lean, powerful body smothering every square inch of mine.

Desperately I tried to roll over, to cover my head, to knee him in the groin, but I couldn't get an inch of leverage.

"And this is how you die, little brawler." He nipped at my neck, making me yelp.

"Take it easy, Darius," Emilio warned from the sidelines. "She's had a rough first day."

"Not as rough as the hunter's planning to give me," I countered, getting to my feet and shaking off the pain. "Kid gloves aren't going to help, guys. Until I can get a better handle on my magic, hand-to-hand combat is my best shot."

No, I might not be able to immobilize a vampire or

shifter without a stake, a blade, or a gun and silver bullets, but if I'd learned anything from the last few weeks I'd spent in the Bay, it was that weapons and book smarts were only as good as the one who wielded them.

This month alone, I'd been jumped by a human while packing a hunting knife in my boot, unable to get to it until it was too late. I'd brought a stake to a vampire club, only to have it taken away by the very vampire trying to teach me a lesson now.

Lucky for me, Darius had turned out to be one of the good ones.

But luck was a poor strategy to rely on, and I wasn't taking any more chances. Not when Reva, Haley, and the others were depending on me.

I cracked my neck and nodded at Darius. "Let's go again."

"I'll take this one," Emilio called from behind me. "Will you talk her through it?"

"If you insist on showing off," Darius said to him, "then I suppose I have no choice in the matter."

"She needs every advantage she can get."

"What advantage?" I turned around to ask Emilio what he was talking about, but he didn't need words to answer me.

He loomed before me, naked, as stunning as a sculpture and just as silent. I hadn't even heard him approach, or strip for that matter, but now he was here, close enough to touch. To smell.

I still hadn't spent a lot of time with him—not up close

—and for a moment I closed my eyes, letting his scent wash over me. It was a heady mix that reminded me of everything I loved about being outside—earthy and woodsy, underscored with a touch of something sweet, like vanilla.

It was lovely and warm and comforting, just like Emilio himself.

I opened my eyes, marveling at him. Not even caring that I probably looked like a crazy fangirl.

The biggest of the guys in all ways, his well-defined muscles rippled in the moonlight, sleek and powerful beneath his golden skin.

Despite his playful smile and the kindness in his eyes, standing here in all his chiseled perfection, Emilio Alvarez was downright *frightening*. The raw power locked away in his body gave me chills.

And he hadn't even shifted yet.

Wordlessly he pointed toward the other end of the yard, gesturing for me to walk in that direction. He was so beautiful it almost hurt to tear my eyes away, but somehow I managed, heading out to the edge of the grass that bordered the woods.

"Is this far enough?" I turned around, simultaneously nervous and excited to see him shift again. I'd only seen it the one other time—the night we'd infiltrated Norah's place to save Asher—and there hadn't been much time to appreciate it.

But I'd already missed my chance tonight, because charging across the lawn, heading right for me, was a very fast, very large wolf.

Out here in the moonlight, clearly in his element, the jet-black wolf ignited a primal fear inside me. My heart hammered against my chest, my mouth turning as dry as sand.

"Tuck and roll, Gray!" Darius shouted. "Do it now!"

The urgency of his command snapped me out of my paralysis. Shoving aside my fear, I dropped to the ground and covered my head with my arms.

There was no time to roll.

Emilio crashed into me like a freight train, sending me sprawling onto my back. Like Darius had earlier, Emilio pinned me down, baring his fangs. I blinked rapidly, sucking in air to try to calm my heartbeat.

I knew he wouldn't hurt me, but holy *shit* those fangs were scary.

"It's a show of dominance," Darius explained. "He's testing you to see if you'll submit or challenge him."

"I'm not exactly in a position to challenge him," I said, trying to squirm out from beneath him.

Emilio growled, a quiet but menacing warning meant just for me. Every hair on my body stood on end.

He really was magnificent.

And clearly the alpha in this situation.

I closed my eyes, indicating my total submission.

After a beat, I felt him lower his head, nudging my cheek with his snout. He was still on top of me, but he'd taken his paws off my arms, relieving the pressure.

"What's he doing now?" I asked Darius, opening my eyes.

"I believe the big softy wants you to pet him."

I let out a shaky laugh, my body still humming with fear and adrenaline. "That I can definitely do."

Slowly, I reached up to touch his head, stroking his coarse fur. It was thicker than I remembered, coated with an oily sheen. I grabbed a fistful, giving him a gentle tug, working my way over to his ears.

Emilio just kept on panting, his eyes no longer holding a challenge.

"Well now he's just taking advantage," Darius said, and I laughed again, reaching up with my other hand and rubbing the tips of his ears.

"Remember our purpose, *El Lobo*," Darius teased. "Everyone loves a good stroke, but we've got a lesson to teach."

Emilio turned his head toward Darius and growled, then tipped his head up, exposing his throat.

"He's showing you his vulnerable spots," Darius said, continuing with the lesson. "His throat, his belly. If you're attacked by a shifter in his animal form, your best chance is to inflict damage where he's got the least protection. Unfortunately, that requires getting close to him. In a situation like that, you'd better be packing magic. Most animals won't give you the option of submitting—they'll simply go for the jugular."

I swallowed hard, remembering Emilio's sharp fangs.

I touched my fingers to my throat, feeling very human, and very breakable.

Emilio finally retreated, and I got to my feet, refusing to

take my eyes off him. He'd cheated me out of seeing him shift into wolf form; no way was I missing the change back to human.

He loped back over to the other side of the yard, stopping by the tree where he'd left his clothes. His wolf form elongated and thickened, bones snapping and reshaping, the thick coat of hair fading.

Moments later he stood before us, all man once again.

"You might want to close your mouth, love," Darius said, helpful as always.

"As long as I don't have to close my eyes." I smirked, fully enjoying the view while Emilio put his clothes back on.

"Not too bad for your first shifter attack," Emilio said, grinning at me as we regrouped at the center of the lawn. "We'll try again tomorrow. I just wanted to give you an introduction."

"Thank you," I said, lowering my eyes. Heat rose to my cheeks. I'd just seen the man naked—twice—and all wolfed out, but suddenly I felt shy. Humbled. In a small, quiet voice, I said, "You really are amazing, Emilio."

"You're not so bad yourself, *bruja bonita*."

"Hey!" I finally met his eyes again. "What happened to *querida*?"

Emilio smiled. Like me, he was blushing. "Just trying a new one on for size."

"What does it mean?" I asked, though I was pretty sure *bonita* meant pretty.

Before he could answer, Darius was there with another

helpful suggestion. "If you two are planning to spend more time rolling around on the ground together, you should probably get over this bashful thing."

"Does it bother you, vampire?" I asked playfully.

"It's sickeningly sweet," he said. "My fangs are getting cavities just being in the vicinity."

"Don't listen to him, *bruja*. He's just jealous that I never gave *him* a nickname."

"Preposterous," Darius said, but he was grinning, the mood among us lighter and happier than it had been all day.

I rolled my shoulders, still feeling pretty good. Feeling like I could go another round.

"You ready to call it a night?" Darius asked.

Emilio headed back to his spot at the side of the yard, but I shook my head. "Not while I've still got some blood left in me."

He didn't ask me if I was certain, didn't nod to let me know he was ready. He simply launched himself at me.

I turned just in time to partially block him, but my shoulder took the brunt of the impact. The pain was intense, reverberating down my arm and my back, making my fingers go numb.

I squeezed my eyes shut, but there was no time for licking my wounds. Darius disappeared in a blur, attacking again from behind. But when he reached forward to grab me, I leaned back, an unexpected move that threw him completely off balance. The momentum carried him forward, and I twisted out of the way, sticking my foot out to trip him. He went down hard.

Wasting no time, I jumped on his back and shoved an imaginary stake between his shoulder blades.

"And this is how *you* die, bloodsucker," I said. "Well, how you get immobilized long enough for me to cut off your head. Now be a dear and hold *real* still while I decapitate you."

I released him, allowing him to roll onto his back.

"Vicious," he said, his eyes sparkling with pride. "I think you're getting the hang of this, love."

"Awesome." I stood up and dusted off my hands.

Who was I kidding? As much as I would've loved to keep this up, I was spent. Unless I wanted to end up in the hospital, I needed a shower, some tea, and a good night's rest before I signed up for any more beatings.

"By this time next week," I said, "maybe I'll be able to walk without a limp."

"You're doing really well, Gray." Darius got to his feet, sliding his hand behind my neck and giving me an encouraging squeeze. "You've got a lot of work ahead of you, but you really impressed me."

"Hmm. Say it again?"

"Anything for you, love. You really impressed me." His teasing smile changed to concern. "Ah, you're bleeding again. Allow me." He dipped his head down and pressed his mouth to my shoulder, his tongue skating across my skin.

SARAH PIPER

His lips closed over the wound, sucking gently. I couldn't hold back my shiver.

After what felt like an eternity, he finally pulled away, his lips red with blood.

Briefly, I wondered what it said about me that seeing him with my blood on his lips turned me on so much.

Briefly, I decided I didn't care.

I met his eyes, but there was no threat there. No super-charged bloodlust.

Only the regular kind of lust. The kind that radiated from his hungry, honey-colored eyes and straight down to my aching core.

God, he's fucking hot…

"Ooo-kay," Emilio said with a laugh. I'd almost forgotten he was there, still watching us from the sidelines. "Well, it's been a blast, but I can see you two have a few things to, ah, discuss. I'll just… I'll go. No worries. I need to check in at the station anyway. Don't wait up."

"We won't," Darius said, still not breaking eye contact with me.

"I, um, I'm going to take a shower," I mumbled.

"You do that, Miss Desario."

"Fine. I will." I walked backward, stumbling and awkward, a stupid smile plastered on my face. I felt like I was in middle school again, giddy that the cute boy from my English class finally noticed me.

But unlike my innocent English class crush, the vampire watching me like he wanted to eat me wasn't a cute boy at

180

all. He was a man, impossibly strong, incredibly sexy, and the best part?

He was all mine.

And we were about to have the entire house to ourselves.

SEVENTEEN

GRAY

I'd just ducked under the hot water when I felt him step into the shower behind me, his intoxicating whiskey-and-leather scent giving him away despite his efforts at stealth.

"Miss me already, vampire?"

"I thought you might need a little help reaching your back," Darius said, stroking a hand down my spine and cupping my ass.

Laughing, I turned and looped my arms around his neck, pressing our wet bodies together. "Pretty sure *you're* the one who needs help reaching my back, because that's my ass."

"This? Right here?" He slid his other hand down and gave me a squeeze, and I sighed in pleasure. Darius did nothing by accident, and his firm, commanding touch was always welcome, especially when we were both naked and wet and slippery.

Gripping me tight, he lifted me up, and I wrapped my

legs around his hips, pressing my mouth to his for a deep, sultry kiss. Hot water streamed down over us, and for a minute I lost myself in his kiss, in his touch, in our own little paradise where hunters and rogue supernaturals didn't exist and our greatest concern was running out of hot water before we finished enjoying each other's company in here.

But that wasn't how the world worked.

I pulled back to catch my breath, and Darius offered a soft smile, blinking tiny drops of water from his thick, dark eyelashes.

"I hope I didn't hurt you too much out there, love," he said, concern shadowing his golden eyes.

"Not too much. Just the right amount." I smiled to let him know I was okay, but he still seemed worried.

"Would you like me to leave?" he asked.

"Well, I *was* going to wash my hair, but since you've already so rudely interrupted, we might as well see where this goes."

"Rudely interrupted? I've done nothing of the sort." He set me on my feet again, then looked over the rainbow assortment of shampoos and conditioners Emilio had brought me, choosing one from the middle. "How are we feeling about…" He narrowed his eyes at the label. "Coconut Sunrise? Good heavens, who names this stuff?"

"I haven't tried that one yet."

"Right. Turn around, then," he ordered, flipping open the cap and squeezing a dollop of shampoo into his hand.

I obliged, tilting my head back and closing my eyes as

his fingers began to work their magic, gently massaging the shampoo into my scalp.

The shower smelled like a tropical vacation—rather, what I imagined a tropical vacation would smell like—and I couldn't recall ever being so relaxed before.

"Does that feel good?" he murmured, his lips close to my ear.

"Mmm. I could very easily get used to this," I murmured.

Everything inside me was melting under his divine touch.

"As could I," he said, gently tipping my head back to rinse out the suds, making sure the water didn't stream into my eyes. "But I'm afraid I can't let you get used to it just yet."

"Too late." I turned to face him again, sliding my hands up over his shoulders.

His eyes were serious again, the space between his brows pinched.

"What's wrong?" I asked.

"I just spoke with my people on the east coast. I'm heading to New York tonight."

My heart sank.

"They've finally made contact with Grinaldi," he explained, stroking my back. "But the old codger refuses to discuss this with anyone but me directly."

I sighed, trying not to show my disappointment and worry. We'd been waiting for news on the Grinaldi front for weeks; it was critical that Darius go.

Still, I didn't love the idea of him heading off alone. What if it was a setup? The vampires who'd attacked us at Norah's had once been patrons of Darius's club, and they'd turned out to be traitors. And we still didn't know where the southern vamps who'd ambushed us at the morgue had come from, or what connections they had to the hunter.

How did Darius know he could trust Grinaldi's people?

"Will you have backup?" I asked.

"Traveling with me, yes. On the estate itself? I'm afraid not, love. Vincenzo Grinaldi is a traditionalist. The presence of my associates would signal to him a lack of trust, ending our meeting before it even began."

"*Do* you trust him?"

"Not in the slightest. But I assure you—no harm will come to me as a guest on his property. His adherence to the old customs is more legendary and unwavering than my own."

"And you're willing to stake your life on that?"

Darius frowned. "Poor word choice, love."

"You know what I mean."

"Yes, I'm willing to *stake* my life on it. Grinaldi is not my ally, but you must remember, Gray—not all vampires are like Hollis and Weston. There is still honor among us—especially in the old families like the Grinaldis."

I blew out a breath. That was something, at least.

"But," I said, "we already know that at least one member of his clan feels differently. And for all you know, that rogue vamp could be Grinaldi himself."

Darius didn't deny it, which only deepened my concern.

"Anything is possible," he said, "and I've done my best to prepare for the worst-case scenario. But my instincts are telling me Grinaldi is just as eager to get to the bottom of this as we are. In fact, I hope I'm able to track down his rogue before his people do; if the Grinaldis find him first, he'll be of no use to us."

"They'll kill him?"

Darius nodded. "Torture first. Then they'll kill him, yes."

I closed my eyes, staving off images of dead vampires. In the last week alone, I'd seen way more than the lifetime recommended dose of decapitated bloodsuckers. "When do you leave?"

"I've still got a few hours." His hand curved down around my ass again, stroking softly.

"Are you trying to distract me from your imminent departure?" I asked.

"No. Maybe. Is it working?"

"Not really." I opened my eyes, my gaze landing on the squishy back scrubber that hung from the shower caddy. In a burst of inspiration, I reached behind Darius and grabbed it.

"Shall I do your back?" he asked.

"No." I shot him a wicked glare. "I'm going to do your front."

Before he could respond, I dropped to my knees, sliding the scrubber beneath them to cushion the hard bathtub.

The hot shower had warmed his skin, and I slid my

palms up his legs, then dragged my fingernails back down his thighs, his slick muscles flexing at my touch.

"Conditions, Miss Desario," he warned, but he was already hard for me, his body's desire overriding his mind's need for control.

"Your willpower is admirable," I said. "But I agreed to your conditions for taking me in your bed. We didn't make any bargains about this."

I brought my lips to his cock, briefly buzzing over the tip.

Darius let out a small sigh of pleasure, but he was still trying to resist me. "Ah, but I'd much rather do this to *you* right now. Perhaps we should switch places?"

The idea of Darius going down on me in the shower sent a rush of heat to my core, and I was beyond tempted to take him up on it, but… No.

This moment wasn't about me. It was about Darius.

It was about him trusting me enough to relinquish his control for just a few minutes and let me give him this pleasure.

It was about breaking down some of his walls, just a little bit.

"You'll like it," he said, still trying to convince me. "I promise."

"I have no doubt about that, Mr. Beaumont," I said, imitating his accent. "However, when that moment happens between us, it will be in *my* bed, and *I* will be taking charge, and your giant ego will be nowhere in sight."

Darius chuckled, and his muscles relaxed beneath my

touch. "You drive a hard bargain, Miss Desario. And I do mean hard."

"I noticed." I fisted his cock, squeezing gently, then stroking him.

"Oh, hell," he whispered, his hands reaching down to touch my face.

Refusing to cede control, I brought him to my mouth and licked the tip, swirling my tongue, loving the taste and feel of his hot, smooth skin.

"You're going to be the death of me, little brawler," he moaned.

I pulled back slightly.

"Would you like me to stop?" I teased, still stroking him. "I don't want to be held responsible for taking down an immortal apex predator with one little kiss."

Darius tipped his face down and growled, the look his eyes hungry and vulnerable as I took him into my mouth again, deeper this time, my hand still wrapped around the base as I worked my tongue over his hot flesh.

"Don't…" he breathed, sliding his hands into my hair. "Don't stop. I can think of no… no better way to… meet my end. That's… fucking brilliant."

My vampire was coming undone, and I was loving every red-hot second of it, licking and sucking him, bringing him closer and closer to the brink.

His hands slid deeper into my wet hair, fisting it tight as I slowed down, teasing him with soft flicks of my tongue, then taking him in deeper, alternating until he was damn near out of his mind.

"You're… killing… me," he grunted.

"Payback for body slamming me," I teased.

"Oh, this is supposed to be… *punishment*?"

"You tell me. You're not used to ceding control," I teased, licking a path from the base to the tip.

"I'm… not," he admitted, his voice wobbly. "You leave me… quite unbalanced."

"In that case, you'd better find something to hold on to." That was all the warning I gave him before I wrapped my lips around him again, sliding down over his shaft as I relaxed my throat, taking him deep.

His knees buckled, but to his credit, he remained upright, and I sucked harder, sensing he was so, so close.

I let out a soft moan, and that was the very end of my vampire's resistance. He came with a roar that echoed off the tiles, his body shuddering as he thrust inside me, harder and faster, his hands clenched so tightly in my hair it made my eyes water and my thighs clench, my own core throbbing at his wild, euphoric outburst.

I'd never seen him so unrefined. So unrestrained.

After a long moment, he sagged back against the shower tiles, and I pulled away, slowly kissing my way up his toned body as I got to my feet. His skin was impossibly smooth, every inch of him perfect and delicious.

When I stood fully upright once again, Darius slid a finger beneath my chin and tipped my face up, leaning down to capture my mouth in a slow, soft kiss that didn't end until my skin was pruned and the water streaming over our bodies had turned as chilly as the autumn air.

EIGHTEEN

DARIUS

Glowing fire, crackling softly. Two glasses of a vintage French burgundy I'd been saving for a special occasion. And Gray, the woman who was quickly forging a path to my heart.

Tonight, I had her all to myself—a rare luxury. Here in my arms, snuggling on the couch before the fireplace, she was safe.

If a more perfect evening existed, I couldn't imagine it.

"Tell me what's happening in there." I traced my lips across Gray's forehead. "What great mysteries are you pondering, what schemes are you hatching, whose demise are you so intricately plotting?"

"Nothing so exciting as all that, I'm afraid." She tucked her feet up beneath her, leaning in a little closer. "I just don't want you to go."

"That makes two of us, love. But I won't be long. Two,

three days at most. When I return, we'll have another shower."

"Yeah?"

"You didn't think I'd stop at Coconut Sunrise, did you? We've still got Peaches and Dreams, Vanilla Vavoom, Let Freesia Ring… I have every intention of working my way through your entire collection."

She laughed, resting her head against my chest. Her hair was still damp, and I pressed my lips to it, inhaling the unfamiliar scent of her new shampoo. Underneath it all, there was still just Gray, the sweet scent of her skin tinged with a hint of lavender and lilac.

I could very easily become addicted.

"Are you staying right in Manhattan?" she asked.

"Yes. I have a flat in the East Village."

"Really?" Gray seemed genuinely surprised by this. "I would've pegged you as a Park Avenue penthouse kind of guy."

"I have one of those, too, but I much prefer the Village. Not quite so stuffy, much better people-watching, interesting restaurants when I'm in the mood for a human meal." I leaned forward and retrieved our wine glasses from the coffee table, passing one to her. "Have you been?"

"Not to that part of town, no." Her eyes misted, but wherever her thoughts had taken her, they brought a gentle smile to her lips. "Calla used to take me into the city every year around Christmas. We'd do a whole staycation thing— play tourist for a few days, check out the tree and all the holiday displays, eat until we nearly burst."

"Did you stay right in the city?"

"No, usually on the outskirts. But one year—not long before she died—she surprised me with a room at the Plaza. She must've saved all year for that, but we had so much fun. Half the time we didn't even want to leave the hotel. We just kept ordering room service in our bathrobes and pretending to be famous."

Letting her eyes fall closed, she sipped her wine, lost for a moment in her own memories.

"What was your favorite thing to see?" I asked gently.

She answered without hesitation. "Central Park. I used to stand in the middle of the Great Lawn and look up at the sky, trying to catch snowflakes in my eyelashes. I'd pretend I was trapped in a giant snow globe." Gray laughed, and when she opened her eyes again and met my gaze, her blue eyes sparkled. "I guess that makes me a total cliché, right?"

"Appreciating something beautiful is never cliché." I swept a lock of hair behind her ear, cupping her face. "I wish I could've seen you there."

"Maybe you did."

"I would have remembered. Believe me."

"I don't know, D. Sometimes it feels like the people who are meant to be in your life keep crossing your path long before you ever actually meet them."

I swirled the wine in my glass, then sipped, pondering her words. Perhaps she was right. After all, she'd been drawn to the Bay for a reason—all of us had, at one time or another. And by demonic intervention or fate or forces far greater, she'd become part of my life, too.

Maybe it was meant to be.

"What time is your flight?" She sat up, reaching for her phone on the table to check the time. "Should we call an Uber? You never know what security at Sea-Tac is going to be like."

"I have a private jet, love. It's the only way to ensure I'm not caught unprotected in daylight. Besides, have you ever traveled commercially?" I shuddered in sheer horror at the thought. "That is a fate I wouldn't wish on my worst enemy. Well, maybe my *worst*. Certainly not my third-worst, in any case."

Gray laughed. "Not all of us are jet-owning gazillionaires."

"Then I suppose it's good you have at least one friend who is." I set down my glass and gathered her into my arms again, kissing the tip of her nose. "And when this is over, I'd like to take you to New York—just the two of us. Would that be alright with you?"

Her eyes lit up, making me wish I'd offered it sooner. That I could offer her such simple pleasures every day for the rest of her life.

"Are you serious?" she asked, and the pure, unfiltered joy on her face served only to remind me how important this mission was. How urgently I needed to speak with Grinaldi and track down his rogue vampire before Gray or any other witch came to further harm.

"As serious as this." With no more than a grin as fair warning, I captured her lush, wine-dark mouth in a kiss so deep and all-consuming, the demon whose bed she'd undoubtedly share tonight would still be able to taste me on her lips.

Unfortunately, my plan backfired. Rather than leaving Ronan a message for later, my kiss seemed to send out a beacon, for the demon in question was suddenly hobbling through the front door with his hellspawn companion, the two of them looking for all the world like they'd been chewed up and spit out by the devil himself.

"Sorry to break up the tender moment," Ronan said. "But we've got bloodsucker problems. Big ones."

NINETEEN

GRAY

"What happened?" I jumped out of Darius's lap and bolted for the front door, taking in the scene. Ronan and Asher were wrecked, bandaged in some places and bruised in others, their eyes red with exhaustion.

Ronan smiled when he saw me, but it was thin and lifeless, and it didn't last. "We got jumped on a delivery to the club last night. About a dozen guys crept up on us."

"They attacked on Black Ruby turf?" Darius rose from the couch, incredulous. "Have they gone mad?"

"Not mad at all, actually," Asher said, kicking off his boots. We followed him into the kitchen, where he rifled through the freezer for a bag of frozen peas and applied them to a nasty-looking bruise on his jaw. "Pretty sure it was strategic on their part."

"They're sending a message," Ronan said. "They would've killed us otherwise. A dozen of them against two of us? We didn't stand a chance."

I touched my fingers to his eyebrow, just below a crudely-stitched gash. "Looks like they tried their best."

Ronan took my hand and brought it to his mouth, pressing a kiss to my palm. His own hand was bandaged, the sight of it igniting a flash of anger inside me. God, how I longed for the day when I'd have full control over my magic. When I could cast a simple tracking spell, find whoever did this to the man I loved, and bring them to their knees in agony.

"It gets worse," Ash said. "The vamps were rollin' with at least four humans."

"*Were?*" Darius's voice went up an octave. "Tell me you're speaking in the past tense because you talked the humans out of their poor choice in friends, convinced them that vampires don't actually exist, and sent them home safely."

Neither demon said a word.

Darius closed his eyes, his face a mask of calm I knew he wasn't feeling. Through gritted teeth, he said, "You killed four humans? Outside my club?"

"Wasn't us," Ash said. "The vamps batted us around first, then let the humans take shots, knowing we wouldn't do more than throw a few punches at them. When they'd had enough of that, the vamps pulled a Judas."

"Did they turn them?" Darius asked.

"Nope." Ash readjusted the peas on his jaw, wincing at the movement. "Staked 'em. We tried to help, but the dudes bled out fast."

"They're setting you guys up," I said. "Vamps don't carry stakes. They want people to think you guys did it."

"No," Darius said. "Not *people*. The bloody Fae Council."

My blood ran cold. If the Council decided to do an inquiry, and Ronan and Asher were found guilty of murdering four humans, they'd be imprisoned. Worse, if the fae felt like making an example of them.

"This is fucked eight ways from Sunday," Ronan said, grabbing two beers from the fridge and passing one to Ash. I helped myself to Ronan's, forcing him to get another. My nerves couldn't handle this conversation otherwise.

"After patching ourselves up at my place last night," Ronan continued, "we spent all day today trying to suss out the situation, see who was behind the attack. Nobody's talking—not the other vamps, not the fae, not the shifters."

"The blood slaves might know something," Ash said, "but we didn't dare approach them. The scene was still too hot tonight to risk it."

"Does Emilio know?" Darius asked.

"His crew showed up this afternoon," Ronan said. "We didn't make contact. We didn't want anyone connecting him to us and making trouble."

I sat on one of the high-backed stools at the center island and took a few swigs of beer, trying to stay calm. Ronan was right—this was fucked.

"I don't understand why the humans got involved in the first place," I said. "Were these guys recruiting?"

"Always." Darius began to pace across the kitchen, his

shoulders tense, his mind clearly working overtime. "There exists a subset of humans who believe that being a vampire is a lifestyle choice—something no more significant than deciding whether to live in the city or the country. They don't realize that for most of us, it was never a choice. They idolize and idealize us based on Hollywood's notion of our immortality, knowing nothing of the pain, the isolation…"

Heat flared in his eyes, and for a moment he seemed to forget where he was, lost in the torment of his own thoughts—thoughts I could only begin to guess at.

After a beat, I finally caught his eye and mouthed, "Are you okay?"

He narrowed his eyes as if the question confused him, then looked away.

"Many of them *want* to be turned," he continued, "thinking it will solve their human problems or elevate them to some special status they couldn't otherwise achieve. Unscrupulous vampires take advantage, preying on desperate humans with promises to turn them and help them through the transition once they've proven themselves."

"Sounds like a gang initiation," I said.

"Precisely," Darius said. "But what the poor bastards don't realize is most of them will end up becoming blood slaves, or just dying."

My stomach turned, my anger at the men who'd hurt Ronan and Ash fading under the harsh light of that truth. They'd simply done what they thought they had to do for a shot at a better life.

Their mistake had been in thinking that becoming vampires *was* their shot. That it was the very best option they had.

Despite so many supernaturals living in plain sight, most humans didn't know our world existed, and they were better off for it. But for the ones who'd come by that knowledge, life quickly became a double-edged sword.

For some, their entire worldview collapsed, and it left them untethered and lost. Others tried to share their newfound knowledge with the world, only to be labeled—and eventually driven—crazy. The path was no simpler for those who tried to assimilate or just peacefully coexist; it was all too easy to start feeling small and insignificant when your neighbor or hairdresser or favorite coffeeshop owner lived on human blood, turned into a wolf, carried out orders for hell, traveled to the summer court, cast spells, or brought people back from the dead.

Ronan tipped back the last of his beer, then let out a sigh. "Any idea who'd want to set us up? Who's sending this message?"

"Or what the message even *is*?" Ash asked. "They never did tell us."

"To be fair, I staked the one doing the talking," Ronan said.

Darius, who'd gone quiet again, finally spoke up. "It's not a message. It's a challenge." He resumed his pacing. "Now that I think of it, it's unlikely they're setting up Ronan and Asher for a Council inquiry at all. I believe this is about me—the demons just happened to be in the wrong place at the wrong time."

"I'm not following," I said.

"By attacking my associates on my turf," Darius explained, "someone is making it known that he—or they, depending on who's pulling the strings—no longer consider my authority valid."

"They mentioned something about you betraying your own kind," Ronan said. "Which led me to think Hollis's people were involved. But other than Weston, Hollis never *had* people."

"What about the rest of the bloodsuckers you guys iced at Bay Coven HQ?" Asher said. "Any one of them could've had friends in high places."

"Or friends in low places willing to join forces against a common enemy," I said.

"But I'm not their enemy," Darius said. "Other than Hollis and Weston, I've had very few confrontations with the vampire population—in Blackmoon Bay or anywhere else. Most, in fact, have been loyal Black Ruby regulars for years. Any customer service issues have been settled amicably."

"It's not about your business practices," Ash said. He finished his beer, then set down the bottle, locking me in an intense gaze that burned all the way down to my toes. "It's about Gray."

"What makes you say that?" Darius asked.

"The first dude said something about Darius turning into a… What was the phrase?" Asher held my gaze, his lips quirking into a grin that made my fingers itch to strangle him. "Oh, right. A witch's lapdog."

Darius huffed, but despite my best efforts to hold tight to my monster-sized grudge against Asher, the image actually made me laugh.

"Oh, you find this funny?" Darius leveled me with an icy stare. "I don't suppose you want me to fetch your slippers?"

"If you don't mind?" I said. "Maybe a newspaper, too? No, wait. A magazine would be better."

"Not the one she smacks you with when you're a bad doggie," Asher said.

"Don't worry, Darius," Ronan chimed in. "If you're a real good boy and you promise not to shit behind the sofa, maybe Gray will let you sleep at the end of our bed."

Darius stepped into Ronan's space, so close they would've been sharing the same air if Darius had actually needed to breathe. "Or maybe she'll stay in *my* bed, hellspawn, and while we're doing everything on that mattress *but* sleeping, you'll be outside in the doghouse, whimpering with your nose pressed up against the glass, watching me do things to her you could only dream about."

Ronan, Ash, and I were laughing so hard, Darius finally had no choice but to join us.

But the good humor was short-lived, the seriousness of the situation quickly chasing away the last of our laughter.

"So what's next with these vamps?" Ronan asked. "Do you trust your staff at the club? People are going to start talking, if they haven't already."

"I do trust them," Darius said. "I'll put in a call to my manager later."

"In the meantime," Ash said, "I'll make a few sketches, see what I remember about the assholes who jumped us. Maybe you'll recognize someone."

"Good call," Ronan said.

"A Council inquiry is the very last thing I need," Darius said. "I'm supposed to fly to New York tonight. Grinaldi finally agreed to a meeting."

Ronan perked up at that. "About time. That's the first bit of good news all week."

"Not anymore." Darius pulled out his phone, trying three times before he finally figured out how to unlock the screen. "I'll need to postpone. I can't go back east until I deal with this."

"What? You can't blow off Grinaldi," I said. "You've been trying to set up that meeting for weeks. We need the intel."

"Gray's right," Asher said. "You need to be there. Ronan and I will track down the vampires and deal with them. We just need to let Emilio do his thing first."

Darius was unconvinced. "The Council—"

"They won't get involved until the police wrap up their official investigation," Ronan said. "And by then, Emilio and his guys will have already proven you had nothing to do with it. Hell, he'll clear our names, too."

"You're missing the point," Darius said. "The Council's greatest weapon against us isn't the threat of imprisonment or death. It's their unbending devotion to bureaucracy.

Once this begins, I'll be tied up in a lengthy investigation that will destroy the last of my credibility, weaken my position, and leave my territory wide open for a power grab, which is precisely what these vampires are counting on. Further, while you may find the 'lapdog' comment amusing, I'm taking it for what it is—a subtle threat against Gray. And *that* leaves me even more unsettled than the thought of jumping through the Council's many hoops."

Both demons glared at me, silently imploring me to talk Darius out of bailing on that meeting. But there was no need for the looks; the three of us were absolutely on the same page.

"Darius, wait." I reached across the counter and grabbed Darius's hands, willing him to understand. "I know you want to keep me safe, but trust me—the best thing you can do right now is track down that rogue. He's our best shot at figuring out where the hunter is keeping the witches and what his ultimate plans are."

"We can figure that out later, after—"

"Without the rogue, we've got nothing but a sketchy vision from the fireplace. It's not enough, and you know it." I squeezed his hands tighter. "Go talk to Grinaldi. Emilio will investigate the scene at Black Ruby. Ronan and Ash will help. Liam's… Liam. But between the four, they're all watching my back."

"And her front," Asher said.

"And as long as Ronan's around," I said, glaring at Asher, "there's at least *some* adult supervision going on."

Darius shook his head. "I don't like it."

"None of us do," Ash said. "But there's too much at stake for us to let even one ball drop. Divide and conquer is the best strategy."

Darius looked deep into my eyes, his concern making my heart melt. I wanted nothing more than to pick up where we left off on the couch, curled up together in front of the fire, enjoying the wine, planning our trip to New York, kissing until the sun came up and Darius had to retire to the basement.

"Are you absolutely certain?" Darius asked, reaching out to cup my face. "I won't go if you don't feel safe. We'll figure something else out with Grinaldi."

I covered his hand and held it to my face, memorizing the feel of his firm touch, remembering the slide of his hand down my backside in the shower earlier. I would've loved to take him up on that offer, to make someone else deal with Grinaldi, to send someone else to investigate the situation at Black Ruby, to hand all of this over to someone —*anyone*—else.

But we were it. Haley, Reva, and the others were counting on us. Sophie was counting on us. And so was every witch who'd yet to cross the hunter's path—every witch who was at risk of dying at his cruel hands. If we had even the slightest chance at getting intel that could lead us to him, we had to take it.

"As much as I hate to say this," I said, "and you might want to get video evidence because I don't plan on ever saying it again, mostly because it's probably never going to happen again, but... Asher is absolutely right."

Darius cursed under his breath, but his honey-warm gaze didn't falter.

"Then I shall take my leave." Leaning in close, he brushed his lips against the shell of my ear, giving me a playful nip. "Now be a good little witch and walk your lapdog out to the car for a *proper* goodbye kiss."

TWENTY

GRAY

The rest of the week passed in an exhausting blur on all fronts—physical, mental, and emotional.

The guys hadn't made much progress in identifying the vampires who'd attacked them. Emilio had been circulating Asher's sketches around the Bay, but unsurprisingly, no one had come forward with information. And they likely wouldn't—especially with control of the territory potentially shifting. No one wanted to wake up on the wrong side of that particular war.

Darius was faring about the same in New York. For the trip that was supposed to take two days at most, he'd already been gone for four. Apparently, Grinaldi was playing games, rescheduling their meeting with one excuse after another.

Here at home, Asher and I had settled into a new normal that consisted of exchanging as few words as possible, suddenly remembering we had somewhere else to be when the other person entered the room, or flat-out ignoring each other. He'd tried to joke with me a few times. I'd tried to laugh. But in the end, neither of us was ready to say the things that needed to be said, starting with our fight the other night, and going all the way back to the night I'd taken his soul and seen all the things he'd spent his life so desperately trying to outrun.

Just about the only good news was my training. Ronan and Emilio had created a workout program for me—a combination of cardio, strength-training, and fighting techniques that already had me moving faster and thinking smarter. I was still ending up on my ass nine times out of ten, but in every match, I fought hard for that one time when I'd get the upper hand, using that to fuel my determination to keep learning, keep improving.

Liam and I had been meeting in the woods in the afternoons, avoiding the realm for now. Instead, he'd been helping me practice releasing my thoughts, allowing me to more easily sense my magic—when it was running low and I needed to rest, when I'd taken too much and needed to dispel it, how to balance my emotions and fears, how to redirect negative energy.

After each session, I'd spend an hour or two journaling in my book of shadows, feeding and nurturing it with my questions, my answers, my observations. The act of writing was a direct connection from my heart to my hand to the page, and with every word I shared, I felt our bond deepening.

The strange, unfamiliar handwriting that had appeared

so feverishly the other night had vanished, though I was no closer to answering its insistent question:

What are the consequences of messing with a demon's soul?

Still, I'd left those pages blank. Even without the glowing blue words, the question still haunted me, waking me at night, slipping into the quiet hours before the dawn, whispering in my head.

I longed to talk to Asher about it, but that would require, well, talking to Asher. Obviously, that wasn't happening.

Alone in the house for an entire blissful hour this evening, I was stretched out on the couch recording the details of today's session with Liam when Emilio finally returned.

He'd just come home from a twelve-hour stint at the police station, and his face was as grim as I'd ever seen it.

"Where's the demonic duo?" he asked.

"I think they're out back working on Asher's bike. What's going on?"

"Round 'em up and put on the coffee. I need to grab a quick shower, but then I've got some news."

I closed my book and sat up fast. "About the vamp attack?"

"No. The hunter." Emilio removed his badge and gun and headed down the hall toward his room, calling out one last directive. "On second thought, forget the coffee. We're gonna need the hard stuff tonight."

TWENTY-ONE

EMILIO

Asher, Ronan, Gray, and I gathered around the dining room table with a bottle of whiskey and last night's leftover veggie pizza, all three of them fidgeting in their chairs as they awaited the news.

I cleared my throat and sucked in a deep breath, picking up on too many scents at once—motor oil and metal from the guys, the tang of the alcohol, onions and garlic overpowering everything else on the pizza, and beneath all of that, the sharp, bright scent of Gray's fear.

I didn't blame her for being scared. Nothing about this situation was comfortable or reassuring, and I was about to make things worse in a lot of ways.

But the now-familiar steel in her eyes shone through anyway, and I couldn't help but feel a little proud of her—of how far she'd come.

"Well. Let's have it," she said, pouring herself the first

shot of whiskey, then passing the bottle to Ronan. "Whatever it is, we'll figure out how to deal with it."

"Always do," Ronan said, pouring his shot and passing the whiskey to Asher.

Classy as ever, the incubus took a swig right from the bottle before handing it to me, then he dove right into the pizza as if he hadn't eaten in a month.

Filling my glass to the brim, I said, "This week has been an absolute shitshow in the Bay. It seems the brawl outside Black Ruby set off a chain reaction of supernatural crimes across the city. Fights, vandalism, arson, you name it. I had to call in a favor and bring in some rookie shifters from Driscol Island PD to help with the caseload, and we're still neck deep. Between that and keeping the human cops out of our hair…"

I trailed off, taking a good swallow of whiskey before continuing.

"Point is," I said, "my tech guy finished isolating the security cam footage from Haley's block the night you guys were jumped. It's grainy as hell, but we got the make, model, and a partial plate on the van the suspects used."

"They're not suspects," Gray said. "They're perpetrators. We know they did it."

"Sorry, *querida*. Old habits." I sipped my whiskey, then continued. "With some help from a contact at the DMV, we were able to get the full plate and ID the vehicle's owner. Forty-nine-year-old named William Landes out in Raven's Cape. Human, as far as we could tell."

"Raven's Cape… That's on the coast, right?" Gray asked.

"Small community just about spitting distance from the shoreline," I confirmed. "Lots of cliffs and caverns out there, so if that's indeed where the hunter is holed up, it jives with your vision."

"Did you talk to this Landes guy?" Ronan asked. "Is he a hunter, too? Or just some asshole looking to make a quick buck?"

"Neither," I said. "That's the bad news."

"Let me guess." Asher reached for a second slice of pizza, shoveling in a mouthful before he'd even finished his sentence. "Dude reported his van stolen months ago, didn't see anything, doesn't know anything, doesn't want any trouble, and we're right back to square fucking one."

"Not even close." I leaned back in my chair and looked up at the vaulted ceiling, wishing it were that simple. Square one would've been a hell of a lot better than *murder* one. "I put in a call to the RCPD as soon as I had an address. They sent a cop out to sniff around the property, get some more details from Landes."

"And?" Gray asked. "Did he cooperate?"

I lifted my glass, gesturing for Ronan to pour me another drink, which I promptly chugged. The photos the department sent over were still burned into my retinas, making me queasy every time I closed my eyes.

No matter how long I'd done this job, it never got any easier.

"The officer found Mr. Landes in a shed behind the

house," I said, "bound and gagged. His eyes had been crudely removed, along with several of his fingers and toes. His throat was slit, though he likely passed out long before that happened." I swallowed hard. "They're estimating he'd been there at least a week, probably longer. Neighbors thought he was in Oregon visiting his mother."

"Shit," Ronan whispered, and I closed my eyes, not wanting to see Gray's face when I said the next part.

"The victim was naked aside from a single piece of jewelry," I said, and by her sharp intake of breath, I could tell she understood. "A silver crescent moon with an eye made of opal, black onyx, and topaz."

No one spoke after that—not even Gray. When I finally found the courage to open my eyes and look at her, she was staring into her whiskey, her brows pinched together, her thoughts veiled.

"I asked them to send me the amulet, *querida*," I said softly. "After they finish with the forensics."

She nodded, but didn't say a word, still fixated on her drink.

Since her big blowout with Asher last week, I hadn't seen her shed a single tear. Not when she was shuffling Sophie's tarot cards, or after a particularly grueling sparring session, or when I'd catch her staring out the window, her mind a million miles away. Not even when she'd dropped a can of soup on her bare toe last night.

But even without the tears, anyone looking at her now could sense the weight of her grief. It washed over me in waves, pulling my heart down like an undertow, pressing in on me from all sides. I could only imagine what it was like for her.

More than anything I wanted to take her into my arms, hold her to my chest, and promise her that this was going to get better. That even though it was my job, it didn't have to be hers. That we wouldn't always be sitting at this table rehashing the most gruesome details of the most heinous crimes, forcing her to relive the traumas of her past in the hopes that we might help someone else avoid the same pain.

I wanted to promise her that one day—maybe soon—we'd be able to eat an entire pan of brownies under a nearly-full moon for no other reason than because we damn well felt like it.

But I couldn't make that kind of promise today. Not until we solved this case. And the only way to do that was to wade right into the thick of it, ugly parts and all.

"I take it you've got someone on point at RCPD?" Asher asked. "Someone you trust?"

I shot a quick glance to Ronan—the only other living soul who knew about my situation with the RCPD. He offered a nod of support, but he wasn't saying a word.

I didn't know whether to be relieved or worried.

Raven's Cape. Just speaking the name again sent a crack right down the middle of my heart.

I used to think a hundred and twenty-odd miles was plenty enough distance to put between that part of my life and this one. That with that kind of distance—and enough time—I might be lucky enough to wake up one morning and *not* feel the hollow ache in my chest. To stare at my eyes in the mirror and *not* see all the old ghosts staring right back at me.

But I'd fled Argentina years earlier with the same stupid assumptions. If moving to a new damn continent hadn't helped, what on earth had made me think a new town would be any better? A million miles, a million years, and I'd still be carrying the same pain, like a well-worn suitcase I just couldn't seem to part with. And now it seemed the past I'd been trying for so damn long to outrun was on a collision course with a future I wasn't sure I deserved, and this time, running wasn't an option.

Not when the people sitting around this table were counting on me to stay. To deal with this. To make things right.

"The situation with the local police is complicated," I said, settling on the easiest and most palatable explanation for all of us. "They've got quite a few shifters on the force—lone wolves who made their own pack some years ago. They're excellent cops, but they're territorial and don't like outsiders. The chief is the toughest of the bunch."

"You know the guy?" Asher asked.

I cut my gaze to Ronan again, then looked down, rolling the edge of my glass over the condensation rings on the table. "Yeah, I know the guy. The woman, actually."

The RCPD chief and I had more history between us than I cared to recount, starting with our shared last name.

But if anyone at this table thought blood was thicker

than water—or whiskey, for that matter—they obviously didn't know my sister.

"From the little bit she was willing to share," I continued, my wording much more diplomatic than it'd been on the phone with her earlier, "I learned that no witches have been reported missing or dead in their jurisdiction, and there haven't been any other supernatural crimes outside the norms of what they usually see. If our man is holing up out there, he's keeping a low profile."

"That's all part of his game," Gray said. "This whole time, he's been leaving us breadcrumbs. First, he takes Haley and Ash, but he doesn't bother hiding the license plate or avoiding the cameras. Then he texts me the picture of Ash in the devil's trap, leading us right to Norah's house, where we're ambushed by vampires who we later learn were ordered to leave me alive. He knew we'd track down the van's owner, and he left us his mutilated body wearing my mother's amulet."

Her scent changed, her initial fear and trepidation receding as a wave of anger rushed in.

"He wants to be found," she said. "He's just baiting another trap, waiting for us to walk right into it."

"Or multiple traps," Ronan said. "Just to cover the bases."

"Of course he is," I said. "And in a perfect world, we'd let him keep playing his game, wait for him to make a mistake. But we can't afford to sit on this. Even one witch's life is too many to risk, and if Gray's vision was accurate, he's holding dozens captive. Maybe more."

"And they're not just Blackmoon Bay witches, either," Gray said. "Again, if we're assuming my vision was accurate, then the majority of his captives are out-of-towners. Who knows how long he's been planning all this." She shook her head, her lip curled in disgust. "Before Sophie died, she and Haley found some of Norah's correspondence with other underground coven leaders, and they learned that a bunch of witches had been murdered recently, starting on the east coast and working westward. For all we know, he could've been behind all of them, killing as he made his way to me."

"It's not out of the realm of possibility," I said. "I checked in with my contacts at a few other PDs between here and Raven's Cape, and they're seeing the same thing. Witches are being murdered or kidnapped, and so far, no one has been able to pick up any decent leads."

"That's because he's leaving all the leads for me," Gray said. "He couldn't kill me the first time, so he's made it his mission in life to hunt me down. To torture me. And eventually, he'll—"

"Hate to say it," Asher said, shoving in a mouthful of food. The man had always eaten like every meal was going to be his last, but now he seemed to be making an Olympic sport out of it. "But I think it's a lot more complicated than one dickless hunter's obsession with our witch."

Gray bristled, but I nodded for him to continue.

"Witches are magical guardians, right?" he said. "So even if they're not practicing, their presence basically keeps the balance."

Gray folded her arms over her chest, narrowing her eyes at him. "What's your point?"

"Think big picture here, Cupcake. If enough of you broomstick riders start vanishing from a community, things are bound to get fucked up. Look at what happened the other night with the vamps. Challenging Darius Beaumont?" Ash licked pizza sauce off his fingers, one at a time. "A few months ago, that would've been unheard of. And look what else has happened this week alone. Emilio said it himself—the Bay is a shitshow."

"Disgusting habits aside," Ronan said, glaring at Ash, "he's right. We don't know who else the hunter is working with, but there's no way he's pulling off so many killings and kidnappings alone. Hell, I doubt he could do it even with a *small* operation. Maybe he wants us to think he's a lone psycho, but logistically it doesn't add up. He'd need more men."

"Hunters have always worked in packs," Gray said, nodding. "Even when they came after me and Calla—two witches alone in the middle of nowhere—they still sent the whole cavalry."

"Do you think Jonathan is still working with his father?" Ronan asked her. "Or the other men who came after you and Calla?"

"I don't… know." Gray's face paled as she considered his question, the pain of her memories etching deep lines across her forehead.

I reached across the table and placed my hand on her forearm, giving her a reassuring squeeze. Beneath my giant mitt, she felt small and vulnerable, but on the inside, our *bruja bonita* was anything but.

I squeezed her again, nodding for her to continue.

"When Sophie died," she said, "I never wanted to believe it was hunters. But even after Hollis confirmed Jonathan was the one who'd paid him for intel about us, I still assumed he was acting on his own—mostly because his actions were so different from the hunters' usual search-and-destroy M.O. The vampire blood, the rune carvings, the kidnappings... I kind of figured he'd gone off the rails. But now?" She met my gaze across the table, her blue eyes clear and determined. "Yes, it's totally possible that he's still working with his family. That he just wants us to think he's on his own so we walk into his trap even more unprepared than we already are."

"And maybe destabilization is part of a bigger play for these fucks," Asher said. "It's kind of brilliant, actually. Take out the witches, let all the supers fuck themselves up in the ensuing chaos, then leave our communities ripe for takeover."

"But takeover by whom?" I asked. "The hunters? How many of them could possibly be left?"

"More than we realized," Gray said. "Sophie had written some things in her book of shadows about it. Apparently, a lot of the coven leadership believe the hunters may be joining forces again. Some of the witches tried reaching out to Norah, but Norah dismissed them, and she forbade Bay Coven members from reaching out to other groups."

"Probably because she's involved," Asher said. "That has to be it."

"This is… insane." Ronan pinched the bridge of his nose, shaking his head.

The feeling was mutual.

Dread settled over us like fog.

I reached for the bottle again, and this time, I didn't bother with the glass, either.

"So where the hell is the Council in all this?" Gray asked. "I get that they're kind of hands-off, but how long can this go unchecked? Humans died at Black Ruby the other night—and that's just one incident, in one town." She looked at Asher, who sat up a little straighter under her scrutiny. "It's not just about hunters and witches and screwing up the supernatural balance," she said. "Humans are going to start noticing us—if they haven't already—and that's the last thing the Council wants."

"The Council can go fuck themselves," Ronan said, eloquent as always. "They checked out a long time ago."

Gray shook her head, her blonde curls brushing her shoulders. "I don't buy that. I know they tend to look the other way for a lot of stuff, but this is big. It's going to affect them eventually, too."

"Not up in those ivory towers," he said.

"Part of what keeps them there is that the supernatural masses keep ourselves in check," she said. "If things fall apart in a big way, that's going to draw human attention on an epic scale. Right now, our biggest safety net is the fact that most people don't believe in us. Once that net comes down, forget about it. Not even the Council will be able to stay in the shadows. As long as they want to maintain a presence and power on the earthly realm, they need us as much as they think we need them."

"They're already aware of the situation at Black Ruby," I said. "But so far, they're keeping their distance. My contact there says they'd rather let us sort it out. The humans who died weren't—and I quote—high profile enough to cause a stir."

"Those *assholes*," Gray said. "I mean, I get that the humans who died signed up for the job, but still. Ignoring what happened sets a dangerous precedent for those who *didn't* sign up."

I took another swig of whiskey, hoping the alcohol would dull the sharp edges of my thoughts. It was bad enough when we were just dealing with a psycho hunter targeting Gray and the witches of Blackmoon Bay. Now, we were talking about murders across the state and country, supernatural crime waves, hunters rising again, and a potential conspiracy…

It was hard to carry on with odds like that.

"Okay," I said, "let's strip all this down and get back to basics. We can't tackle all of this at once."

"Emilio's right," Gray said. "Right now, our primary objective is still Haley and the others. We need to find Jonathan. The rest will have to wait."

"Agreed," Asher said.

"So now that we've got a lead in Raven's Cape," Ronan asked, "what's our next move?"

"The hunter likes to play games?" I said, grabbing the whiskey and topping off everyone's glass. "Good. We're going to give him one right back. First step? Baiting a trap."

"What's the bait?" Asher asked.

"Not a what—a who." I raised my glass and touched it to each of theirs, then sent a silent prayer to Darius in New York, hoping his negotiating skills were as sharp as when he'd practiced law. "The gutless vamp who betrayed him."

TWENTY-TWO

DARIUS

Tonight wasn't the worst of my immortal life, but it certainly qualified as a top-ten cock-up.

After leading me around by the fangs all week, Grinaldi had finally summoned me to his estate for our meeting, only to shuffle me off on one of his staff for a tour of the grounds, followed by a dinner during which Grinaldi didn't appear and I did not dine, and a game of billiards with his eldest sired son, Francisco, who'd barely spoken as I proceeded to embarrass him at the table.

By the time he bowed out of his entertainment responsibilities, I was so out of sorts I nearly called off the meeting altogether.

But of course, one thought of my little brawler back home, and I knew I'd wander the grounds of this ridiculously sprawling compound for a decade if it meant securing even a shred of information that could help us track the hunter—that could help us keep her safe.

Now more than ever, we needed to locate the Grinaldi-sired vampire whose blood was responsible for Sophie's death. Not only were we counting on him to reveal the hunter's whereabouts, but the rogue was a critical component in Emilio's latest plan to draw the hunter out of hiding.

I was still in the billiards room, gazing out the window at the lush, moonlit woods that surrounded the property, when my host finally deemed me worthy of his time.

"Darius Beaumont," he said as he entered the room, his tone and expression as neutral as his home was ostentatious. "It has been some years, friend."

I took in his polished appearance, but the immaculately-trimmed gray hair, tailored Italian suit, and French cologne did nothing to hide his age. He'd been close to seventy when he'd been turned, trapped forever in a body that had already outlived its prime in his own era. Despite his immortality, Vincenzo Grinaldi looked bone-tired, the brutal savagery of time wearing him down as a river wore down a canyon.

"Indeed it has, friend." I briefly lowered my eyes, a silent acknowledgment that this was his home, and I was his guest.

No matter how badly I wanted to wring his neck.

"Shall we relocate to the south parlor?" he asked, already turning toward the hall without awaiting my answer, and neither apologizing for nor explaining his lateness. "I've taken the liberty of inviting some fresh... cocktails."

I followed him into an intimate but gaudy room with gleaming white marble floors, deep mauve walls, and uncomfortably old-fashioned upholstered furniture better suited to a Victorian woman's bedchambers than the home of the most powerful vampire family on the eastern seaboard.

But keeping his guests in a constant state of unease seemed to be Grinaldi's primary driver, and to that end, the room was perfect.

I sat on a dainty floral-print settee as he settled into an intricately-carved rocking chair across from me and called for our "cocktails" to present themselves. Two nude women entered the room on silent footsteps, one kneeling at Grinaldi's feet, the other at mine.

Both had pale, milky skin and waist-length dark hair that covered their small breasts. Their faces were painted heavily; I suspected it was supposed to make them look older, but it had the opposite effect.

The woman before me, who couldn't have been a woman by more than a year if that, extended her arm toward my mouth and bowed her head.

My stomach twisted. Old traditions or not, the practice was horrific.

"*Cin cin,*" Grinaldi said, sinking his fangs into the mirror image of the woman at my feet. Briefly, I wondered if they were sisters.

Neither of them made a sound.

Both trembled in fear.

Using my influence, I sent the woman before me what I hoped was a gentle reassurance. She seemed to relax.

When Grinaldi finally had his fill, he shooed the woman away.

His mouth stained with her blood, he grinned at me and asked, "Will you not partake?"

"Thank you," I replied. "But no. I do not wish to sully the taste of my last drink."

He held my gaze a moment, considering. It was extremely rude of me to refuse his offer; I hoped he found my excuse plausible enough to let it go.

"Very well," he finally said. He clapped twice to draw the woman's attention, then shooed her away in the same manner as the other. She exited without a backward glance.

Unfortunately, I knew my polite refusal to drink from her hadn't spared her any pain—it only postponed it.

I tried not to think about that.

When we were finally alone again, Grinaldi said, "I understand you've taken a witch under your protection. Could this be the 'drink' who has spoiled you for all others?"

"It is," I said.

There was no point in denials with Vincenzo Grinaldi. The man was, among other things, a brilliant judge of character. Of course, that only made our current predicament that much more puzzling. How had one of his own clan managed to betray him?

"A witch of some significance, I'm told," he said.

I raised an eyebrow, wondering what he'd heard, and

more importantly, from whom. The less he knew about her the better.

"A witch of some *determination*," I said. "She's the reason I've requested this meeting, and I greatly appreciate your accommodating me."

"Go on."

"Her best friend, along with several other witches in the area of Blackmoon Bay, Washington, were murdered with the assistance of a vampire bearing the scent of your clan. We've since learned that this vampire was working closely with a hunter. Their motive remains a mystery."

"A hunter? Nonsense." Grinaldi waved a hand in the air as if swatting a fly. "The witch-killers disbanded decades ago when the last powerful families died out. None remain."

"Current events would suggest otherwise."

"Hmm." He nodded slowly, pondering the information. Or at least pretending to ponder it. "If that's true, why is this the first I'm hearing of it?"

"With all due respect, I've been trying to reach you for weeks."

Tension crackled in the air between us, but I would not —*could* not—back down. Not from this.

He seemed to sense this, finally sitting back in his chair. Slowly, methodically, he began to rock. Back and forth. Back and forth. The chair creaked and moaned under his weight, but still, he didn't stop. He rocked for so long that I worried he'd fallen asleep. I was about to wake him when he cleared his throat.

"I realize, Mr. Beaumont, that I've wasted a great deal of your time. I do not wish to continue. Let us drop this pretense and speak plainly, as old friends ought to."

"I would appreciate that," I said.

"As you are already aware, one of our own has betrayed us. We don't believe that any of the attempted conversions have been successful, but nevertheless, it is against our code."

"And against Council law," I added, "considering the attempts were non-consensual."

Grinaldi shifted uncomfortably in his rocking chair, but he didn't deny it.

"Have you spoken to anyone on the Council about this?" I asked.

Grinaldi's eyebrow twitched—the only sign the question had even remotely unsettled him. "If that is a threat, Mr. Beaumont—"

"I assure you, it isn't. You asked that we speak freely, so that's what I'm doing. It's a concern, plain and simple."

"Yes, but I don't see how it's a concern of *yours*."

"You've got a rogue vampire on your hands, one who's aiding and abetting a murderer. The witch under my protection is in danger, as are others in Blackmoon Bay and potentially elsewhere."

"Since when are vampires and witches such strong bedfellows?"

"Since their presence maintains a delicate power balance. Their disappearance could easily create a situation dangerous for humans, which could ultimately create a situation dangerous for all of us." It had already begun. The episode in front of Black Ruby could not have happened otherwise, and Emilio had been updating me all week on other crimes unfolding in the Bay.

I shared a little of the information with Grinaldi, just to drive the point home.

"So you can see why the Council might have cause for concern," I said.

"They might have at one time, yes," he conceded. "But those impotent fools have long since turned their backs on such matters. Frankly, I'm not sure why they insist on perpetuating this charade of power and control when it's quite clear they've lost both."

I raised a curious eyebrow. The Council was imperfect at best, but they were the closest thing to a government we had. If Grinaldi had insights about their inner workings—especially if something had gone afoul—I wanted to know.

Unsurprisingly, Grinaldi waved away my implied inquiry, turning the tables back on me. "If you wish to bring concerns to the Council, perhaps you should begin with those unfolding in your own backyard."

"I beg your pardon?"

"Word is you've been—shall we say—shitting in your own sandbox."

The image was crass and so far from his normal manner of speaking that I had no doubts he'd heard the exact phrase from someone else.

"I'm not certain I know what you're referring to," I said.

He leaned forward in his chair, pinning me with a cold

glare. "I'm referring, Mr. Beaumont, to the slaughter of numerous vampires at the behest of your witch. You are supposed to set the example, not give in to your baser instincts."

My mind was reeling. The fact that word of our recent conflicts in the Bay had reached Grinaldi—and via an unknown source at that—suggested that the situation with the hunter and the witches was only the tip of a much larger, much more dangerous iceberg.

Just like Emilio, Gray, Ronan, and Asher feared.

"I am loyal to family over species, Mr. Grinaldi," I said, refusing to offer any details beyond that. "Rather than misdirecting me with thinly-veiled threats and vague accusations about which you're severely uninformed, I would appreciate it if you would answer my questions about the vampire your family seems to have lost."

"Family over species?" He sneered at me, his eyes full of disdain. "I never thought I'd live to see a greater vampire name a common witch his kin."

Rage ignited in my chest, pushing me to my feet. "Nor I to see a respected family such as yours allow a rogue to dirty your name and elude your capture, yet here we are."

He glared at me another moment, then gestured for me to take a seat once again.

"Forgive me," he said. "It was not my intent to ambush you with rumors and speculation, nor accuse you of disloyalty."

I narrowed my eyes, scrutinizing his face for any signs of treachery, but finding none.

As strange as it was, I believed him.

"Apology accepted." I reclaimed my spot on the settee.

"Please," he said. "Continue. I shall endeavor to be more forthcoming, if you agree to do the same."

"Very well." I folded my arms across my chest. "Since it would seem you're not of a mind to do it yourself, I plan to track down your rogue vampire and bring him to justice myself."

I thought he might forbid it, or at the very least attempt to dissuade me. But Grinaldi did neither, saying only, "Her, Mr. Beaumont."

My eyes widened.

"Yes, the rogue you seek is a female," he said. "Should you find her, I trust you'll return her to me alive?"

His comment came out more like a question than a demand, and I pressed my advantage.

"So you can let her run wild again? Sink those fangs into a few more witches in my community? I don't think so."

"I can assure you that will not be the case. We simply prefer to handle our affairs internally, as I'm sure you're well aware."

I was. The punishments for betrayal and disloyalty in the Grinaldi family were legendary.

I considered his request. Given the fact that his rogue was directly tied to several murders and Grinaldi had yet to report her to the Council, he was in no position to negotiate.

However, there might come a time when I needed a favor, and Grinaldi—for all his faults—was a powerful ally to have in your corner.

"Once I've finished questioning her," I said, "and I've deemed that she's answered those questions truthfully, and she has done everything in her power to help us locate the hunter responsible for the deaths in my community, I will return her to you alive, assuming I find her in that condition to begin with and she does nothing to warrant immediate… termination."

"I have your word?" he asked.

I inclined my head, lowering my eyes. It was all the promise he needed.

"Her given name is Fiona Brentwood. I don't know what she calls herself now." Grinaldi relaxed into his rocking chair, much more forthcoming now that he believed he'd handed his problem off to me. "She'd been living in Westchester when she'd first captured my youngest son's attention four years ago, but she was originally from a small town near the Catskill Mountains called Phoenicia."

Phoenicia.

Gray's hometown.

"She was born twenty-three years ago," he continued, "but was turned at the age of nineteen, not long after she and Everett began dating."

I nodded, doing some quick mental math. I'd already assumed the rogue was a somewhat recently-turned vampire. The older members of Grinaldi's family had always been loyal.

But her age put her at just two years behind Gray. With both of them being from the same town, they'd almost certainly known each other in school.

Which meant that Grinaldi's rogue also knew Gray's hunter long before she'd been turned.

"May I ask who turned her?" It wasn't the most critical piece of information, but it might help me understand her a bit better. And if I could get inside her head, I might just be able to predict her next move. "Was it Everett?"

Grinaldi stopped his rocking, his fingers tightening over the arms of the chair, his eyes never leaving mine.

I was beginning to regret asking the question.

"In any case," I continued, hoping to redirect the conversation and regain the ground I'd just lost, "I suppose I'll start with—"

"*I* turned her, Mr. Beaumont." He finally broke his gaze, turning toward the window at the other end of the room. "And lest you think any less of me than you already do, I assure you—she wanted it."

My mouth soured at his words. How many vampires had used that as a justification for turning the lives of innocent humans—particularly young women—into horror shows? Into nightmares from which there was no escape but death?

I shook free of the thoughts. I wasn't here to save Fiona, or any of the others he'd turned during his long reign. I was here to save the witches rotting away in some prison we'd yet to locate. I was here to save Gray, a woman who'd come to mean more to me than Grinaldi—with his endless parade of servants and "cocktails" and sired children lining up to do his bidding—could possibly understand.

"And your son?" I prompted.

232

I hadn't really expected him to divulge additional details, but he continued without hesitation.

"He has not spoken with me since." A flicker of sadness crossed his features, aging him another ten years in an instant. "Everett did not want this life for her, but *she* wanted it, and she believed it was her decision to make. It had been a source of contention between them for months —all of us, including the staff, had heard their many battles, and we all began speculating on when they might finally part ways."

"When did it happen?" I asked.

"About six months into their relationship. She'd been living with us by then, and I found her in the study late one evening, reduced to tears after a particularly brutal argument. When I tried to comfort her, she told me that he'd finally broken up with her—that he'd told her if she wanted to become a bloodsucker, she'd have to find another vampire to turn her. He wanted no part of it, and no part of her."

"So you offered to turn her?" I asked.

Ignoring the question, he said, "She was quite fragile, you see, and I'd grown rather fond of her. I worried she might harm herself or stumble into the clutches of a vampire who would take advantage of her desperation. I tried to reassure her that her stay in our home was not contingent upon her relationship with Everett—she was welcome to remain as long as she wished, and no harm would come to her under our roof."

"Obviously, she took you up on your generosity."

Grinaldi nodded. "She seemed content for some time. She had her own quarters, and Everett went away to university that fall, so she didn't have to worry about running into him. But a desire rooted as deeply as hers does not merely fade with time, and it wasn't long before she fell into a dark melancholy."

I leaned forward on the settee, enraptured by the story. It was quite obvious my assumptions about Fiona's turning had been wrong; Grinaldi was speaking of her not as a plaything or an insignificant human, but as a daughter-in-law.

One he cared for, deeply and sincerely.

"She began to drop subtle hints about becoming one of us," he continued. "And finally, she asked me to do it. I refused, explaining to her about our custom—we were twenty strong at that point, and until one of our line passed, we could not make another. Of course, this only made her more determined. She begged, she threw tantrums, she threatened to... to take her own life." His voice broke on the last word, shocking me with its raw pain.

"I'm... sorry," I said, equally shocked to find that I'd actually meant it.

"As am I." He offered a faint smile, perhaps the first genuine moment we'd shared. "You asked me, Mr. Beaumont, if I'd offered to turn Fiona. The answer is no. She simply... wore me down. So, when one of our clan was killed during a skirmish in Buffalo last fall, I finally turned her. Two weeks later, she was gone."

"And you never heard from her again?"

"No. You know, the worst part of this ordeal isn't that she betrayed me or broke our rules. It's that she broke my heart." He closed his eyes, and I saw his real age, the mask he'd worn for centuries finally dropping away. Behind his customs and pompousness and power, Grinaldi was no more than a tired old man, the last of a dying line struggling to bear the infinite weight of a heart besieged with regret.

Like so many of our kind.

It was a harsh reminder that with very few exceptions— Fiona notwithstanding—vampires did not choose this life. It was chosen for us, leaving us to march onward as best we could, or simply wither and die.

I sensed our visit had come to its end. Looking upon Vincenzo Grinaldi with new eyes, I offered my final farewell. "Thank you for your time and hospitality, Mr. Grinaldi. I shall be in touch about Fiona soon."

He surprised me once more by bowing his head in respect, and without another word, I allowed myself to be led by another of his servants to the main entrance, my throat unexpectedly tight with some unnamed emotion.

Stepping out into the cool upstate New York night, I was overcome with the need to gorge myself on the scent of fresh air and moss and living things, and I took several deep breaths before sliding into my waiting town car.

"To the hotel, sir?" My driver asked, navigating us out of the wooded area that camouflaged the Grinaldi estate.

"Not yet, Michael. We need to make a detour."

"Where to?"

"Phoenicia. The county courthouse, please."

"As you wish, sir." He spoke a new command to his GPS unit, which promptly recalculated our route. "Though they're almost certainly closed for the evening."

"Oh, I'm counting on it."

TWENTY-THREE

GRAY

One week after I'd kissed Darius goodbye in our driveway, I awoke in Ronan's bed from a dreamless sleep to the rich whiskey-and-leather scent of my vampire.

"Darius?" I whispered, sitting up and opening my eyes. His scent still lingered, but he wasn't here.

Ronan was gone, too. In his place, I found a small gift box sitting on the pillow. It was wrapped in glossy white paper embossed with roses and tied with a gold silk ribbon, as lovely and tasteful as the man I suspected had left it for me.

Forcing down the urge to tear into the present, I carefully unwrapped the box. The paper alone was a gift—thick and luxurious, the roses as soft as velvet—and I wanted to save it.

As butterflies swirled in my stomach, I opened the box and reached inside, pulling out a small white notecard written in the most elegant handwriting I'd ever seen:

A promise of more to come…

Love, D

Beneath the card sat a small but heavy object wrapped in tissue. I took it out of the box and removed the wrapping, revealing a crystal snow globe no larger than a plum. It looked handmade; the scene inside was intricately crafted and painted, the whole of Manhattan miniaturized in a perfect likeness. When I shook it, tiny white and silver snowflakes swirled, capturing the city in a glittering storm.

It was mesmerizing. It was beautiful. It was perfect.

Tears blurred my vision. Not just from the thoughtful gift and the sweet note and the giddy excitement that filled me when I imagined traveling to New York with Darius one day, but because the gift meant he'd safely returned from his trip. It meant that he was here, right now, under this very roof.

I didn't care if it was the middle of the day and he was sound asleep. No one could stop me from slipping into the basement and climbing into his bed, wrapping him in my arms, and covering him with happy, tear-stained kisses.

I brushed my teeth and twisted my hair into a messy bun, then headed out into the kitchen, practically bouncing on my toes.

I was so happy Darius was home safe that not even Asher's ever-present scowling could ruin my mood or steal the smile from my face.

"Good morning," I said, beaming. "Would anyone like fresh coffee? I'm about to make a—"

The rest of the words died on my tongue when I saw

their grim faces, the three of them standing around the center island, staring at me.

Concern lingered in their eyes.

"What happened?" I breathed, pressing a hand to my heart. "Is Darius…?"

"He's fine," Ronan assured me, though the tightness in his voice suggested otherwise. He nodded toward the door that led down to Darius's room in the basement. "He's waiting for us."

"He's awake?" I asked.

"Hasn't slept since he got back."

"You need to tell me what's going on," I said. "You're freaking me out."

"It's better if we show you, *querida*," Emilio said.

"Let's go." Ronan reached for my hand, but instead of squeezing it like I expected, he pressed a hawthorn stake to my palm, folding my fingers tightly around it. "Darius wants us all down there when she wakes up."

TWENTY-FOUR

GRAY

Holding a stake of his own, Darius was waiting for me at the bottom of the stairs, his jaw clenched tight, his normally immaculate wavy hair untamed. He smiled when he saw me, his eyes sparkling for the briefest instant, unleashing a curl of fire in my chest.

But our happy reunion would have to wait.

"There's someone you need to see," he said, cupping a hand around the back of my neck and gently steering me into the main room of the basement.

It was set up like a family room, with thick beige wall-to-wall carpets, two black leather sofas, and a big flat-screen TV mounted on the wall, currently tuned to an Alaskan survival show on mute.

At the other end of the room was a dry bar and four cocktail chairs. Chained to one of them was a woman with long, straight, chestnut-colored hair, wearing an ankle-length black dress, a threadbare cardigan, and one sneaker.

Her skin looked ashy in the flickering blue light of the television, but I recognized her immediately.

"Fiona Brentwood?" I whispered. Apparently, the snow globe wasn't the only gift he'd brought back.

He'd also picked up a time machine.

That's how it felt as I stared into the sleeping face of a girl I hadn't seen since my junior year of high school.

"Careful," he said, brushing his knuckles down the back of my arm as I approached her. "She's bound and sedated, but she's still a vampire, Gray."

I nodded, keeping my stake at the ready just in case. Her hair was a little longer than when I'd last seen her, her skin unnaturally flawless, but otherwise she looked exactly as I remembered her.

Still sedated, she rested calmly, not moving a muscle.

Not even to breathe.

She no longer needed to.

Little Fiona Brentwood is a vampire.

I couldn't wrap my head around it.

She'd been an awkward kid back then, two years our junior, a little too loud, way too clingy. She had a huge crush on Jonathan, which I found endearing, but he couldn't stand her. She'd tag along everywhere we went—to the Shop-'N-Save on early dismissal days, where she'd offer to pay for our ice cream or candy. To the Palace Theater for a Sunday matinee. On our bikes to the wooden playground not far from school, where she'd do flips on the parallel bars while he and I sat under the fake drawbridge kissing until we ran out of breath.

Jonathan was perpetually annoyed by her.

I used to feel bad about it, inviting her along for pizza or a hike up Duckback Mountain on the weekends. He'd go along with it, but he always said the same thing afterward: *I just want you all to myself once in a while, Sunshine. What's wrong with that?*

I loved it when he called me Sunshine. *Rayanne*, he used to say. *My little ray of sunshine.* In my immature, starry-eyed mind, I thought he was just being romantic.

Goosebumps rose on my arms.

Without warning, Fiona's eyes opened.

"Shit!" I jumped back, my heart leaping into my throat.

Her lips curved, but her smile was small and sad, tinged with something that looked an awful lot like regret. She wouldn't look me in the eye. "Hey, Ray-Ray."

"Hey, Feefs," I said automatically, the nickname I'd given her coming back as easily as the one she'd given me.

Guys! I got my mom's credit card! Wanna go to Java House?

Her voice echoed through my memory, and I stared at her open-mouthed, struggling to reconcile the sweet-but-goofy kid I'd once known with the beautiful vampire sitting before me now.

The vampire Darius had captured.

The Grinaldi rogue who'd teamed up with Jonathan to murder my best friend.

Holy. Shit.

It'd taken all those minutes for the initial surprise to wear off, and when the fog finally lifted, the reality of the situation struck me like lightning, fierce and destructive, a raw bolt of power shocking me into action.

I lunged for her, grabbing a fistful of her hair and jerking her head backward, pressing the tip of my stake to the soft underside of her chin.

I waited for a pair of strong hands to land on my shoulders, an arm to slip around my waist, a calm voice of reason to talk me down. But none of the guys made a move to stop me. They simply stood by my side, rock-solid and supportive, their own stakes held tight.

"Tell me he *made* you do it," I said, my teeth clenched so hard my jaw ached. "He threatened your family and forced you to turn, forced you to give him your blood. Tell me he preyed on your feelings for him and lured you into his trap. Tell me he left you no other choice."

My arms trembled, my chest heaving like I couldn't get enough air. I wanted it so, so badly to be true—that he'd forced her. Because then I might be able to make sense of it. I might be able to channel all of my rage, all of my grief, all of this churning, roiling, boiling fury into making sure Jonathan died in the most painful, horrific way imaginable.

I might even be able to forgive her.

"Tell me!" I screamed.

But even with a stake pressed uncomfortably against her throat, she still shook her head. "All he's ever wanted was to reclaim his magical heritage. He told me he needed a vampire to do that."

"And you *volunteered*?"

"I loved him enough to make the sacrifice. I still *do* love him, even after everything."

Stake her, a voice inside me urged. *Paralyze her. Light a match. End her.*

The darkness slithered inside me, a twisted black serpent desperate for release.

Unleash me and watch her burn, burn, burn...

God, I was so tempted. It wouldn't take much. Just a stake to the throat, then I could get one of the guys to take her out back and decapitate her. Or burn her.

Burn her!

I could almost taste the smoke...

I closed my eyes, shaking it off. I couldn't end her. Not until we found out what she knew. Not until we finished making—and executing—our plan.

I took a deep breath and opened my eyes, forcing the serpent inside me back into its cage.

I flicked my gaze to Darius, who stood unmoving beside me, his arms at his sides.

"How did you find this... this *filth*?" I ground out the word, tightening my grip on her hair. Fiona didn't make a sound, didn't whimper or beg. Her eyes were flat, her expression neutral.

It was like she'd already given up, which pissed me off even more.

As far as I was concerned, she wasn't allowed to give up or take the easy way out. Not after what she'd done to Sophie.

"It's a long story," Darius said, "but after I spoke with Grinaldi, I decided to start in Phoenicia. Public records pointed me to the location of her family home, where I'd hoped to gain some additional insights. Imagine my surprise when the vampire herself answered the door, smiling as though I were a neighbor delivering a fresh-baked apple pie."

"My mom was expecting a visitor," she said simply, like that was the only part of the story worth commenting on.

"Did this visitor know there was a monster in her midst?" I asked. "Did your mother?"

Again, she shook her pathetic head. "After I left Jonathan, I... I had nowhere else to go. My mother had no idea what I'd become." Her voice dropped to a whisper. "What I'd done."

For the first time since she'd opened them, her eyes glazed with emotion. Her calm detachment was slipping away, revealing the broken girl beneath the mask.

Suddenly she was fourteen again, crying in the girls' bathroom because Jonathan had told her to get lost.

"I just want to be his friend, Ray-Ray. I don't get why he's so mean to me."

My heart skipped, an old, familiar ache pooling in my gut.

Pity.

I wouldn't fall for it, though. Sophie was *dead* because of her. I was beyond compassion. Beyond even the most basic form of human decency.

"Why?" I demanded, my throat burning as I shouted in her face. I didn't need to elaborate; she knew damn well what I meant.

Why had she gone along with his plans?

Why had she helped him kill my best friend and so many others?

Why had she given her life up for a monster?

Fiona took a moment to consider my question, not blinking, not breathing, not doing much of anything but staring up at me with the same light brown eyes that had once looked at me as if I were her big sister—someone she admired, envied, loved, and hated all at once.

When she spoke again, her voice was high and sharp.

"Do you know what it's like to love someone so much you'd die for them, even knowing they'd never do the same for you? To love them so much your heart breaks every time they say your name because you fear each time will be the last? Do you have any idea what that's like?"

My heart squeezed in my chest, but I refused to give her an inch. Refused to let her manipulate me into thinking we had anything in common other than one very unfortunate, long since outgrown crush.

"No, Fiona. But I *do* know what it's like to love someone so much you go to sleep every night praying you don't dream, because if you dream about them, waking up feels like losing them all over again. I know what it's like to replay the memory of someone you love saying your name a thousand times a day because you fear today might be the day you finally forget the sound of their voice. And I know what it's like to watch someone you love die right before your eyes because someone like you decided to take something that never belonged to them in the first place."

My eyes burned right through her, and I was suddenly overcome with the strange and inexplicable urge to bite her. I wanted to jump into her lap, sink my teeth into her skin, rend the flesh from her bones.

Magic pulsed across my palms, and her eyes widened.

Obliterate her…

Darius stepped up behind me, putting his hands on my shoulders. I felt the lightest touch of his mental influence brush against my mind, almost as if he were asking permission to be there.

The sensation was odd, but not unpleasant—like going outside with wet hair in the winter, but on the inside of my head.

I closed my eyes and took in a breath, letting down the walls I hadn't even realized I'd erected, inviting him in. His presence washed over me, cool and soothing.

"What can you tell us about his plans?" Darius asked Fiona, still keeping his hands—and his thoughts—on me.

"I don't know what his endgame is," she said.

"That's easy," Ronan said, speaking up for the first time. Until that moment, I hadn't realized how quiet they'd all been. "The hunters' endgame is always the same. They want to eradicate witches and steal their magic."

"Not Jonathan." Fiona shook her head. "He's not like his father and the others. He… took a different path."

"Elaborate," Asher said.

"Well, the way he explained it, his father's generation is old-school. Pitchforks and torches, root out the witches, burn them to the ground, that sort of thing."

"That sort of *thing*?" This, from Emilio, whose low growl sent shivers down my spine. He stepped up close to her, grabbing the chains at her chest. "Do you think this is just a game, vampire? Witches—women and *girls*, some of them younger than you—are being murdered. Kidnapped. Tortured. All because they're born with something through no choice of their own that the hunters decided belongs to them."

Emilio, who'd been the strong and silent partner behind me through this entire ordeal, was shaking with rage. I'd ever seen him so angry.

Fiona had the grace to lower her head.

Emilio finally backed off, coming to stand beside me. Despite his anger, when his eyes met mine in the dim space, they were soft and kind, melting me just a little bit.

"Go on," Darius told her.

"Jonathan... He's big on technology. Inventions. Experimentation. When one fails, he just comes up with something else. He's always testing new ways to track down witches—not just from magical hotspots, but high-tech stuff like cell phone records and internet tracking, social media posts, credit card records, municipal security cameras. He's even hired private investigators a few times."

My blood ran cold at her words. All this time, we assumed it was the magic. For so many years, it had *always* been the magic.

But if what she was saying was true...

God, how many other hunters were doing the same thing? Ditching the old ways in favor of electronic footprints and readily-available spy tech? How could any witch hope to disappear—to go truly underground—in a society where privacy was quickly becoming a currency not everyone could afford to trade?

"How did he track me?" I asked. I didn't have credit cards or anything else in my real name, and I didn't use social media. Even my cell phone was untraceable. At least, I'd always thought it was.

"You were different, Rayanne." Fiona looked up at me, her eyes flaring with jealousy. "He always said you two shared a special connection. He never liked to talk about it with me, though. You were his white whale." At this, the ghost of a grin crossed her lips, almost as though she were glad he'd finally caught up with me. "He's been looking for you for a long, long time."

I fought off a shiver. Darius tightened his hands on my shoulders, and Emilio stepped closer, sliding an arm around my waist.

"Enough, bloodsucker," Asher said, his lip curling in disgust. "Your boyfriend's witch-killing days are over."

"Killing?" Fiona shook her head. "Oh, no. He's not trying to *kill* witches. He's trying to turn them." She sat up straighter in the chair, her chains clinking as they weighed down her shoulders. "And he's not just using vampire blood, either. He's experimenting with all kinds of hybrid techniques—shifter blood, fae magic, demonic possession. The witches who died... that was accidental."

"But... Why?" Ronan asked. "What's the point of all that?"

Fiona tried to shrug, but the chains prevented it. "I guess to prove that he can. His father never forgave him for letting Rayanne live. He never said it outright, but I always got the sense that everything he did in his adult life was all just some elaborate scheme to win back his father's approval."

His father. Dirty Beard. The man who'd slit Calla's throat while I watched helplessly from the root cellar.

Once he'd finished with my mother, he'd ordered his son to take care of me. Only, Jonathan wasn't able to hurt me then—not physically. Calla had cast a protective spell around me, rendering me impervious to any attacks. The only thing Jonathan could do was spit at me and make threats.

Last time I expect a boy to do a man's job, his father had said, smacking the back of his head. *Leave her, fool boy. Unless you want to burn.*

The guys fell silent again, their minds undoubtedly playing out their own versions of the horror show she'd just painted.

Technology. Inventions. Hybrids. Experiments.

The words spun through my head, blurring at the edges. What did Jonathan hope to accomplish? If his experiments worked, and his father finally gave him that elusive approval, what then? Would they team up, hunt down more witches, set their little half-breed army on the loose?

Every time we got a little closer to the true path, four more branched off in its place, darker and more tangled than the last.

"Where is he?" I asked her. "Where does he do these experiments? Where is he keeping them?"

"That, I don't know." Fiona shook her head, releasing an unnecessary sigh I was certain was for our benefit. "He never took me there. After he told me about his experiments, I freaked out. I told him I couldn't do it anymore."

"Really?" I asked. "We're supposed to believe that?"

"Say what you want about me, but I never signed up to hurt or kill anyone. I thought he was just trying to get his magic back. I didn't want any part of that other stuff."

"There is no magic to get back," I told her. "Hunters don't have magic. That's the whole point. They're just trying to steal it."

"They say the same about witches," she said.

"What happened when you told him you wanted out?" Asher asked.

She closed her eyes, shuddering. "He said it didn't matter what I wanted. If I bailed on him, he'd go after my family. My mom. My little brother. I couldn't let that happen."

"So you stayed?" Asher asked.

Fiona nodded. "But things were different between us after that. He stopped telling me about his plans, where he spent his time, what he was working on. He'd come to me for more blood, and that was it. But it was obvious things weren't going according to plan in Blackmoon Bay. He was unraveling. I couldn't... I couldn't stay. I confronted him again, told him I was absolutely done this time."

"What did he say?" Asher asked.

"Nothing. Not one word. Just nodded and opened the door, waiting for me to walk out. His silence was worse than any outright threat. I've spent every day since wondering if today's the day he's going to come after me, or worse—my family." Her eyes flicked to Darius, glazing with what I was certain were fake tears. "I lied when I said I thought you were a visitor. I thought you were one of Jonathan's men, finally coming to end me. Truthfully, I was relieved. I can't... I can't keep living like this."

"Cry me an ocean, Fiona," I said, breaking free from Darius and Emilio. "Who exactly are we supposed to feel sorry for here? You? Your mother? Your brother? What about the witches he's killed? What about the friends and family left to pick up the pieces?"

"You don't have to like me, Gray." she said, lowering her head once again. "You can spend the rest of your life hating me—I get it. But if I were in your shoes right now, I'd spend less energy blaming me for a past that I can't change and more energy trying to figure out how to stop him before one of his experiments actually succeeds."

"That's good advice, Feefs," I said. "You're wrong about one thing, though. I don't hate you. Hating someone requires giving a shit about them in the first place."

"We were friends once," she said, her eyes softening.

"That was a long time ago."

"For what it's worth, I... I'm sorry."

Her voice broke on the last word, tears streaking her face. For a fraction of a second, my heart hurt for her. She'd spent her entire life loving a man who never loved her back.

A man whom I suspected was incapable of loving anyone but himself. She'd sacrificed her humanity for him, and in the end, he'd probably betray her anyway, just like he'd done to me.

So maybe I should've felt sorry for Fiona. For the girl I went to school with, the one who followed us around and wanted so, so badly to be liked.

But this *thing* in front of me was not Fiona; as far as I was concerned, that girl died. She was merely a vampire who'd colluded with the man whose family killed my mother. She'd helped him murder Sophie. Because of her actions, he was able to kill and hurt and kidnap other witches. He was hurting them still.

And then, when she finally decided to grow a shred of a conscience, instead of trying to make things right, she turned tail and ran.

Now she wanted me to believe that she was actually sorry?

Burn her…

"Fiona?" I said, and she nodded, a faint hope flickering in her eyes.

"Your blood is the reason my best friend is dead. So as far as I'm concerned, you can take your apology to hell." Magic flamed to life in my hand, encasing the stake in a blue glow. In a blur so fast I barely saw it happen, I slammed it straight through Fiona's thigh, reveling in the sound of her agony.

Her leg trembled, then stopped, the poison from the hawthorn wood quickly working into her bloodstream.

I had no idea what effect, if any, my magic would have on her. But *damn*, that had felt good. Better than good. Fucking amazing.

"You have no idea what it's like!" she shouted, her body twisting as she began to lose control of her muscles. "It's so easy for you, isn't it? To have friends. To have people who care about you no matter what."

"It's *never* easy as long as people like you are out there, destroying lives for no other reason than your own life didn't turn out how you wanted it."

"It's not fair," she said, her voice growing faint.

"Nope. But you got into bed with the devil anyway."

"Yeah? And how long were *you* in his bed before you led him straight to your mother's house?"

Her words should've cut me deep, but they didn't. They couldn't. Those particular grooves in my heart were well-worn, sliced open and scarred over so many times by my own incessant guilt that I could no longer feel them.

"I was a dumb kid who didn't know any better," I said. "I was in love with him."

She leveled me with a final glare, her movements slowing as the paralysis spread up her torso and along her arms. Through gritted teeth, she choked out three final words, and they lodged deep in my heart, far beneath the magic and the scars and every last regret, where a tiny seed of empathy bloomed in the darkness.

"So. Was. I."

TWENTY-FIVE

GRAY

When I was a little kid, I loved to spin.

Even during the harshest upstate New York winters, I'd stuff myself into my snowsuit and tromp out onto the frozen Arctic tundra of our yard, looking for a prime spot. Once I found it, I'd extend my arms out, tip my head back, and twirl, round and round and round so fast not even the snowflakes could catch me. When I couldn't take another second of it, I'd drop onto my back, stare up at the sky, and hold on for the ride.

It was the only time I felt completely out of control, no sense of my body or my mind or whether some great mystical hand would reach down from the clouds and pluck me right off the earth.

Back then, the feeling was addicting.

I was no longer spinning, but lying in the grass behind the house and staring up at the sky now, I felt the same loss of control, as if I'd been twirling around for days and suddenly decided to hand over the reins of my life to some great unknown force whose intentions were still a mystery.

But unlike the games of my happy childhood, this one wasn't fun. It wasn't a rush. My entire life seemed to be unraveling in the wind, and no matter how hard I tried to hold those threads together, they kept on slipping through my fingers.

"In the mood for some company?"

I'd come out here to be alone, but the sound of Emilio's gentle voice was like a hug I didn't even realize I'd needed, and I smiled.

"That depends," I said, peering up into his warm brown eyes. "Did you bring brownies?"

"You know, *querida*, they say it's the thought that counts. And I'm definitely *thinking* about brownies. Fair enough?"

"Fair enough." I sat up and patted the grass.

Settling in next to me, he leaned back on his hands and said, "Can I ask what you're thinking?"

"I'm thinking that sometimes the world feels too big." I blew out a breath, forcing some of the tension out with it. "Or maybe I'm just too small."

"Maybe a little of both, yeah?"

"Maybe." I rested my head on his shoulder, closing my eyes and inhaling his sweet, earthy scent. It calmed me, as always. "Where are the guys?"

"The demons are in the kitchen arguing over whose turn it is to make dinner and whose to wash dishes. Darius is downstairs keeping an eye on... our guest."

Our guest.

I still couldn't believe that little Fiona Brentwood—Feefs—was the vampire that had helped Jonathan. She'd been such a tiny, peripheral part of my life back then, I never could've imagined that one day she'd have the power to completely alter its course.

Yet she did alter it.

I closed my eyes, remembering all those times she trailed after Jonathan, her eyes full of hope. What if he'd paid more attention to her? What if they'd started dating instead of he and I? If only she'd gotten her wish... Maybe she never would've become a vampire. Maybe Sophie would still be alive. Maybe Jonathan would've been so focused on Fiona he never would've discovered that Calla and I were witches. Maybe Calla would still be alive, too.

If only. What if. Maybe. Three of the most dangerous phrases in the English language.

"So, does our plan fall apart now that we know our bait is a teenaged girl?" I asked.

"Fall apart? No. But Fiona definitely changes things. Not because she's a teenager, though. Or a girl, for that matter."

"Then what changed?"

"You tell me."

Gazing into his deep, soulful eyes, I knew exactly what Emilio wanted me to say—that unlike the evil, traitorous vampire we'd envisioned, Fiona wasn't some opportunistic bloodsucker looking to make a fast buck at the expense of witches. I may have stabbed her with a stake, but she was still a victim. If we used and manipulated her to our own ends, we'd be no better than the hunter who was holding the witches captive.

On some level, I understood that. I really did.

But whether she was coerced or not, Fiona still played a part in killing Sophie and the other witches in the Bay, and who knew how many others before that. No, maybe I didn't want to see her tortured for it, and maybe I was starting to feel slightly guilty about staking her—okay, more than slightly—but I wasn't ready to let her off the hook.

"So you believe her, then?" I asked, avoiding his question. "About why she went along with it, even after learning about his plans?"

Emilio held me in his gaze for a long time before he finally responded, and when he did, his voice was soft and sad. "People do all sorts of misguided things when they're trying to protect the ones they love, *querida*. Let's just say I know something about that."

His eyes misted, and he looked away, suddenly fascinated by a blade of grass at his side.

I swallowed the tightness in my throat and reached for his hand, hooking my pinky around his.

Since Emilio had come back into my life after Sophie's murder, he'd been so focused on helping us try to hunt down Jonathan and piece together this whole insane puzzle, I'd almost forgotten that it hadn't always been this way. That he hadn't always been here with me. That he'd had an entire life before I was even *born*, likely filled with love and heartache and sacrifice and pain. I saw it some-times—the ghost of some old memory flickering through his big brown eyes—but I'd never found the right time to ask.

Maybe, like Asher, he just couldn't talk about his past.

Maybe he felt like he had a lot to atone for, too.

Whether he was to blame or not, my heart ached when I thought about him suffering in silence. I had no idea what he'd been through, only that I wanted to ease his pain the way he'd so often eased mine.

I leaned in close and pressed a soft kiss to his cheek, close to the corner of his mouth, my lips lingering just a beat too long.

When I finally pulled back, he was blushing.

"Not that I'm complaining," he said, his lips curving in a shy smile, "but what was that for?"

"You're a good man, Emilio Alvarez. I hope you know that."

His smile faltered, but he didn't say anything. Just put his hand on my back, strong and reassuring, the warmth of his touch spreading out across my skin.

I rested my head on his shoulder again, releasing a deep sigh. "Did anyone ever tell you that you have a seriously calming effect on people? Especially crazy-ass witches?"

"No, *mi brujita loca*. Only you." He laughed, but the moment was cut short by the emergency ringtone on his phone.

"*Jesús, María, y José*," he grumbled. "What now?"

"I guess you need to get that, huh?"

"Yep." He fished the phone out of his pocket and hit the answer button. "Alvarez. What've you got?"

His golden face paled, his eyes suddenly wide with horror as they locked onto mine.

"What's wrong?" I mouthed.

"Thanks," he said into the phone. "I'll get there as fast as I can."

"More vampires? Another witch missing?" My heart was in my throat. "Emilio, what's happening?"

"Your house in South Bay," he said, the shock still plain on his face.

"What about it?"

"It's on fire."

TWENTY-SIX

GRAY

They wouldn't let me go to Blackmoon Bay.

Ronan tried to make me a cup of mint tea, but he didn't do it right—not like Emilio always did. Darius alternated between checking on me, interrogating Fiona, and apologizing to her for my actions, as if he still couldn't decide whose side she was really on. And Asher did what Asher did best lately—stayed away from me, locking himself in his room, probably obsessing over his sketchbook.

I paced. I jogged around the yard. I showered. I paced some more. Nothing could calm the anxious energy zipping through my bloodstream as we waited for news from Emilio.

It was several hours before he finally returned to us, walking through the door like a ghost, his face covered in black soot, his hair gray with ash, his eyes red.

"Is there anything left?" I whispered.

Emilio took my hands in his, gently shaking his head.

"I'm so sorry, *querida*. Your house… It's gone."

Gone.

Such a small word for such an immense, irrevocable declaration.

Calla was *gone.*

The house I'd grown up in was *gone.*

Sophie was *gone.*

The house she and I had shared was *gone.*

How could anything so solid, so real no longer exist? How could something be here one moment, close enough to touch, and then just… not?

I dropped onto the couch and closed my eyes, trying to process this devastating news.

Emilio told us that no one had been hurt, and for that, I was truly grateful.

But the house… It was still the loss of something I cared deeply about. A place where I'd made some of my best memories—a place where I'd hung my heart. And though none of us had talked about timelines, deep down I'd always hoped I'd be able to return someday, even if that someday was a year from now.

A fool's hope, perhaps, but one I'd still held close.

Ronan was still paying my rent, and he'd been checking in on the place regularly during his shifts, making sure it looked lived-in and cared-for so it wouldn't become a target for vandals. At some point, I'd planned to sort through Sophie's things—to set some of her artwork and clothing aside for Haley, maybe pick out a few things for Jael. Sophie would've wanted me to donate the rest of her art supplies to one of the local schools, and her clothes and shoes to the women's shelter down near the precinct.

I'd thought about selecting a few of her favorite things to keep with her ashes once we got those from the funeral home—maybe a piece of jewelry, a knickknack or two—at least until I was able to make that trip to Colorado to scatter them.

I'd even decided to keep her annoying fox clock; I wanted to think about her and smile every time it chimed.

But the clock had probably melted, and her clothing had probably vaporized, and now I'd never have the chance to do any of those things I'd planned.

Maybe it was a stupid thing to get upset over when I was sitting here in this beautiful cabin with people who cared about me, fed and clothed and warm, unharmed, a solid roof over our heads, but it broke my heart just the same.

In so many ways, losing the house felt like losing her all over again. Like I'd disappointed her all over again.

"How… How did it happen?" I finally asked. "Electrical or something? Old wiring? Gas leak?"

"This wasn't an accident, Gray," Emilio said, taking a seat next to me. "It was arson. Somebody set that fire."

Somebody set that fire.

"Gray?" Ronan sat on my other side, his brow furrowed with concern. "You okay?"

"She's in shock," Emilio said.

"Just breathe, baby." Ronan rubbed my back. I was dimly aware of his soft murmurs, of Emilio's hand on my thigh, of Asher coming out of his bedroom to find out what was going on.

But all I could smell was smoke. I tasted it on my tongue. Felt the heat of the flames consuming my house. Heard the hiss and pop of the wood as it finally gave in to the destruction.

My eyes glazed with tears, and I closed them, trying to catch my breath. To swallow through the lump in my throat. To calm myself.

Asher had told me I needed to stop hiding under a blanket and crying every time things didn't go my way. I'd taken his comments to heart. I hadn't cried since that night —not once.

I didn't want to cry now, either. Not in front of Asher. But no matter how hard I tried, I just couldn't hold back the dam.

It poured out of me in a heaving sob, my body shaking with it, my tears falling like a rainstorm.

Asher took one look at me, then turned around and grabbed his helmet off the island where he'd left it, heading right for the front door.

"Asher?" Ronan called, but the incubus didn't stop.

"I can't watch this," he said.

"Really?" I glared at him, shocked at his cruelty. At his heartlessness. "Sorry if my tears are annoying you, demon. Instead of teaching me how to fight, maybe you should teach me how to turn my heart into a block of ice."

The words burned my tongue on the way out, filling me with shame. I hated myself for speaking to him that way, but I was hollowed out inside, broken and defeated, every piece of me in agony.

Asher glared right back at me. "You think I don't *feel* things?"

"No, I think you're a master at dealing with your emotions. That's why you spend your nights drawing ghosts in your sketchbook and pushing everyone who's still alive away."

Asher scoffed and shook his head, his eyes saying what his mouth wouldn't.

He couldn't stand the sight of me.

Not that I blamed him. Not after what I'd just said. The realization sent forth a fresh tsunami of tears, and I closed my eyes, trying to find the words to apologize. To explain. To take it all back.

"Asher?"

Ignoring me, he turned on his heel and marched out the door. Seconds later, the roar of his motorcycle rattled the front windows.

It felt like my heart was chained to the back of that bike, dragged along behind him for hundreds of miles as he sped away into the night.

"It's okay, Gray," Ronan said softly. "We'll get through this."

Emilio cupped the back of my head and I buried my face in his chest and let the two of them wrap me in an impossibly tight hug, the warmth of their bodies the only thing keeping me from shattering into a million unfixable pieces.

TWENTY-SEVEN

GRAY

I doubted any of us would sleep tonight, but when I finally emerged from Ronan's bedroom an hour later, all was silent.

I stared blankly at the cold fireplace, strangely drawn to it.

Even after learning that a fire had taken the home I'd shared with my best friend, even after it had destroyed my childhood home, even after it had burned my mother's body and everything I'd ever known, I still wanted to make another one. To stare deep into the flames and feel the heat licking my face, knowing that it hadn't gotten me. Not yet.

I knelt down at the hearth, adding a few logs and kindling, coaxing a new fire to life.

The flames flickered and danced, and my mind went to Jonathan.

Tonight had been his doing—I felt it, deep in my bones. I was also certain he'd known I was no longer living there. So, what had he hoped to accomplish by burning down an empty house? Was he just trying to unsettle me with a reminder of the fire his family had started in my home a decade ago? Did he think his actions might sufficiently weaken my mental state and make me an easier victim?

Or was this some clue, some piece of the larger puzzle we'd yet to figure out?

Keys jangled in the front door lock, startling me from my churning thoughts. I looked up just in time to see Asher walking in, cradling his helmet against his chest as if it were full of water he wouldn't dare spill.

Sweat and grime coated him from head to toe, his face smudged with black streaks. His boots thudded heavily as he walked across the wooden floor to join me at the fireplace.

"Hi," I said, getting to my feet but unable to meet his eyes. I hated fighting with him. Hated that I was taking everything out on him. Hated that no matter how close we'd gotten, something always came right back between us again.

"Gray," he said softly, "I shouldn't have—"

"No." I held up a hand to stop him. "I was out of line. I had no right to bring that up—especially not like—"

"I hate that she haunts you, too. I know she does. It's killing me." His words were a whisper, and I finally met his eyes, my heart squeezing at the pain I found there. I wanted to tell him it was okay, that it wasn't his fault—the woman's death *or* my nightmares—but when I opened my mouth to say it, Asher shook his head, silently begging me once again to let it go.

Frustration burned in my gut. If we could talk about it together, maybe we could help each other through it.

But I wouldn't add to his pain. Not tonight.

"You went to the house, right?" I asked, but I didn't need him to confirm. He reeked of fire, and his boots were coated in wet ash.

"I'm sorry." Asher cleared his throat. "I tried to salvage…" He trailed off, holding out the helmet for me to look inside, but now I couldn't tear my eyes away from his eyes, red-rimmed and defeated, so vulnerable it hurt to look at him.

"I looked and I just… I couldn't," he went on. "Everywhere I turned it was just rubble and ash." His voice broke, and he turned his head and coughed into his shoulder. I moved to touch him, but he shrunk away from me, holding the helmet between us like another barrier, never letting me get too close. Not when it really counted. "Just take it, Gray. Please."

Nodding, I finally accepted the offering, peeking inside to see what he'd found.

Three smooth, palm-sized stones sat at the bottom of the helmet, their carefully crafted designs and sweet messages no more than a multicolored swirl of paint that bubbled and curled at the edges.

But they were still hers. Sophie's. My breath caught, and I reached inside and pulled them out, pressing them to my chest.

The house Sophie and I had shared for so many years had been destroyed tonight. Before this moment, all I had of my best friend were her book of shadows, her tarot deck, and memories so beautiful they hurt to look at.

But now I had these, the very last of her creations.

I looked into Asher's ocean-blue eyes, tears slipping down my cheeks, my heart cracking wide open, and I nodded. It was all I could manage.

"I'm so sorry, Gray," he whispered again, setting down the helmet so he could cup my cheeks. He caught my tears with his thumbs, pressing a gentle kiss to my forehead. "This was all there was. Please don't cry."

The helmet no longer between us, I leaned against his chest.

"You can never really know love until you know yourself," he said, running a hand over my hair and down my back. "It was written on one of the stones—I saw it the night you did my cards."

I remembered the exact stone, turquoise and white and lavender, the words painted in Sophie's tiny, perfect letters.

I couldn't even speak.

He pressed his lips to the top of my head, whispering into my hair. "Tell me how to make this better."

I shook my head. The tears kept falling, but not for the reasons Asher thought.

It wasn't the fire or the loss of Sophie's things. It wasn't the way her beautiful art had been reduced to a smudge of paint on the rocks he'd brought back for me.

It was that he'd brought them back for me at all.

TWENTY-EIGHT

GRAY

The dirt was cool and damp beneath my bare feet as I picked my way through the tangled path. Since my last visit, the flowers had become so overgrown it was nearly impossible not to crush them.

"Sorry," I kept saying. But they never said anything in return, and eventually, I made it to the meadow and the lake, the water nipping at my bare toes.

The brambles were gone.

I hadn't meant to come to the realm. I'd fallen asleep on the couch next to Asher, and somehow, I ended up here.

I wasn't afraid, though. Jonathan's presence was gone—at least for now. There just me and a million stars floating in the fathomless lake of my unconscious mind. I tried to count them, but I kept losing my place.

"How many times have I told you," a familiar voice said, "you won't find the best rocks on the shore? You have to wade in there. Work for your art, girl!"

270

Sophie…

My heart swelled, and I turned around to see my dearest friend, her red hair shimmering in the starlight, her smile bright and contagious.

"Are you going to hug me, bitch, or is this about to get *super* awkward?"

I laughed, throwing my arms around her and pulling her close. The scent of her strawberry shampoo washed over me, so real it brought tears to my eyes.

"I miss you," I said, squeezing her a little tighter. I knew it wasn't Sophie—not her form, not her soul—just an image my magic conjured up because I'd fallen asleep thinking about her. About our home. About everything we'd lost.

But right now, none of that mattered. She was my best friend. Her death didn't change that. It didn't end our relationship. A part of her would always live on in my soul, so who was to say this image, this memory, this mirage wasn't any more real than her physical form had been? Who was to say she *wasn't* communicating with me on some level?

Stranger things had happened in the realm.

"Can I sit with you?" she asked. "I brought my cards."

I beamed. "Of course you did."

We found a comfortable spot on the shoreline, close to the water's edge. The water was warm and dark, rippling gently every time one of us dipped our toes in.

"So, what's new?" she asked brightly, and my smile faltered. I didn't want to tell her about the house. About everything we'd lost tonight.

But somehow, she already knew.

"It's just stuff, Gray."

"I know. But it reminded me of you."

"As if I'd ever let you forget me." She rolled her eyes and stuck out her tongue, her funny faces slowly coaxing my smile back to life.

Sophie shuffled the cards—the same deck she'd always used—then laid out five cards in a row between us, face down.

"Are these cards about me or about you?" I asked, stopping her from flipping the first one. "I'm asking in advance so you don't make me guess after the fact."

"Nice try, Gray." Sophie grinned. "The cards work in mysterious ways. Who are we to question their methods? When the universe has a message to share, the intended recipient is always revealed at the intended time, no sooner, no later."

Now she was starting to sound like Liam. I opened my mouth to tell her as much, but changed my mind. Liam, Death, the unknown quantity… You kind of had to meet him in person to understand.

I realized, with a shudder, that maybe she already had.

"Ready?" she asked, and I nodded, half expecting the Death card to appear.

But the first card she turned over was the Six of Swords reversed. In it, a creature escaped a burning city in a hot air balloon affixed to a boat with six swords. The impression I got from the reversal was one of being trapped.

"Way to kick things off, universe," I mumbled.

Sophie turned the next card. This one was upright—

Seven of Swords. With his legs in the air, a harlequin balanced a sword on his feet, another dangling from the end by a frayed rope, perilously close to falling into his open mouth. Five additional swords lay around him.

"Someone is trying to trick us," I said. "A cunning, dangerous foe. I don't know—I just get the feeling that this guy is sitting here doing these death-defying tricks, all the while distracting us from what's really going on."

"That's my feeling, too," she said.

"Coupled with the poor guy trapped in the burning city, I'm already not liking where this is going."

"Let's look at the rest," she said, and I nodded, gesturing for her to turn them all over at once.

She flipped the Eight of Swords next, followed by the Nine, then the Ten.

A shiver rolled across my scalp and down my back. Every instinct inside me was telling me to bolt. Escape. Get out. Run. Leave.

The Eight had turned up the night I'd seen Reva in the flames, and that night, I'd felt like someone was trying to force her to do his bidding—likely the hunter. Clearly under the influence of some other force, the woman on the card was a breath away from falling out the window to her death, impaling herself on the eight swords below.

The Nine was the nightmare card, featuring a creature riddled with anxiety sitting upright in bed, gnawing nervously on her own hand as an imp gnawed on her shoulder. Behind her, nine swords hung on the wall.

The Ten in this deck was particularly creepy, and it

always unsettled me a bit when it turned up. But tonight, it felt downright terrifying. It had turned up in my reading for Asher the night he'd crashed at my place, and I'd thought it was referring to something in his past that he'd yet to release. Now, it felt like another imprisonment, a man shoved into a tiny wooden box, his body run through with ten swords. He tried to stop them with his hands, to resist the sharp blades, but he couldn't. The end was inevitable.

Something was coming to an end, but unlike a peaceful transition or a necessary release to make way for the new, this one was going to hurt.

Imprisonment. Trickery. Coercion. Nightmares. Painful endings.

Everything about the reading made me itch to flee.

"What do I do?" I asked. "What is this about? The witches?"

"I don't know, Gray. But judging from your reaction, I'd say this message was intended for you."

I jumped to my feet, no longer able to sit still.

Run, a voice echoed in my head. A breeze rolled in across the lake, raising goosebumps on my arm. *Get out now.*

"But I'm not trapped here!" I said, though I had no idea who I was speaking to.

The message in the cards put me on edge, but there was no danger in my realm right now. Everything was at peace. I was sure of it.

"I'd better go," Sophie said, packing up her cards.

"But you just got here."

Sophie smiled, but she was already fading. Fresh pain blossomed in my chest. I wasn't ready to say goodbye.

"Please," I whispered. "Don't leave me. Not this time."

"You are going to be okay," she said calmly. It was the same thing Calla had said to me before she'd bound my magic, saying goodbye for the very last time.

"Don't," I tried again, reaching for her hands. "Not yet."

"I have to," she said. "And so do you."

"But I want to stay with you."

"You can't," she said softly. And then she was gone, her final words floating on the lake breeze. "Don't lose your way, Gray."

* * *

It felt like I'd been walking for hours, yet I still couldn't find the path that would lead me out. Somehow, I must've ended up on another path, one I didn't recognize, choked with sharp, treacherous vines that cut my bare feet as I wandered through the dark.

I hoped they weren't poisonous.

Unlike the soft, cool earth I was used to on my usual path, the ground here was rocky and uneven; it was a wonder anything could grow in it at all. Somehow, the trees were even larger here, with huge black trucks wider than cars and branches that blotted out the night sky. The longer I walked, the darker the woods became.

Mist crept in among the tree trunks, slithering around my ankles. But instead of the cool touch I'd been expecting, this mist burned my skin, seeping into the cuts in my feet and setting my nerves on fire.

I glanced around for a boulder or log, anything I could climb on top of to escape this deadly vapor, but there was nothing but tangled vines and giant, sinister trees in all directions. I tried to walk faster, hoping I'd find another path, but that only made it worse; the mist seemed to be chasing me, thickening around my ankles, slowly working its way up to my calves, my knees, my thighs. Panic buzzed through my limbs, but there was nowhere to run, no escape.

I thought of the man in the Six of Swords, trapped in his burning city.

Taking a deep breath, I forced the panic back down, reaching instead for my magic. It swirled inside me, warming my skin, but no matter how hard I tried to call it forth, it wouldn't come.

The mist kept climbing, wrapping around my hips, my waist, my chest, squeezing me as if it were a giant python. I coughed and gasped, but I couldn't get enough air. Mist filled my lungs, burning my throat, making me gag.

The realization sank in my gut like a stone.

Whatever devilry had invaded my realm, there would be no escaping it.

I couldn't breathe. I couldn't even gasp.

I dropped to my knees, and then fell forward, my face smashing into the rocky soil. The mist swept over me fully, enshrouding me in a blanket of white so thick and impenetrable, it was as though I'd never even existed at all.

I was just... *gone*.

TWENTY-NINE

EMILIO

Why am I on the floor?

I looked around my bedroom, trying to get my bearings. It was dark outside, which meant I'd slept the day away. My mouth tasted like I'd eaten a full ashtray, and a hacking cough burned my lungs.

I was also naked, and my clothes were in tatters on the floor around me, which could only mean one thing.

At some point in the middle of the night, I'd shifted.

An injury was the only explanation. I healed faster in wolf form; unconscious shifting was my body's self-defense mechanism.

So, what the hell had set it off?

Gingerly, I got to my feet, checking myself over for any signs of injury, but other than the cough and that horrid taste in my mouth, everything seemed fine.

The fire at Gray's place must've done a number on my system—more than I'd realized last night.

Desperate for some coffee, I threw on a T-shirt and sweats and headed out into the main area of the house, surprised no one else was around. They were all late risers, but by sundown, I'd usually find *someone* sniffing around for food.

I thought about banging on some doors, but figured coffee was more important. Caffeine first, then a group wakeup call.

After that, we needed to hash out the next phase of our plan, including what—if anything—we were going to do about Fiona.

I walked past the living room and peeked over at the couch, wondering if Gray and Asher were still cuddled up. I'd found them there late last night, and covered them with a blanket, but like everywhere else in the main area, the couch was empty.

I wondered if they'd decided to work out the last of their differences in a way that required a little less conversation.

In that case, maybe I *wouldn't* go banging down his door just yet.

Chuckling to myself, I headed for the kitchen, but before I got much further, a strange sensation crept up my spine, raising the hairs on the back of my neck and stopping me cold.

I whipped around, certain I was being followed.

But I was alone.

I scanned the living room, convinced I wasn't imagining

things. Something was off—I could feel it. I could almost *smell* it.

"Guys?" I called out. No answer.

I knocked on Ash's door, but he didn't respond. When I peeked inside, I found his room empty, his bed still made up from yesterday.

Gray's room was empty too.

Ronan must've heard the racket—he emerged from his room, coughing like the devil.

"Damn, this sucks," he said, clearing his throat. "What's—"

"Gray with you?" I asked him.

"No, I thought she was with Ash. They—" I didn't hear the rest. I was already bolting down the basement stairs.

Ronan followed, close on my heels.

"Darius?" I called down.

He was just coming out of his bedroom, looking as bleary-eyed and wrecked as Ronan. He was also coughing.

"Where's Fiona?" I asked.

He looked around in utter confusion, his brows knitting together. "She was… right here."

"Gray and Ash are gone, too," I said, heading back upstairs. The three of us scoured the place, even checking the yard and the woods around the perimeter, but there was no sign of them.

My gut felt like I'd swallowed a handful of sharp rocks.

"Do you think it was Fiona? How late were you awake?" I asked Darius, trying to piece together the timeline.

"That little bitch," Ronan said. "All that bullshit about how sorry she was."

"I don't believe it was her," Darius said.

Ronan scoffed. "You don't *want* it to be her. There's a difference."

"She was in restraints. I had my eyes on her until well after sunrise. It's only an hour after sunset now. That wouldn't have left her much of a window to escape."

"Maybe she had help," Ronan said.

"From whom?"

"Jonathan," I said. "You heard her last night—she still loves him, even after everything."

Darius shook his head. "I could buy that, but he didn't know she was here. No one did. I kidnapped her from her mother's home in New York, sedating her immediately. She's been in my presence ever since—no calls, no nothing."

"But no one else knew we were up here," I said. "No one else but Liam even knows this place exists."

"Someone else obviously did," Darius said, letting loose another cough. "Or someone tracked us."

Ronan's cough started up again, too, the sound making my own throat tickle.

Again, that strange sensation crept across my skin.

What is that smell?

I closed my eyes, trying to place it. It was faint, barely detectable even to me, but it was there, lingering just below the familiar scents of Gray and the guys and the home we now shared, like some kind of chemical tinged with magic.

I took a few more whiffs, opening my eyes and following the scent to its source.

Bingo.

I was standing over the coffee table, looking down at three black rocks, partially coated in what looked like swirls of red and bluish-gray paint.

I picked one up and brought it to my nose. Before I even took another whiff, I felt the burn in my nostrils and coughed.

"I've smelled something like this before," I said. "Pretty sure it's fae. What are these?"

"Asher brought them back from Gray's house last night," Ronan said. "After the fire. They were Sophie's. She used to paint rocks from the Bay."

Once he'd said it, I remembered seeing them in a basket on Gray's kitchen table the night I'd gone over there to investigate Sophie's murder.

The memory clawed a gouge in my heart.

"Well, that answers the question of why Jonathan set that fire," I said. "He knew she'd want something from the house. These were the only things that didn't burn, so he had them spelled."

"With what?" Darius asked.

"I'm guessing a tracking device and some kind of time-release poison gas."

Despite everything Fiona had told us, everything Gray believed about him dropping breadcrumbs, we'd still underestimated him.

"And you're certain it's fae magic?" Darius asked.

"Has to be," Ronan said. "That's the only way someone could've detected a signal from in here. Nothing else would've gotten through *our* fae magic."

"Exactly. And once we were all unconscious," I said, "it would've been easy for him to waltz right in here and take them."

We all fell silent after that.

The bastard had come into our home. He'd put his hands on our friends. He'd taken them right out from under our noses.

"Fuck!" Ronan exploded in a ferocious roar, grabbing the rocks and whipping them at the window. They crashed through the glass, landing somewhere in the yard.

I crossed the room and put my hands on his shoulders, pulling him in for a hug. He was trembling with rage, his chest rattling from the last of the poison, all of it conspiring to wreak havoc on his system.

I met Darius's eyes across the room, gesturing for him to get his vampire ass over here.

I pulled back from Ronan, holding his shoulders and looking him dead in the eye. "Listen to me, Ronan. We'll get them back. I fucking promise you, we'll get them back."

"*El Lobo* is right." Darius put a hand on each of our shoulders—a rare show of affection from the normally cool vampire. "Failure is not an option. Not when it comes to Gray and Asher."

Ronan met his eyes, nodding once.

I pulled him in for one last hug, then left them alone, heading into my bedroom to gather up a few things.

When I returned, Darius was sweeping up the broken glass while Ronan taped cardboard over the windowpanes.

"Pack your shit, boys," I said, dropping an empty duffel bag on the kitchen counter. "We're going to Raven's Cape."

"You think he's still there?" Ronan asked.

"Absolutely. He could've killed us last night, but he didn't. He left us alive for a reason." I grabbed a bunch of waters and some fruit from the fridge, shoving it all into the bag. "It's a game to him, remember? Killing us would've ended it. He *wants* us to go after him. He left the amulet on William Landes so when the time came, we'd know right where to look."

"I suppose the time has come," Darius said. He looked as if he'd aged ten years in the last ten minutes.

"You're saying he wants a face-to-face?" Ronan asked.

Another cough roared its way out of my chest. When I caught my breath again, I said, "No two ways about it."

He scratched his thin beard, his eyes lost in thought.

When he looked up at me again, they were black as night.

"Then I say we give this motherfucker *exactly* what he wants." Ronan's wave of sadness and unchecked rage had receded, replaced now by an unwavering determination. The malevolent glint in those demon-black eyes set my teeth on edge, making me grateful we were on the same side. "And *exactly* what he deserves."

THIRTY

GRAY

"She's probably dead," a woman's voice said, flat and defeated.

Panic shot through my limbs, making my hands and feet tingle. *Dead?* Was she talking about *me*?

I tried to open my eyes, to open my mouth to talk, to flex my fingers and toes, but I was completely paralyzed. The only thing I could feel other than the tingling in my limbs was the raw burn in my chest.

I wanted to cough, but I couldn't get my lungs to work.

"You probably killed her," she went on. "Just like you killed the other ones."

Her voice seemed vaguely familiar. Where the hell *was* I?

"No."

Rough hands gripped my shoulders, hauling me into a sitting position and shaking me hard.

Pain rushed at me all at once, forcing my eyelids open. I

had just enough time to suck in a gasp of air before the grip released, dropping me on my back. I was lying on some kind of table, but everything was still blurry, the two figures before me no more than smudges.

Am I in a hospital? How long have I been unconscious?

"See?" the man said. "Not dead."

He leaned down close, his head hovering over my face like a balloon as I tried to blink him into focus.

"Ronan?" I mumbled, though I already knew it couldn't have been him. Ronan never would've touched me that way.

The cough finally worked its way out of my chest, leaving me breathless and sore.

When I finally stopped hacking, I looked at the man again, slowly bringing him into focus.

Dark red hair. Eyes the color of new spring grass.

And a smile that twisted like a knife in my gut.

"Afraid not, Sunshine."

THIRTY-ONE

GRAY

"Hello, Rayanne," Jonathan said. "You look even better in person than you did in your realm. You've grown up to be more beautiful than I could've ever imagined."

My skin crawled, bile rising in my throat as he grinned at me, his eyes wild with unchecked menace.

How many hours had I stared into those eyes? How many times had I run my fingers through that dark red hair, laughing about how much I envied it?

It was hard to believe I'd loved him so much.

Now, I just wanted to end him.

My eyes darted around the room, trying to get a sense for where I was. It wasn't a hospital—that was for sure. The room was cold and damp, its stone walls rough and rounded, one side completely open to a corridor. There were no windows. The only light came from glass orbs lining the walls.

Somewhere in the distance, the ocean whispered against the shoreline.

I was in a cave on the coastline, just like I'd thought when I'd connected with Reva in the flames.

My heart quickened. If my vision had been correct, maybe the guys would figure out where I was. Maybe they'd put together all the rest of the clues and track me down. Maybe—

"I understand you might feel a little speechless," Jonathan said, crashing into my thoughts. "Though I hope you change your mind about that. We have so much to catch up on! What has it been, ten years?"

When I didn't respond, he turned to the woman behind him.

Fiona Brentwood bowed her head, her shoulders slumping.

Had she brought me here? Where were the guys? I thought Jonathan had somehow taken me from my realm last night, but if Fiona was here…

God, none of this made any sense. How did Jonathan even know she was at our house? How did he find me there?

"Ten years. Right, Feefs?" he said.

Fiona nodded, but she'd fallen silent, too.

I watched her a moment longer. I had no idea how either of us had come to be in his clutches, but one thing was certain: whether she still loved him or not, Fiona was not here of her own free will. Shame and fear rolled off her in waves, her body trembling. Every time he spoke, she jumped.

I tried to catch her eye, but she refused to look at me.

"Rayanne, honestly." Jonathan sighed, clearly getting annoyed at my lack of enthusiasm over our little reunion. "You can't think of a single thing to say to me after a decade?"

When I find you, I will burn you…

"Why am I not dead?" I finally asked.

"Dead?" he looked positively aghast. "Why on earth… Wait, are you talking about all that unpleasantness at your mother's house? Oh, Sunshine. I was young and spineless back then. Just following Daddy's orders. But, you know, we all have to grow up and become our own people eventually." He laughed, his wild eyes dancing. He was totally unhinged —a cartoon villain I just couldn't seem to outsmart. "Like most men in his generation, my father lacks imagination and foresight. Fortunately for you, I have plenty of both."

I blinked up at him, unsure what to say. Everything about him seemed to be hanging on by a very thin thread.

Behind him, Fiona remained as still as a statue.

His smile dropped. "Get up, Rayanne."

"You can't turn me," I said, sitting up on the table and swinging my legs over the edge. I was still dressed in my clothes from last night, including my bra and underwear, which was a relief. But whatever Jonathan was planning, I didn't want to be on my back when it happened. "Witches can't survive the change."

"Not yet," he said. "But I'm working on perfecting the technique. Until then, I need something else from you. Don't look at me like that," he said, swatting the air and rolling his eyes. "Do you honestly think I'd go to all the trouble of retrieving you if I was going to hurt you?"

"Where are the others?" I asked. "Haley, Reva—"

"Why do you care about those witches? We have everything we need now that you're here."

"Are they even… alive?" I whispered.

"That's what you're worried about?" He rolled his eyes. "Yes, they're alive, Rayanne. Probably not at their personal best at the moment, given that they're sleeping on wet rock and haven't seen the sun in quite a while, but they're being fed and watered and you really have nothing to worry about there."

"Can I see them?"

He pursed his lips. "I don't think that's a good idea. Not right now."

I blew out a breath. It wasn't much, but something told me he was telling the truth—that they were alive, and they were here. Which meant I might be able to find them and get us all out of here. I just had to keep playing along until I figured out what the hell to do.

I swayed in place, the edges of my vision dimming. I was hungry, and probably dehydrated, and doing my best to hold on to any shred of hope I could find.

"What do you want, Jonathan?" I finally asked.

He shrugged, as if he were simply asking for another

glass of water or a dollar for the candy machine. "I think you already know the answer to that."

Inside me, my magic stirred, humming faintly in my blood as if it had just awoken from a long nap.

He won't touch us, the voice said.

I wanted to believe it. But how could I? How could I believe he wouldn't touch me after everything he'd already taken from me?

"I already gave you absolutely everything I had," I said, my voice breaking. "And you just... you led your father and his men to my house. You let them kill my mother. You tried to kill me." At this, I finally met his gaze. "How could you?"

I swear I saw regret flicker through his crazy green eyes, but the instant I blinked, it was gone.

"The problem with giving someone *absolutely* everything, Sunshine, is that eventually, you run dry. And then what have you got to offer?"

His jaw ticked as he stared at me, but I didn't think it was from clenching his teeth. In fact, the longer he talked, and the closer I scrutinized him, the more I realized there was something seriously off about him. It wasn't just his jaw; all the muscles in his face twitched, as if his skin didn't fit right anymore. His left eyelid drooped, and when he laughed, one side of his mouth sagged.

None of it was obvious or severe, but I'd spent a lot of hours gazing into those eyes, studying the lines of his face. Kissing him. Yes, we were both older now, but still. Whatever was going on with him had nothing to do with age.

"Aww, don't look at me like that," he said, mistaking my morbid curiosity for something else. "It turns out, you didn't actually give me *everything*. You were holding out on me, Rayanne."

Holding out on him? What was he talking about now?

He gestured for me to stand up, and I did, hoping if I didn't give him too much trouble right off the bat, I could buy myself a little time to figure out a plan. To see if I could wake up that sleepy magic inside.

He grabbed my hand, yanking me out into the corridor and into an adjacent alcove, this one much smaller than the room I'd been in, with a metal gate over the front. I peered between the bars, but the room beyond was pitch black.

"What is this?" I asked.

"You tell me."

God, what was with the games?

"Give me a hint," I said.

"Okay, but only one." Grinning, he banged his fist on the metal gate. "Come out, come out, little mouse."

Seconds later, a figure emerged from the darkness, her movements slow and stiff, her eyes milky white.

My stomach lurched, the room tilting beneath me.

"Ring any bells, necromancer?" Jonathan laughed, but I barely heard him, all of my attention on the poor creature before me.

She leaned against the bars, her arms reaching through them, hands grasping at nothing but air. A low moan wheezed through her chest.

Her face was rotten in some parts, bruised in others

where someone had obviously beaten her. Her clothing was in tatters, and while she'd been thin is a rail before, now I could literally count the ribs through her pale skin.

A blue unicorn hoodie hung off her shoulders, torn and dirty and stained with old blood.

My eyes blurred with tears, but I couldn't look away. I owed her that much.

I'm so, so sorry Bean. You deserved better.

"I see your memory is coming back to you. I knew it would, Rayanne. You always were the smartest girl in school. And the prettiest. It's really too bad you turned out to be a witch." Jonathan had been rambling for so long that when he finally shut his mouth, it took me a beat too long to realize why.

I turned to glance at him over my shoulder. He was holding a gun, pointed right at Bean.

"Don't!" I shouted, but it was too late. He'd already pulled the trigger.

Bean caught a bullet in the chest. She stumbled back from the impact, but she didn't fall. Didn't drop. Didn't die. Seconds later, she was at the gate again, reaching through the bars for something she'd never, ever find.

"Amazing," he said, that twisted smile contorting his face.

I lowered my eyes, unable to watch the sick spectacle a moment longer.

"What do you *want*?" I whispered. It was all I could manage without throwing up.

"Easy-peasy." Jonathan grabbed my chin, his hand reeking with the sweet, metallic tang of gunpowder as he jerked my face up, forcing me to meet his eyes. "I want you to teach me how to make more."

THIRTY-TWO

LIAM

Though only hours had passed on the material plane since the vampire notified me of Gray's disappearance, it felt as though I'd been stalking the edges of her realm for months, desperately seeking the faintest sign that she was still alive. Still within reach.

My human vessel was exhausted. I'd been going back and forth among the Shadowrealm, Gray's magical realm, and the material plane, scouring the corners of the globe and beyond, hoping I'd find something. Anything.

So far, I'd come up empty. It seemed as if Gray had simply ceased to exist.

There was a time when this would have simply upset my plans, forcing me to move on to another Shadowborn, perhaps in another time and place. That would've been disappointing, but not devastating. I was used to waiting. I could wait eons.

But Gray Desario had come to mean something to me.

Whether that was the result of compromising myself by spending too much time in my human vessel, unable to escape the vestiges of all its earthly concerns and emotions, or there were some other forces at work well beyond my immediate comprehension, I couldn't say.

I could only say that when I thought of her now, something deep inside me ached in a way that brought back more memories than I cared to admit.

Memories of a time when I, too, walked the material realm. When I, too, willingly enslaved myself to the whims of my earthly concerns and emotions.

But that was neither here nor there.

Weary and losing hope, I shed my bone-tired human vessel in favor of a great grey owl, eager to rest in the black trees that surrounded her realm. Leafless and tall, they afforded an excellent vantage point from which to survey the vast lake and the dark tangled forests beyond.

It was here, perched upon the tallest branch in the tallest of these trees, that I finally felt the tug of her essence.

There—at the edge of the lake—a flash of blonde hair caught my attention, and I launched myself from the branch and spread my wings, soaring down to the shoreline.

I lacked the energy to quickly transform back into Liam's vessel, so I opted for the shadowy form—human enough in its abilities that we could at least speak.

"Liam!" she cried out the moment I landed.

The breeze picked up, blowing her hair into her face,

whistling through my robes with a chill I'd never before felt here.

I wrapped my hands around her shoulders. Beneath my gloves, beneath her human skin and muscle and bone, I felt the hum of her magic, electric and warm, scented with lavender and lilac and something new I didn't quite recognize.

But there was no time to waste.

"Gray, I need to know where—"

"Raven's Cape! He's—" She cut off abruptly, her eyes wide, her face twisting in abject pain. The gruesome, tortured sound that escaped her lips nearly brought me to my knees.

"Gray!" Desperately I reached for her, but it was too late. Just as swiftly as she'd arrived, my Shadowborn vanished into the mist, leaving me with nothing but the memory of her hair blowing in the breeze and the heartbreaking echo of her final scream.

THIRTY-THREE

RONAN

I was fucking *gutted*.

The woman I loved had been taken. The best friend I'd give my own life for had been taken. And all we had were a bunch of stale breadcrumb clues left by a madman, the trail quickly running cold. I was running on fumes, and I wasn't sure how much more I could take.

"I'm not picking anything up here but shifters," Emilio finally said. "My sister's team must've done quite a number on the place."

We'd arrived in Raven's Cape last night. Driving around town in a nondescript rental van we'd picked up in Black-moon Bay, we'd done a general sweep of the area, trying to get the lay of the land and make some kind of plan.

This morning, Emilio and I had left Darius in a dark motel to wait out the sun while we headed over to William Landes' place.

Apparently, it was a wasted trip.

"This is bullshit," I said, slamming a fist through the living room wall. "We're chasing a ghost."

"We just got here," Emilio said. "We need to be methodical about this."

"*You* be methodical. I need to do something."

"Do what, exactly?" he asked.

I shoved a hand through my hair, ignoring the sting in my now-bleeding knuckles. "I don't know. Put myself out there. Let him know I'm here."

"You mean, use yourself as bait?" Emilio shook his shaggy black head. "Not happening."

"We're out of time and up against a wall and the whole place is on fire. So unless you've got a better idea, Alvarez, this is our plan B."

He eyed me warily, the skin around his mouth drawn tight. I'd never seen him look so tired.

In a voice heavy with defeat, he said, "I hate every fucking thing about this, Ronan."

"You and me both, brother." I clamped a hand over his shoulder. "But we can't let our girl die in there. And Asher needs our—"

"Shh!" Emilio's ears cocked back just a half-second before I heard the footsteps, too.

Unfortunately, it was a half-second too late for both of us.

"Hands where I can see them, boys," a woman's voice said from behind us, clear and commanding and absolutely *not* fucking around. Her accent was Argentine, and though

I hadn't turned around to look at her yet, I knew her hair was jet black, her skin golden and smooth, her brown eyes soft and expressive.

Just like her brother's.

"Both of you," she barked. "Back up slowly and keep those hands up high."

We did as she ordered.

When she finally permitted us to turn around, I nearly gasped. I felt like I'd been yanked twenty years into the past, right back to the last time I'd seen her. The last time Emilio had seen her.

She was just as I'd remembered, other than the fact that she was now carrying a gun, pointing it right at her brother's chest. Three men as big and broad as Emilio flanked her. All of them were wolf shifters.

"Elena," Emilio said, unable to keep the raw emotion from his voice. Tears shone in his eyes. "It's… good to see you."

Something told me the feeling was *not* mutual.

"Didn't I tell you not to step foot in my jurisdiction, *wolf*?" She flashed a feral grin. Then, without warning, she clocked him on the side of the head with the butt of her gun.

Emilio dropped like a bag of rocks.

"What the hell?" I shouted.

"Shut up, demon," she barked.

I took a step toward her just as I caught the blur of another cop in my peripheral vision. I tried to duck, but it was too late—he cracked me right on the skull.

The last thing I heard before the pain surged and sucked me under was the sharp bite of Elena Alvarez's final command.

"Cuff them and put them in the truck. Make sure no one sees them."

THIRTY-FOUR

GRAY

"That was unwise, witch."

I was flat on my back on the stone floor outside Bean's gate, Jonathan staring down at me, his foot planted squarely in the middle of my chest.

My entire body screamed in agony, as if he were holding me down in a tub of acid. I couldn't scream. I couldn't even breathe.

Somehow, seeing Bean had unleashed something in me, and I'd slipped briefly into the realm. But I'd barely been there a second when Jonathan yanked me back out again.

My shield must not have held.

Now, I wanted to die.

"Please," I finally managed.

"Do you promise to behave yourself?" he asked.

I nodded and held my breath. It was all I could do to keep my body from imploding on itself.

Jonathan crouched down and jammed a needle into my arm, injecting me with a liquid that warmed my veins.

And then… bliss.

The pain ended. I didn't have the stomach to ask him what he'd injected me with, or what he'd done to cause so much pain in the first place. All that mattered now was that the pain was gone.

Jonathan grabbed me by the arms and hauled me to my feet. "Walk with me, Rayanne."

I did as he asked, letting him lead me further down the corridor. Every few feet, we passed another dark alcove, but I kept my eyes on the ground, not wanting to see what else he might've chained up inside.

The pain had completely receded, but somehow, he'd woken up the serpent inside me. I felt it uncoil, slithering in my gut, warming. I welcomed it.

I knew now it was simply biding its time. When I absolutely needed to call on it, it would respond. It would be ready. *I* would be ready.

The thought gave me courage. Hope.

"We're more alike than we are different, you know," Jonathan said, reaching for my hand.

I rolled my eyes. Really? That's the angle he was going for here?

"How do you figure?" I asked, shoving my hand into my pocket, out of his reach.

"You were meant to be alone, just like me."

"I'm *nothing* like you."

"No? I see your struggle. I live it. Every day, torn in half, wanting to do what's right, not knowing your true path. Fighting it."

The darkness roiled inside me, responding to his words.

As if he could sense the surge in my power, he said, "That's it, Sunshine. Let the darkness fill you, fuel you. Fuel *us*. We could be a team."

I shook my head. "You said so yourself, Jonathan. I was meant to be alone."

He stared at me with pity in his eyes, like he was the only one in on some sick, elaborate joke. In the silence that followed, I realized just how hollow my words sounded now—just how empty that old refrain had become.

For so long, I'd believed it. But after everything I'd been through with my rebels, how could I say that now?

Alone? I was the farthest thing from alone I'd ever been.

We came to a stop at another gated alcove, and Jonathan wrapped his fingers around the bars of the gate, turning to face me.

"In my experience, Rayanne, people who make bad choices aren't necessarily bad people. They just lack the proper motivation."

A chill ran down my spine at his words.

What was he plotting now?

He opened the gate and hit the light switch on the inside wall. "I believe you know my guest?"

"Asher!" I gasped. The sight was all too familiar.

He sat in a chair at the center of the room, shirtless like he'd been in Norah's attic, only he wasn't chained. The ground and cave ceiling were rough and bare, no signs of devil's traps or other magical workings. His skin was unmarred.

But he looked exactly as he had that night in the attic. Wounded and defeated from the inside out, his eyes bloodshot, his head lolling forward.

"Have you changed your mind yet, Sunshine?" Jonathan asked. "Or do you need another minute?"

"What… What did you do to him?" I sputtered.

"Nanotechnology. Have you heard of it?" He didn't even give me a chance to respond before plowing on. "It's brilliant, actually. All sorts of medical and military applications. For now, just picture hundreds of mechanized particles mobilizing in his bloodstream like a tiny robot army, each soldier's armor engraved with the precise symbols necessary for holding a demon indefinitely." Jonathan laughed. "Well, not *indefinitely*. Only until his body gives out and his soul slips into Oblivion."

My heart was frantic, banging against my chest, pumping raw adrenaline through my veins. The voice inside me grew louder.

He must die. Destroy him.

A vision shot through my mind, bringing me back to that night in the woods when I'd reconnected with my book of shadows. In my memory, I saw the bright green pulse of the earth's magic glowing in my hands.

Of course!

The cave was natural, the rocks beneath my bare feet part of the earth. If I could connect with it, I might be able to draw on some additional magic, further enhancing my own, just like I had that night.

"My father was short-sighted," Jonathan went on, "but I've always had more of a long-term vision."

The bigger implications of Jonathan's plans began to crystallize.

He was unhinged—clearly. But he was also brilliant.

He'd invented an *internal* devil's trap, impossible to eradicate without a complete bloodletting. Even if I took Asher's soul out like I'd done at Norah's, it wouldn't matter —I wouldn't be able to put it back into his body. Not as long as his blood remained tainted.

And this monster was planning to weaponize it.

Horror didn't even begin to describe it.

I closed my eyes, envisioning my feet turning into tree roots, digging down deep beneath the cave floor. Deeper, deeper, deeper still, until they finally reached a great, glowing well at the center of the earth.

The words came to me easily then, and I whispered them inside my mind, again and again.

> *"Great green Earth, mother of all*
> *Hear my plea, heed my call*
> *Grant me the strength to see this through*
> *Lend me your magic, pure and true*
> *Bind us together, you and me*
> *Above and below, so mote it be."*

Not the most elegant verse, but it was honest, and I felt

the earth warm beneath my feet. Still visualizing my roots, I imagined dipping them into the great pool and drinking deep, filling myself with green, glowing, strong magic.

Jonathan clapped once, startling me, but not breaking the connection. "Oh, and just in case you're still dreaming about *another* one of your knights in tarnished armor storming in to rescue you, allow me to disabuse you of that notion."

My heart thudded in my chest.

"Every last one of your allies has been captured and eliminated," he said.

I narrowed my eyes, my hands clenching into fists at my sides. The earth magic surged inside me, twining with my own, twin serpents of green and black. "I don't believe you."

"No? Have you ever heard the sound a wolf makes when he's being skinned alive?" he asked. "It's not howling, exactly. More like… What's the word? Braying? Oh, eventually he shifted back into his human form, but I think he regretted that choice, *mi querida*."

I flinched at the sound of Emilio's words, so gentle and kind in his voice, so twisted in Jonathan's.

"And the crossroads demon?" he went on. "He wanted you to know how much he loved you, of course. But if that were true, he would've found a way to save you instead of getting himself and his friends killed on your behalf, right? No matter. He's back in hell where he belongs. I'm sure they were very happy to get him back."

He's lying, he's lying, he's lying…

"By the time I got to your vampire, I was kind of out of ideas, honestly. So I harvested his blood, then I set him on fire. Efficient. I have to respect a man like that, though. He didn't even scream until I lit that match."

He planted those images inside my mind, and now they spread like a poison, filling me with rage.

"What do you *want* from me?" I screamed.

"I've already told you. I want your power. I want you to teach me how to do what you do. The system would be much more efficient, if you think about it. I wouldn't need to recruit new soldiers if I could simply resurrect them. It's the ultimate form of recycling."

"I don't know how to teach you," I said, and that was the honest truth. "I'm still learning the power myself."

"Then you need to figure out a way to give me that power altogether, Gray. It never should've been yours in the first place. It's wasted on you. All of you."

I'd heard of certain witches being able to "borrow" power from others, or channel certain powers from supernaturals—like vampire influence, for example—but that was usually temporary. I had no idea how to give Jonathan what he wanted.

"I don't know how," I said.

"Not even to save your friends? Damn. I thought I was a cold-hearted bastard. But you? You've got ice in your veins, Sunshine." He pressed his lips together, biting back his obvious frustration. "Well, you got him out of one devil's trap. Can't hurt to try again. Maybe we'll all learn something new today."

SARAH PIPER

He shoved me into the cell, slamming the gate and locking it shut behind me.

I went down hard on my hands and knees, grunting with the impact. Tiny green sparks skittered across my hands, but Jonathan hadn't seen them.

"Well," Jonathan prodded. "Get to it, witch."

"You're just going to stand there and watch?"

"I prefer the term *observe*, and yes, I am going to do just that. Observation is a crucial part of any experiment, and I'll continue to do just that until I can devise a way to transfer your power."

Great.

Getting to my feet, I dusted myself off and slowly circled Asher, my eyes locked on his as I pretended to analyze the situation.

In reality, I just needed a little more time. The magics were still fusing inside me, filling me with immeasurable power.

I leaned in close to Asher's face, breathing in his fiery demon scent.

"Careful, witch," Jonathan called out. "I need to see what you're doing."

"I need to see his eyes," I said.

"Explain."

"The soul is the root of my magic," I said, which was at least partially true, but Jonathan didn't need to know the details. I just had to feed him enough bullshit to keep him distracted long enough to figure out how the hell I was going to fix Asher. Magic or not, if I didn't neutralize that devil's trap, he'd die. "Eyes are the window to the soul. Ergo, I need to see his eyes."

Jonathan seemed satisfied, at least for the moment. "Carry on, then. But no tricks, Sunshine. I'm serious."

Turning my attention back to Asher, I studied his ocean-blue eyes. Despite his obvious pain, they were still sharp and clear.

"You okay?" I mouthed.

"Been better," he whispered. "Are you here to kiss me again?"

I smiled. "In your dreams, buddy."

"Every single one."

Relief rushed through me. Asher was still Asher. That meant he was still okay. That he still had a chance. That *we* still had a chance.

"Hell of a mess, huh?" he whispered. "Any ideas?"

"One. But it's kind of crazy."

"I like crazy."

I gave him a quick wink. Then, before I could change my mind, I spun on my heel and charged toward the gate, slamming a burst of magic into Jonathan's chest.

He went down hard, flat on his back on the cold stone.

"Over and out, asshole."

"Holy shit!" Asher said. "I knew you had it in you! Is he dead?"

I shook my head. "I don't have the juice to kill him. That's just a variation on a hold spell. He's unconscious for now, but we don't have much time."

And with any luck, he'd be confused and groggy when

he came out of it, not remembering that I was the one who put him down.

I was counting on it.

I had other plans for Jonathan. But first…

"Speaking of quickies," I said, turning back to Asher and taking his face into my hands. I brushed the hair from his eyes, offering him a gentle smile. "Let's see what we can do about this nanotech predicament."

THIRTY-FIVE

ASHER

Gray's smile was a light at the end of a long, dark tunnel.

"Still determined to win me over with your outlandish stunts, incubus?"

I coughed out a weak laugh. "Yeah, well, I couldn't remember what flowers you liked, so I figured this was the next best thing."

"Hmm." She stroked my cheeks with her thumbs, making me shiver. "And here I thought Emilio was the softy of the bunch."

I reached for her hands, covering them with mine. Her touch was so warm and soft, I didn't want her to stop.

But she needed to get out of here before that fuckstick woke up.

"Gray, you have to—"

"I have to help you. That's what I'm doing right now." She pressed a kiss to my left eyebrow. Then to the other.

Each caress, each kiss, sent a burst of warmth to my chest. "So stop fighting me."

I closed my eyes, letting her cover my face with her soft, perfect kisses. Letting her strengthen me, just a little.

"This isn't how I wanted things to happen between us," I said.

Gray laughed softly. "Well, maybe you should've thought of that before you decided to get locked up in here and pumped full of nano-soldiers, because now you don't have a choice."

"No, but *you* do." I turned my head away from her and coughed.

Gray stood up, taking a step back. I didn't know whether to be relieved or disappointed.

But I should've known better. She wasn't going anywhere.

Keeping her blue eyes locked on mine, she slid out of her pants and underwear. I hadn't even fully processed this when she straddled me on the chair.

Oh, fuck. The wet heat of her core radiated through my pants, kicking my heart rate up a few notches.

I clenched my teeth, fighting off a rush of pleasure. I appreciated the temporary energy boost, but this was fucking dangerous.

"What are you *doing*, Gray?"

She rocked her hips forward, brushing against the fabric of my pants and the firm ridge of my cock beneath. Another wave of warm, healing energy pulsed through my chest, keeping the devil's trap particles at bay and filling me with a burst of new energy.

Also, a hard-on.

Fucking hell.

"We've been dodging this since we met, Ash," she said. "So unless you can look me in the eyes and *swear* to me this isn't what you want, I'm not stopping."

I cradled her angel face in my hands, my thumbs stroking her silky-soft cheeks. Goddamn, she was breaking my heart. "You know I can't, Cupcake."

"So what's the problem?"

I laughed. "You mean, aside from the fact that we're locked in an underground cave prison by your totally unhinged ex-boyfriend—excellent life choice there, by the way—and no one knows where we are or how to get to us, and I'm dying a slow death by some kind of devil's trap blood transfusion, and he might be back at any second to force you to transfer your power so he can unleash his crazy on the world?" I fingered a lock of her hair and took a breath. Chances are I wouldn't live to see tomorrow, so what was the point of holding back this last bit? I could only manage a whisper, but I had to say it. Now or never. "I'm, uh… I'm pretty sure I'm falling in love with you, too. So… there's that."

Her eyes widened, but she didn't say anything right away. Her silence felt like a punch in the gut.

For a minute, I worried I'd ruined everything. That telling her was an even bigger mistake than falling for her in the first place.

But then she leaned in close, her lips brushing mine in the dark, squalid damp of that room, giving me just enough hope to hang on a little longer.

"Then let me do this for you," she whispered, and I was gone, melting beneath the hot press of her mouth on my neck. Her kisses were like the best kind of fire, burning a path across my skin, lighting me up inside and out.

With one hand, she reached down the front of my pants, fisting my cock in a tight, perfect grip that made me moan.

It took everything in me to grab her hand and stop her.

Gray growled in frustration. "Damn it, Ash, we don't have time. What is your problem?"

"If I hurt you—"

"You won't."

"You can't know that."

She stilled, finally considering my words. After a beat, she blew out a breath and said softly, "I remind you of her, right?"

Every muscle in my body stilled.

I didn't have to ask her who she meant.

"No, you don't." I reached for her face again, not bothering to hide the ghosts in my eyes. She knew them. She'd always known them. "She's…"

"She's what?" Gray whispered.

"She's… not a story for nice girls." I dropped my hand, hoping she'd let it go. Hoping that *I* could let it go. Leave it in the past where it belonged before that memory finally did me in for good.

Gray slid her hands into the back of my hair, stroking my skin.

"I don't know what happened to you before," she said softly, even though I knew she'd seen it. She might not understand the details, but the night she'd tried my soul on for size, she'd witnessed me killing the first woman I'd ever really loved—witnessed it through *my* eyes. My memories. Much as I thought I could spare her by not talking about it, it'd probably haunted her dreams as often as it haunted mine.

"Gray—"

"It's different with us," she said.

"You *want* it to be different," I said. "Believe me, Cupcake, so do I. But that doesn't make it so."

"Maybe it does." She shrugged, the corner of her mouth lifting in a smile. "Intention, right? That's what magic is."

"But—"

"Listen. I've healed you before. That night in the woods, with the cougar? My magic, coupled with the earth magic, was enough to heal you with one kiss. Well, I'm even stronger now, and if you'd stop being such a stubborn dick about things, you'd be getting a hell of a lot more than one kiss."

It sounded logical, but it was still a risk.

"Look," she said, finally getting pissed. "It's the only thing I can think of to try. If my magic can heal you, maybe it's enough to strengthen your blood and your immune system to destroy those damn nano-bots."

"Maybe it is," I said. "But at what cost?"

"What if there are no costs with us? What if there are only benefits?"

"I want a guarantee."

"You don't get one. Not in this life. Not for anything. You get hope. And when you do, you fucking take it, because hope is as precious a gift as anyone can offer."

I opened my mouth to argue, but she cut me off with a kiss, and that was the end of my protests.

No more talking. Fearing. Guessing.

She let out a soft moan, her energy already seeping into me, filling me once again.

I broke our kiss, pulling back to check her for any signs of distress. "You good?"

"No. You stopped kissing me. That's not good. That's the exact opposite of good."

She reached for my cock again, already rock-hard for her. Hell, ever since I'd met her I'd been walking around half-hard every fucking day, so this wasn't all that much of a stretch.

But her touch? Her touch was fucking incredible.

Gray arched her hips, positioning herself right up against me. Her liquid heat was a siren song I couldn't resist.

It also felt like a last hurrah, even though we hadn't even had our first.

"Why do I get the feeling you're about to do something really stupid?" I asked.

"You mean, have sex with you?"

"Stupider."

"Asher?"

"Yeah, Cupcake?"

"Shut up and fuck me before you die and ruin my whole day."

I laughed, tugging my pants down and freeing my cock. "You win, Gray."

She lifted her hips, then lowered herself down over my length, inch by mind-blowing inch until I was buried to the fucking hilt.

"Asher," she breathed, rocking her hips in a gentle rhythm. The sound of my name on her lips sent chills racing down my spine, and I matched her movement, thrusting inside her.

Hot. Fucking. Damn.

I'd never felt anything like her before. Her skin. Her heat. Her magic. It flowed into me, singing through my veins, energizing and strengthening me until I felt like I could tear this whole place to the ground with my bare hands.

It was beautiful and perfect and crazy and hot as hell, and I never wanted it to end.

But this wasn't a fairy tale. This was our reality. Time was not on our side, and despite our banter and teasing and all the back-and-forth, we couldn't drag this out another minute.

She seemed to sense the direction of my thoughts, and without a word, she sped up her movements, riding me harder and faster, losing herself in the hot slide of our bodies coming together, closer and closer and closer until I couldn't hold out another second.

Neither could she.

"Ash!" She fisted my hair, tugging hard as her body clenched around me, her hips bucking wildly as she threw her head back, gasping in pleasure. I felt the pulse of her orgasm at it overtook her, pumping me into a frenzy as we both tumbled hard and fast over the edge.

Biting her shoulder to keep myself from screaming out her name, I dug my fingers into her hips and slammed inside her, coming in a white-hot burst that left me dizzy and seeing stars.

We gave ourselves about a minute to come back to reality. It was all the time we could spare.

"Gray, I—"

She pressed her finger to my lips, following up with another kiss I felt all the way down to my damn toes.

"Did it work?" she ask, slowly pulling away. "Are you back to normal?"

I nodded. Before I could elaborate or even ask about *her* physical state, she was in motion once again, newly energized and more determined than ever.

"Save your energy," she said, sliding down off my lap. Her bare thighs glistened with sweat. "You're going to need it."

"Yeah, I kind of figured." I watched as she slipped her pants back on, wishing all of this had happened under different circumstances. Wishing I could take my time, kissing those bare thighs all the way up to the top. "Care to elaborate?"

"I'm working on a plan to get Jonathan out of here. Once that happens, I need you to promise me something."

I pulled up my pants, readjusting myself inside. "Anything, Cupcake."

"Find the witches—he's keeping them in here somewhere. You have to get them out. Fiona, too." Gray looked at me, her blue eyes so fierce and beautiful there was nothing I wouldn't have promised her just then. "The guys… The guys are okay. I can feel it."

"They're fine. They're great. They're already out looking for us. That motherfucker is just trying to get under your skin."

"Yeah, well, that's not happening. Not anymore."

"That hold spell won't last forever," I said, nodding at the lump of him outside the gate. He was already starting to show signs of life again, groaning softly, his leg twitching.

"You take care of everyone else," she said. "I'll deal with Jonathan."

"I want to help you end this, Gray."

"I know, and… and I love you for that." She paused for a moment, taking a deep breath, and then she leaned in and kissed me again, a slow and lingering kiss that absolutely melted me. When she pulled back, her eyes were glassy with tears, but she didn't let them fall, determined to tough it out till the bitter end. "But I'm afraid my fight with Jonathan is just beginning."

THIRTY-SIX

GRAY

Sophie had always been an all-in, ride-or-die kind of girl.

If she ordered ice cream, it was a banana split with extra hot fudge and two cherries instead of one. She once worked double shifts at Illuminae for an entire month in exchange for borrowing another bartender's car, just so we could drive to the coast for a few hours to watch the sun set over the Pacific. She laughed hard and often, and if you didn't, she made it her mission in life to change that.

And when it came to tarot, while most people favored the gentle guiding energy of The Star, or the inner-child exuberance of The Sun, or even the charming naiveté of The Fool, her favorite card had been the one that sent nausea-inducing waves of fear through the rest of us: The Tower.

In it, a sinister beam of moonlight—or in some decks, lightning—struck a massive brick tower, blasting the top to bits. Desperate to avoid the destruction, several people threw themselves from the tower's highest windows, some of them dashing themselves on the rocks below.

It represented shocking, sudden change or destruction, and the personal transformation that often followed. Sophie was all about sifting through the rubble for the gems that life's most painful lessons often provided, and she believed that the Tower card heralded great opportunities for us, as long as we were open to receiving them.

"Don't fear the storm, Gray. Be ready for it."

How many times had she said that to me when the Tower turned up in one of my readings? How often had that shocking, life-altering, foundation-crumbling Tower card energy graced my life? How many lessons had it taught me, forcing me to rebuild again and again as I stood in the ruins of something I once held so dear?

Before I'd even learned to walk, my birth mother died. Calla had adopted me, given me a home, taught me about magic, and loved me as her own, only to be murdered before my eyes, savagely brutalized by Jonathan's family. Jonathan murdered Sophie, my best and most cherished friend. I'd learned that I was a Shadowborn, a necromancer who could manipulate souls. I'd discovered that someone had signed my life away in a crossroads deal, and that the man I most trusted in this world was the demonic guardian charged with delivering my soul upon my death. My house had been destroyed, also by Jonathan's hand. I'd become his prisoner, along with countless others—women I might've been able to save if only I'd figured it out more quickly, acted differently, been another person altogether.

Lightning. Smashed bricks. Dashing myself on the rocks below, trading one pain for another.

So many tower card moments, shaking down the foundations of everything I held true, forcing me to stand in the ruins of an old life and rebuild, again and again and again.

But through all that devastation and loss, I'd also made friends. Reconnected with my magic. Built another home with people I cared for deeply.

And I'd fallen in love. I was *still* falling in love.

I pressed my fingers to my lips, the cinnamon taste of my demon lingering, and I smiled.

I used to think the Tower card was a warning. You couldn't always know where the lightning would strike, or how much damage it would do, and you definitely couldn't stop it. But if you heeded the card's advice—if you readied yourself for the storm, as Sophie always said—you might be able to lessen the impact of your impending fall. To prepare yourself to get up once again, crawl out of the rubble, and begin the long, slow process of putting your life back together.

But maybe Sophie and I had been wrong.

Maybe the Tower wasn't about figuring out how to survive the fall and thrive in its aftermath, but deciding what you were willing to sacrifice so that someone else might.

I thought of Asher, his chestnut hair sticking up from where I'd run my hands through it, his sea-blue eyes telling me more than words ever could.

When he looked at me like that, I felt him in my very

soul, warm in all the places it had connected with his, binding us forever.

I thought of Haley and Reva and the other witches, imprisoned somewhere in this cave. I thought of Fiona, broken and afraid, still waiting for the chance to find her inner strength. I thought of all the beings Jonathan had hurt, and the ones he'd yet to get his hands on.

I thought of Ronan's protectiveness and his strong, steady heartbeat, and the dizzy way I'd felt the first time he kissed me. I thought of Emilio's soulful eyes and infamous brownies and his boundless empathy. I thought of Darius's commanding touch and the tender side of his heart he'd only shared with me.

And I thought of Liam, guiding me through the strange, dark, beautiful landscape of my magic. My soul.

His words came back to me now, echoing from another time, after another man had tried to hurt me—Travis, the man from the alley. The man who'd killed Bean.

The man's blood is literally on your hands, Liam had said, trying to stop me from trapping Travis's soul in the Shadowlands.

I knew what I had to do now, and I knew what it would cost me.

But when this particular tower crumbled to the ground, if I could give the people I cared about a fighting chance at surviving the fall, it would be worth the price.

Jonathan was coming to, confused and wobbly as he got to his feet. "What... What's happening?"

I chanced a final glance at Asher.

I knew he didn't want me to go through with this, but I also knew he'd back me up, no matter what. I offered him one last blazing smile, and he returned it with a crooked smirk and a wink I felt all the way down in my bones.

Then, he slumped forward, groaning in fake pain.

Jonathan stumbled over to the gate.

"No more bullshit, witch," he hissed, and again I thought of Travis. Of Liam's advice.

The combination of blood and soul is like a magical key to a very ancient, very complicated lock. In possession of both, Shadowborn have the ability to banish the souls of the living to the Shadowrealm.

At the time, he was trying to save me from making a grave mistake.

Now, those words were my saving grace.

"I… I'm sorry, Jonathan," I said, forcing a weakness into my voice that sounded pathetic, even to me. I lowered my head, as if I were ashamed and exhausted. "I can't… I can't fix him."

"Then I guess he dies."

"Please," I whispered, getting down on my knees. "I'm begging you. Let him go."

"And give up my leverage? I think not."

"You don't need leverage. I don't want to play this game anymore. You've killed most of my friends. Destroyed my home. My mother's dead, I have no family. Everyone I've ever loved is just… just gone." I met his eyes, channeling all of my hatred, my anger, my grief into a look of complete and utter resignation. "I'm done."

He considered my words, his face softening. "In some ways, I'm sorry to hear that, Rayanne. I was looking forward to playing the game a bit longer." His grimace took over once again, his mouth crooked, his eyelid twitching. "In other ways, time is of the essence."

"Jonathan," I said, releasing a weary sigh. "I'm spent. I've got nothing left. So if you have a price, name it and let's end this."

He unlocked the bars and swung open the gate, already greedy and dumb at the thought of getting his hands on my magic.

"I want all of it," he said, leaning against the stone wall. "The power to raise the dead, to take souls… hell, Rayanne, if you've got the power to snap your fingers and make a dollar bill appear in your pocket, I want that, too."

At his words, the indigo flames ignited, swirling gently across my palms, and I gasped in horror as though he were responsible for the magic rather than me.

His eyes widened eagerly. He was practically salivating.

"I hate you," I whispered, letting a tear slide down my cheek.

"Unfortunate, yet irrelevant."

I held my palms out in front of me and lowered my eyes, certain the deception in my gaze shone as bright as the moon.

The anticipation.

The *thrill*.

For so long, I'd underestimated him. We all had.

Now, he was underestimating me.

"Okay," I said meekly. "I think… I think I just need two ingredients to make this work."

"What do you need?" he asked.

Without a second thought, I lunged at him, slamming into him with the full force of my magic, the full brunt of my strength. He hit the ground harder than before, his eyes wide as the back of his head bashed against the rocks.

I leaped onto his chest, pinning his arms as I lowered my mouth to his neck. I bit hard, ignoring the wet, coppery slime of blood in my mouth as I tore out a chunk of flesh.

Blood gushed from the wound, coating my skin.

Jonathan gasped and sputtered, his legs kicking feebly beneath me, but I wasn't done yet.

Calling upon the blackest magic in my heart, I watched my blue-green flames turn black and oily. Then I yanked the tattered fabric of his soul free from the confines of his physical form.

It writhed and twisted as I took it inside me, but unlike Travis's soul, there would be no escape for the hunter. No last-minute swell of guilt, no sudden attack of conscience, no sage advice from Death, trying to keep me from condemning my own soul in the process.

My own soul no longer mattered.

We are, all of us, bound for darkness.

I grinned wickedly, finally answering Jonathan's question. "Your blood and your soul, hunter. *That's* what I need."

* * *

What fresh hell awaits Gray in the Shadowrealm, and how will Asher and the others escape their brutal prison? Find out in *Demon Sworn*, the third book in the Witch's Rebels series. **Get Demon Sworn now!**

If you loved reading this story as much as I loved writing it, please help a girl out and **leave a review on Amazon!** Even a quick sentence or two about your favorite part can help other readers discover the book, and that makes me super happy!

XOXO
Sarah

ORIGINS OF THE WITCH'S REBELS

I was primarily inspired to write this series by three things: my fascination with Tarot, my love of all things witchy, and my desire to see more kickass women telling stories for and about other kickass women.

I've always enjoyed books, movies, and TV shows about witches, monsters, and magic, but I never found exactly the right mix. I wanted a darker, grittier Charmed, an older Buffy, and most of all—as much as I love the brothers Winchester (who doesn't?)—I *really* wanted a Supernatural with badass bitches at the helm, hunting monsters, battling their inner demons, and of course, sexytimes. Lots and lots of sexytimes.

(Side note: there's not enough romance on Supernatural. Why is that? Give me five minutes in that writers' studio…)

Anyway, back to The Witch's Rebels. We were talking about badass bitches getting the sexytimes they deserve.

Right.

So I started plotting my own story and fleshing out the character who would eventually become our girl Gray, thinking I had it all figured out. But as I dove deeper into the writing, and I really got to know Gray, Darius, Ronan, Asher, Emilio, and Liam, I discovered a problem. A big one.

With so many strong, sexy guys in the mix, I couldn't decide which one would be the hero to win Gray's heart. I loved them all as much as she did!

I agonized over this.

It felt like the worst kind of love triangle. Er, love rhombus? Love—wait. What's the word for five of them? Pentagon! Yes, a love pentagon.

Pure torture!

But then I had my lightbulb moment. In the face of so much tragedy and danger, Gray fights hard to open herself up to love, to trust people, to earn those hard-won friendships. Her capacity for giving and receiving love expands infinitely throughout the story, so why the hell *shouldn't* she be able to share that with more than one man?

There was no reason to force her to choose.

So, she doesn't. And her story will continue!

You, dear reader, don't have to choose either—that's part of the fun of reverse harem stories like this. But if you happen to have a soft spot for a particular guy, I'd love to hear about it!

Drop me a line anytime at sarah@sarahpiperbooks.com and tell me who's winning your heart so far! I'll tell you mine if you tell me yours! *wink wink*

MORE BOOKS FROM SARAH PIPER!

Paranormal romance fans, I've got even more sexy books ready to heat up your bookshelf!

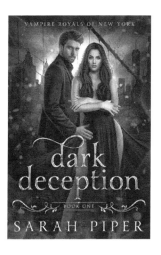

VAMPIRE ROYALS OF NEW YORK is a scorching paranormal romance series featuring a commanding, dirty-talking vampire king and the seductive thief who might just bring him to ruin… or become his eternal salvation. Sizzling romance, dark secrets, and hot vampires with British accents abound!

TAROT ACADEMY is a paranormal, university-aged reverse harem academy romance starring four seriously hot mages and one badass witch. Dark prophecies, unique mythology, steamy romance, strong female friendships, and plenty of supernatural thrills make this series a must-read!

ABOUT SARAH PIPER

Sarah Piper is a Kindle All-Star winning urban fantasy and paranormal romance author. Through her signature brew of dark magic, heart-pounding suspense, and steamy romance, Sarah promises a sexy, supernatural escape into a world where the magic is real, the monsters are sinfully hot, and the witches always get their magically-ever-afters.

Her works include the newly released Vampire Royals of New York series, the Tarot Academy series, and The Witch's Rebels, a fan-favorite reverse harem urban fantasy series readers have dubbed "super sexy," "imaginative and original," "off-the-walls good," and "delightfully wicked in the best ways," a quote Sarah hopes will appear on her tombstone.

Originally from New York, Sarah now makes her home in northern Colorado with her husband (though that changes frequently) (the location, not the husband), where she spends her days sleeping like a vampire and her nights writing books, casting spells, gazing at the moon, playing with her ever-expanding collection of Tarot cards, binge-watching Supernatural (Team Dean!), and obsessing over the best way to brew a cup of tea.

You can find her online at SarahPiperBooks.com and in her Facebook readers group, Sarah Piper's Sassy Witches! If you're sassy, or if you need a little *more* sass in your life, or if you need more Dean Winchester gifs in your life (who doesn't?), come hang out!

Printed in Great Britain
by Amazon

74644123R00201